ICING ON THE CAKE

ICING ON THE CAKE

AMANDA UHL

HARPETH ROAD
PRESS
Nashville

HARPETH ROAD PRESS

Published by Harpeth Road Press (USA)
P.O. Box 158184
Nashville, TN 37215

Paperback: 978-1-963483-53-6
eBook: 978-1-963483-52-9
Library of Congress Control Number: 2026936723

Icing on the Cake: A Delightful, Uplifting Romance

Cover Design by Sarah Hansen
Cover Images © Shutterstock, Adobe, Depositphotos

Harpeth Road Press, April 2026

In memory of my dear friend Joyce, a gentle listener who shared her super plotting skills to craft this story and taught me to seek the rainbow during every storm. I miss you.

CHAPTER ONE

Eating dessert for breakfast was a small but delicious perk of owning a restaurant.

Bethany Parker stood behind the worn wooden counter of Grandma Lou's Kitchen and Pantry and forked a generous portion of her grandmother's famous chocolate cake with buttercream frosting into her mouth. She closed her eyes and swirled the flavors on her tongue. Rich and creamy and buttery. And the ingredients—vanilla, espresso, and coconut milk—in just the right quantities, created an exciting zip that sent a flutter through her small frame. But wait, had she used a smidge too much cocoa powder?

She had to get the recipe right. This was the one that could save her, or rather her struggling restaurant, from certain doom. The one Bethany had been trying for more than a month to duplicate and had finally, *finally* in the last few weeks, mastered. The one that would single-handedly bring her business back from financial disaster to . . .

"That must be some chocolate cake."

The drawling voice was deep and confident and masculine, a hint of laughter hidden in its rich depths. How had she not heard the door chime?

She popped her eyes open and froze, her tongue still stuck to the silver fork.

Oh my God. Oh my God. Oh my God.

A man stood in front of her. An impossibly tall, drop-dead gorgeous hunk of a man. A larger-than-life, muscled blond Adonis who looked like he'd stepped out of a magazine cover because . . . well . . . *he had* stepped off a gazillion magazine covers. And a television to boot.

What the heck was Hank Haverill, star of the hit television show *Apollo*, fitness buff, and God's glorious gift to every woman in the country, doing here—right now—in the middle of Grandma Lou's Kitchen and Pantry? What was he even doing in America? Wasn't the show filmed in London?

She yanked the fork from her mouth and shoved it behind her back. "Uh, sorry. Did you uh, need something?" *To use the phone or, or . . . a bathroom? Maybe he'd been in an accident, or his car needed gas and his pregnant wife's water had burst on the way to the hospital? But Hank Haverill didn't have a wife—did he?*

He smiled and his deep-set blue eyes seemed to carry a message of their own. *Hey, baby,* they whispered, *take a walk on the wild side.*

"Wait, what did you say?" Bethany asked.

He flashed his charming dimples, which she had only ever seen—and drooled over—on a flat-screen television. "I said, I need a place to hide."

"Whatever for?" She straightened her shoulders and tucked the fork in the back pocket of her jeans.

His face fell, removing the dimples. His eyes no longer

whispered anything. "I'll explain later. Just let me hide . . ." He pointed to the kitchen. "Back there."

She looked where he was pointing as if she didn't know where her kitchen was. "You want to hide in my kitchen?"

Geez, she sounded like a parrot. But why would a television star need to hide in her kitchen? She scanned him from the top of his golden head to the bottom of his Italian leather loafers. Had he stolen something? But that was dumb. His shoes alone cost more than her monthly rent. He didn't need to steal anything.

He tapped his foot and turned in a circle. "Unless you have another good hiding place around here?"

Maybe he'd been accused of murder and was on the run? "What have you done?"

"Done?" He puckered his lips like he had eaten a sour pickle. Hank Haverill did not look quite as handsome as he had earlier. "I haven't done anything."

A howling noise filtered through the door like the screech of a high wind. Bethany glanced through the window at a dozen women, maybe more, some distance away, running and yelling like the sky was falling on Grandma Lou's. What were they carrying on about?

She zeroed in on her divinely sculpted customer, and like someone had turned the lens on an out-of-focus camera, everything snapped into place. Hank Haverill, the television star, was in her restaurant, looking at her with growing desperation, for one reason and one reason only. *To stop that gaggle of adoring idiots from finding him.*

Bethany slapped a hand over her mouth. Had she spoken aloud?

"Not a gaggle. One woman—my publicist. The rest of them are harmless."

"Harmless?"

"Listen, I'd love to chat, but as you can see and hear . . ." He tipped his thumb toward the window and scrunched his face into a no-way-will-I-let-them-find-me-here frown. "I don't have the time. So, pardon my invasion, but I promise I'll buy you dinner when things calm down if you don't tell them I'm here. Please."

Hank used both hands to boost himself over the countertop. She had just enough time to move the decorative stand filled with snickerdoodles out of the way before he slid across and onto the floor, then dashed into her kitchen. It was like a scene straight out of his television show.

Impressive move. But really? These Hollywood stars thought they owned the world.

She turned to lock the front door, the swift motion swinging the "no dogs allowed" sign. It banged against the antique wood like an omen signaling she was a second too late. Pandemonium in the form of at least a dozen excited fans rushed inside like a mini tornado.

"Where is he? Is he here?" several women asked Bethany, going in and out of the bathroom. Others weaved in and around the tables and chairs. A few stragglers leaned over the counter to ogle the baked goods.

A tall woman in sleek brown trousers and a white silk top touched Bethany's arm with cream-tipped nails that had to be fake. Her hair bounced around her head in blonde ringlets. "Sorry for the intrusion, but I'm looking for Hank Haverill—and I do mean the actor. Did he come in a moment ago?"

A crashing sound filled the room, and the stand of snickerdoodles went flying to the floor. The ladies stepped back trying to get out of the way. Cookies crunched under their feet.

Bethany leaned forward and grimaced at the mess. She couldn't change the sign on the door to read "no dogs or adoring Hank Haverill fans allowed." Could she?

CHAPTER TWO

"Ooh, snickerdoodles." A large woman in a yellow and white polka dot dress leaned on the counter. "I apologize for the little accident. Do you have any more?"

Bethany glanced at the surviving two in the display case. "Yes, I do."

The woman's gaze followed hers. "I'll take them. And one of those chocolate supernatural whoopie pies too."

"Save some for the rest of us." Another woman in a white straw hat elbowed her out of the way. "I want a whoopie pie."

Maybe Hank Haverill hiding out in Grandma Lou's wasn't such a bad idea after all. "Give me a moment to clean this mess and I'll be right with you."

Bethany swept the broken cookies into a dustpan, doing her best to ignore Hank's adoring fans who chattered like birds around a feeder.

When her grandparents opened the Cleveland restaurant in the 1950s, in the suburb of Tremont, they couldn't have known it would grow into such a vital neighborhood fixture. Grandma Lou had started by cooking a few of her favorite recipes for hungry neighbors and friends. Soon, the restaurant had turned into a popular gathering spot where those in need could be assured of a free or reduced-cost meal. Her parents had continued the tradition and had even added a pantry stocked with donated goods. The business was part restaurant with paying customers, and part charity, and Bethany worked hard to keep it that way.

She glanced at the decorative clock above the counter. It was later than she thought. The fork and the knife pointed at eleven. In minutes, her friends would be arriving, and Bethany could bet they would be hungry. She had a pot of tomato soup and grilled cheese ready to go.

"Ladies, please move over there." She gestured with her empty hand to a long table in one corner.

All but the woman in the white silk top complied with her request. She tilted her nose in the air like she was royalty and Bethany should bow. "I don't think you realize who I am." She shook her long blonde hair and raised perfectly shaped eyebrows over impossibly long eyelashes. "I'm Elizabeth Fortenay, Hank's publicist."

Ah, the woman Hank wanted to avoid. Bethany tried to think if she'd heard the name before but couldn't come up with anything. "That's nice. If you'll excuse me a moment, I need to empty this." She held up the dustpan.

Elizabeth stepped back as if it were poison, glaring at Bethany, who discarded the broken cookies into the trash and set the dustpan behind the counter. Elizabeth craned her neck toward the kitchen, but the bell over the door jangled, and they both turned to look.

"Miss Bethany, Miss Bethany." Two small voices rang out from little girls with dark pigtails and denim dresses. Her friend Rosie's daughters raced toward her, wrapping their arms around her legs and squeezing tight.

"Hi, girls." Bethany smiled and crouched, hugging them close. Her smallest but best customers smelled of sunshine and cotton candy and innocence. This was by far her favorite part of the day.

The oldest child, Tia, unwound herself from Bethany's leg and handed her a drawing of a bunny eating a carrot. Her younger sister, Tana, shook a piece of paper in Bethany's face. "Look at mine! Look at mine!"

"They're beautiful." Bethany looked at each picture. "Where's your mother?"

"She's coming," Tia said.

The girls' mother, Rosie Ortiz, pushed the door open with a jingle.

"Hello, Rosie. Your table's waiting." Bethany pointed to the side. "I've got fresh tomato soup today to go with grilled cheese and . . ." Bethany glanced toward the empty display case, which should have held their favorite snickerdoodles. "Chocolate chip cookies."

"Gracias, Bethany." Rosie smiled, white teeth flashing next to her chestnut hair. She smelled like furniture polish —she must have come straight from cleaning houses. When her husband left the family destitute, Rosie had begged Bethany for a cleaning job in exchange for food, since Rosie barely made enough cleaning houses to pay the rent. Despite her own financial issues, Bethany hadn't hesitated —it was what her parents and grandparents would have wanted. Turned out, giving Rosie a job was the best decision Bethany had ever made. Over the past two years, Rosie had become a big help in the kitchen, and she and the girls had become dear friends. "Sounds wonderful. C'mon girls. Let's get out of Miss Bethany's way. She has other customers to serve today."

"Yes, Mama." The girls rushed to their usual table in front of the window.

On a normal day, the place would be almost empty until the lunch crowd arrived at noon. Which was why Rosie and the girls had taken to showing up around eleven. Bethany turned to fetch their lunch, only to be confronted by Elizabeth, hands on her hips, lips pursed, eyes narrowed, and an I'm-used-to-people-catering-to-me aura surrounding her.

"Excuse me, but I was here first. I'm looking for Hank Haverill. Has he been in your restaurant?"

"I'll be just another moment." Bethany studied Elizabeth from the corner of one eye and made her way behind the counter. She removed the fork from the back pocket of her jeans and shoved it next to the register. So this was the reason for Hank Haverill's mad dash into her kitchen? He'd run from Ms. Fancy Pants? Bethany could admit that her sour face was something to run from, but Hank probably never had to deal with it since he had to be her number one client. So why hide?

She dished steaming soup into her fanciest china bowls and set them on a tray, then headed back around the counter, her gaze sliding again to Elizabeth. She did not look like someone who would cause a grown man to hide in the kitchen. She looked perfect with her flawless complexion, long legs, and golden hair—like someone used to getting attention.

Bethany breezed by Elizabeth and placed the food in front of Rosie and her daughters. "Here you go, girls."

Elizabeth was the kind of woman who made Bethany feel frumpy. Not that she had anything to be ashamed about. Her dark hair was shiny and clean, even if it looked like she had a perpetual perm. No major blemishes marred her olive complexion. Except, Bethany enjoyed a good donut now and then. This woman looked like she existed on a daily diet of carrots and celery sticks.

Bethany took a deep breath, crossed her fingers, and turned to find Elizabeth standing behind her. "I haven't seen him." Why she lied, Bethany wasn't sure. Hank hadn't looked like he'd needed her protection. But there was something about Elizabeth that made Bethany's skin itch.

She made her way back to the counter, where she placed the cookies on a tray and served and collected money from the other ladies. Elizabeth trailed her.

"Well, that's just great." Elizabeth articulated each word as if it tasted nasty on her tongue. "I've got a camera crew ready to go, and he's disappeared again. I don't know how he expects me to generate the publicity needed to open his new center if he can't even show up for an interview."

"Wait a minute." Bethany turned from the counter, her stomach diving like a bird spotting prey. "What new center?"

"Fitaholics, of course. We'll open by the end of the year."

"Where do you plan to open this business?" Bethany struggled to take a breath.

"You mean, you haven't heard?"

Bethany must have shaken her head because Elizabeth continued speaking. "He'll open a full-scale fitness center—right here in this spot."

The room spun and Bethany clung to the counter so she wouldn't collapse at Elizabeth's feet. "Oh my God. He's bought the building from the bank." She pulled out a stool and fell onto it.

Elizabeth smirked like a cat with a bowl of cream. "Yes, isn't it amazing?" Her voice sounded like she called from the top of a mountain. "Hank needs to diversify. A fitness center's the perfect extension of his image. Not to mention the price was right."

Bethany closed her eyes, as if that would make the whole horrible nightmare that was Elizabeth Fortenay and Hank Haverill vanish. She counted her fingers, but Elizabeth still stood in front of her, a gloating tilt to her lips.

Bethany stood, narrowed her eyes, scrunched her face. Her brother, Travis, called it her I-ain't-taking-bullshit-from-anyone face. Bethany knew it as the face she made when life threw her a sucker punch, and she needed to grow some balls and fight back. She didn't much enjoy being sucker punched. She didn't much enjoy having to fight for justice for herself or others. But quite often, she'd discovered that her life required an uppercut, or in this case, a kick in the fancy pants.

She lowered her voice so Rosie wouldn't hear. "Listen, my family has had our business in this building for more than seventy years. It's a neighborhood fixture, and it's historic. And it's needed in this working-class community— many people count on it for survival." She turned her head toward the kitchen. "He can't just tear it down."

Elizabeth cocked her head and widened her eyes. "Oh, he won't tear it down. He plans to do millions of dollars' worth of renovations. It will be just what this suburb of Cleveland needs to revitalize the neighborhood. Tremont isn't exactly a thriving metropolis, you know."

"But," Bethany said, thankful her skin tone would hide the dull red that had to be flooding her cheeks, "what will happen to Grandma Lou's?"

Elizabeth shrugged her elegant shoulders. "That's none of my concern. You'll have to ask Hank—if I can ever find him. C'mon, girls." She motioned the other women toward her. "He's obviously not here. Let's go back outside and look around."

"But I'm not finished. I planned to order a sandwich," the lady in the yellow polka dot dress said, wiping a bit of whoopie pie from her chin.

"You were *not* invited along to order sandwiches." Elizabeth's tone was as frosty as her eyes. "You're here to be ready for the camera, if I can ever find Hank to start the interview. Now, let's go."

Hank's fans filed out the door, one by one, their shoulders slumped.

When they had vanished, Bethany turned toward the kitchen. "Good thing *I* know where the coward's hiding."

CHAPTER THREE

Bethany stormed into the kitchen, nostrils flaring, but she didn't have to look for Hank. He leaned against the freezer, a chocolate-cherry macaron cookie in one hand, his golden hair sticking up in every direction like . . . Bethany frowned. Had he been napping?

"These are quite good." He took a massive bite of the cookie. "Did you make them?"

Bethany blinked at the empty spot on the tray of cookies she had frosted earlier. "I did."

He finished the cookie in another bite and offered her a lazy smile. The afternoon sunlight streaming through the kitchen window caught the blue of his eyes and the blond of his hair, casting him in a glorious glow, like some sort of archangel. Which he was *not.*

"That cookie was delicious. You wouldn't have a glass of milk, would you?" Hank used the back of his hand to wipe crumbs from his mouth. She couldn't help noticing how his forest green V-neck T-shirt molded to his chest like a second skin and showed off a generous sprinkling of blond chest hair.

"Not at this moment." She pressed her lips together. It didn't matter if half the women in America were after him and he looked like the god of light; he owned her building. Her parents had been forced to mortgage the place after a few lean years, and Bethany had been working to pay it off. But when her scheming ex-fiancé had emptied her savings account and fled, she'd missed the monthly payments, and the bank had pursued foreclosure. Hank was the mysterious investor who had purchased the deed from the bank, making him her landlord. What kind of man would throw out a business that had served the community in a historic neighborhood for decades on some whim to build yet another fitness center?

It was ludicrous. It was outrageous. It was downright arrogant.

"That's a shame." He licked the chocolate on his lips.

She gritted her teeth and moved toward him. "Yes, it is."

He did not live here. Did not understand the needs of the neighborhood. Did not know how hard her immigrant grandparents had worked to build a successful business. Did not know how much her parents had struggled to keep it going so they could pass it on to her and Travis. Did not know about the homeless community she and Travis called friends, who visited the pantry and ate in the restaurant each week.

This man reeked of health and Hollywood. He was the farthest thing from homeless she had ever seen. He wouldn't know a good deed if it clobbered him over his handsome head.

"Well . . ." He stretched his long arms as if to taunt her, showing off the definition in his biceps. "I do appreciate you letting me hang out in your kitchen."

He had no idea how much they had struggled over the

last year to keep the lights on and the bills paid, only to have the bank foreclose on the mortgage.

"Funny." Bethany stood in front of him and folded her arms across her chest. "I wouldn't label *hiding* in my kitchen as hanging out."

How annoying: She had to look up to see Hank's expression. It went from innocence to puzzlement to understanding.

"Oh, I've upset you."

"Yes." She blasted him with her grimmest stare. "Although 'upset' is too weak a word for what I'm feeling." She pointed her finger at him. "How dare you come into *my* restaurant, hide in *my* kitchen, eat *my* macaron cookies, and have the audacity to ask for a glass of milk from *my* refrigerator."

He studied her pointed finger, an odd glint in his eyes. "But milk and cookies go so well together."

"Why are you hiding in my kitchen?"

"Well . . ." He came closer. Too close. He smelled of chocolate and spice and everything nice.

Bethany stood her ground even when he gave her another heart-stopping grin. She would not be wowed by Hank Haverill in her kitchen. She refused to be.

"There weren't a lot of places to hide." His voice was as smooth as her grandma's buttercream frosting.

"Actually, I don't particularly care why you were hiding. I want to know if you're planning to put me out of business."

"Not if you're good." He flashed an amused grin.

"Don't play with me. Your publicist said you're planning to open a fitness center in this spot."

"Elizabeth has a lot of grand ideas. She wants the best for me."

He smoothed a hand down his hair, but despite his best efforts, a portion still stuck in the air. He looked tired—like he'd not slept in weeks, even though Bethany was certain he'd napped in her kitchen. Seeing his weariness made her want to lick her palm and flatten it against his hair like her mother used to do for her and Travis, God rest her soul.

Bethany stuffed her hand behind her back so she wouldn't be tempted. *Always mothering,* she could hear Travis say. It was her worst failing. That and a certain stubbornness that kept her in Tremont when so many had left. "So you're not going to open some place called Fitaholics?"

"I don't think so. Does that earn me a glass of milk?"

He looked so sweet and boyish, like a child begging for a toy, that Bethany almost laughed aloud. But she couldn't afford humor. "What do you mean by you 'don't think so'?"

He shoved a hand inside his pant pocket, and Bethany followed the movement until she realized where she was looking. Hank caught her staring and smirked as her cheeks grew even hotter. He was obviously used to women ogling him. She snapped her gaze back to his face and clenched her teeth until her jaw hurt.

"I'm an actor not a businessman. I'm pretty sure I'd grow bored with a fitness center sooner or later. But I have financial advisors who make recommendations. They recommended I buy the building as it's undervalued. So I did."

"What will you do with it?"

He moved toward the dining room. "I haven't decided. If I can get a glass of milk and that soup and sandwich I heard you talking about," he called over his shoulder, "I'll continue renting to you until I figure it out."

Bethany followed him. A squeal sounded from the front room.

"Oh, my goodness," Rosie said. "You scared me. For a second, I thought you were—"

Bethany rounded the corner in time to hear a loud thump and see Rosie slump against the table.

"Mama? Mama? You okay?" Tia and Tana shouted.

Bethany reached around Hank and shook Rosie's shoulder. "Rosie, you okay? Wake up, Rosie."

Rosie moaned and raised her head. "What's in those cookies? I swear, for a moment, I thought I saw . . . *¡Ay, Dios!* It's him. Girls, that there's Apollo from TV. What's he doing here?" Rosie looked at Bethany like she'd awakened on Mars.

"Well . . ." Bethany was at a loss to explain why Hank Haverill had turned up in her kitchen.

"I came for the cookies and milk, like you." Hank gave them his thousand-watt, dimpled smile.

Rosie fanned her chest. "*Dios mío.* Take a seat."

Hank pulled out the chair and folded his long legs into it.

"Bethany, honey, get the man some milk and cookies."

Hank tipped his head back and roared with laughter, and for a moment, the sight was so mesmerizing that Bethany couldn't move. The god of light was in her restaurant about to pound some milk and cookies.

The good Lord really did have a sense of humor.

CHAPTER FOUR

"Do it again, Mr. Hank. Please do it again."

Tia (or was she Tana?) squealed, the noise the most joyous and real sound Hank had heard in some time—maybe years. They stood on either side of him as he sat at the table, their little hands tugging on his arms. The stuffed mouse he'd nabbed from a shelf in the store earlier and nicknamed "Lanky" for his long tail reappeared behind Tia's left ear.

"It's here! Hi, Lanky," Tia said, petting the mouse.

"How'd he do that?" Tana said to her mother.

"It's magic." Rosie beamed at him across the table. She hadn't stopped smiling since she'd recovered from her earlier faint. Hank wished he could bottle Rosie's expression and pull it out during the long, lonesome times, when his days seemed to run together with no end in sight. That seemed to be happening with more frequency. He ran a hand across his faint stubble. He needed food, sleep, and a shave, in that order.

"Now, girls, let's let Mr. Hank enjoy his lunch." Rosie motioned Tia and Tana to their chairs. "Taste the soup."

She gestured to their white bowls and large silver spoons. "You too." She nodded at Hank with another of her broad smiles. "You can't go wrong with Miss Bethany Parker's soup. There's a whole lot of love cooked in there. It's the best there is."

The mention of the owner's name—Bethany Parker—had Hank glancing toward the counter. Since she'd served them lunch, her small hands hadn't stopped moving: stocking shelves with products and refilling trays with cookies and cupcakes and putting them on display with easy precision. Her curly dark hair was pulled into a ponytail that emphasized the prettiness of her oval face and rosebud lips, which turned down when she looked up and caught his stare.

Hank forced his gaze back to his soup and picked up his spoon. Ever since he'd first spied her, eyes closed and savoring a bite of cake, he'd found his gaze returning to her time and again, maybe because she'd seemed to enjoy that cake more than him.

He plunged his spoon into the soup and stirred. The smell of tomatoes wafted upward, tickling his nose, and causing his mouth to water. He couldn't remember the last time he'd enjoyed a simple home-cooked meal.

"Careful now," Rosie warned her children. She moved the bowls closer to them so they wouldn't slop. For someone who looked to be in her early twenties, Rosie sure had the mother thing down. Hank found himself moving his own bowl closer.

He raised the spoon to his mouth and blew on it before tasting. He closed his eyes. Rosie hadn't lied. Creamy toma-toey goodness tingled on his tongue. The soup was one of the best he'd enjoyed. A glimmer of an idea surfaced but he closed it down quickly. He couldn't afford complications.

He was here for a day or so. Just enough time to inspect the building and give his advisors the thumbs up on Fitaholics. And if Elizabeth had her way, he would do an interview or two while he was at it.

"Are you sleeping or eating?"

Hank popped his eyes open to see Bethany standing in front of him with a plate of sandwiches and a glass of ice water, her lips pursed as if she didn't know quite what to make of him.

"I was savoring it, that's all." He wiped his mouth with a napkin and offered her what he hoped was a sincere smile. "It's good."

The smile didn't work. At least, her expression still looked fierce. Why wouldn't she lighten up? Maybe she preferred ladies—most women he knew would have been all over him by now.

"Sure it's good. I made it from scratch this morning." She turned to Tia and Tana, and her tone softened. "Grilled cheese?"

"Yes," they chorused.

Hank didn't blame them. What looked like three kinds of cheese oozed from crusty Italian bread. He waited for Bethany to give him the remaining sandwich. It had been years since he'd enjoyed a grilled cheese. He would have to hit the gym tomorrow, but today he was playing hooky, so . . .

"Here you go." Bethany offered the golden goodness to Rosie.

Hank couldn't stop his gaze from following the plate.

Without another word, Bethany set the ice water in front of him, then turned and headed back to the kitchen. Hank scratched his head. What did a guy have to do to earn a grilled cheese in this joint? He pulled a fifty-dollar bill from his wallet and set it in the middle of the table.

Rosie tapped her hand on his. "Don't worry. Bethany won't let you go hungry. That woman has a heart of gold."

As if in agreement, the bell on the door chimed. Rosie's eyes lit up like she'd hit the lottery. "Well, hey there, Travis." She turned to Hank. "That's Bethany's brother."

Hank eyed the man who came through the door. He didn't look much like Bethany. While she was short, Travis was tall. Her hair was brown and curly with a tint of gold, while his was close-cropped and black. He wore an easy smile in contrast to Bethany's scowl.

Travis drew closer, pausing at their table. "Man is it nice outside. A bit breezy, but there's no better place to be than Cleveland in August." He spotted Hank and his eyes widened.

Okay, maybe Bethany and Travis *were* siblings because Hank swore that was the same surprised look Bethany had given him earlier, from the same eyes. They shared the same olive skin tone too. There was something striking about the brother and sister. An interesting combination of genes, which had Hank wondering about their ethnic heritage. African-American and Scandinavian, maybe?

Travis's lips formed a perfect O, and Hank suppressed a groan, straightening his shoulders and plastering on his public face.

"Apollo? Oh, man. It *is* you. For a second, I thought I was seeing things—but it's—you're the actor from the TV show, right? I've watched a few episodes. 'Forged in Fire,' man. I love that."

Hank sighed. As if he didn't know he was on a TV show with a ridiculous slogan. As much as he loved his superstardom, on some days, it was plain tiresome. He hadn't escaped the spotlight as he had hoped when he'd hidden from Elizabeth and his fans. "Hi." He nodded but couldn't prevent his gaze from sliding to the soup. Would it be rude if he took a bite? He picked up his spoon and plunged it into the bowl.

"What are you doing here? Not that I'm not excited to see you. I'm, wow, I'm in shock, I think." Travis trailed off, looking at Rosie, a question mark on his face. Now that Hank had a chance to study him up close, he could see brother and sister shared the same wide forehead. Hank suspected Travis might be the younger by quite a few years.

"Travis, don't bother our famous customer," Bethany called from the kitchen, her voice like a commanding officer. "C'mon back. Bring the supplies with you."

Travis threw him a conspiratorial grin. "I suppose you met my sister?"

Hank nodded.

"I'd better not keep her waiting. She'll bean me with a loaf of bread. But hey, before you leave, think I could grab a selfie with you? This is about the most exciting thing that has happened to our little restaurant since a neighborhood dog ate a bunch of cupcakes."

Hank grinned. Travis Parker was a friendly sort. He appeared to represent the sweet half of the restaurant, while Bethany added the spice. "Sure—if you can nab me one of your sister's grilled cheese sandwiches?"

"You got it." Travis whipped out his cell phone, crouching next to Hank to snap the promised selfie.

"You two are pathetic." Bethany appeared behind Travis like a ninja. "No need to bribe Travis for food. No one goes hungry in this place. Travis, I cleared off the shelves in the back if you want to put the stuff there."

Travis offered Hank a last jaunty wave and a shrug,

which Hank interpreted as "what's a man gonna do?" and headed out the door.

Bethany set a fresh plate of grilled cheese triangles in front of Hank with a clunk and wiped her hands on her apron—a grandma's apron, decorated with red and yellow roses.

Hank almost laughed aloud. There was something old-fashioned about Bethany. A throwback to another time—she was the kind of girl who expected a boy to keep his distance on their first date—to hold doors and offer jackets and send flowers. So not his type. He frowned. Why was he thinking about whether she was his type or not?

"Do I have something in my hair?"

He came to with a start. "No. Sorry, I was thinking."

"Oh, that must be hard." She laughed, all smooth and husky and rich, like a shot of whiskey.

He should have been insulted. But Hank found himself hanging on every last, luxurious syllable like they'd wash him clean. He shook his head as if to toss off his strange reaction to Bethany.

"Not at all." He reached for his water glass and took a long, slow sip. His gaze caught hers above the rim, and he refused to look away. If she wanted to flirt, he was the master. She didn't stand a chance. He set his glass aside and wiped his lips on his napkin, then stretched his arms behind his head, and winked. "I was just blown away by your cooking."

Hank couldn't miss how her gaze followed his movements before her cheeks took on a slight pink, and she turned toward Rosie and the girls with an eye roll. "Actors. You can't believe a thing they say."

"Bethany, shame on you," Rosie said. "I just got done telling him what a softie you are."

Bethany waved a hand, but Rosie kept talking, turning to Hank with another of her sunny expressions. "Bethany makes the girls' lunch every day. And we're not the only ones she cooks for. Seems like she feeds half the neighborhood around here."

"You're exaggerating." Bethany shook her head. "We have plenty of extra."

"That's not what Travis says." Rosie smirked. "Travis says—"

"You know Travis likes to exaggerate." Bethany waved a hand again as if she could conjure an off switch. "We're fine."

"Miss Bethany lets me make cookies." Tia clapped her hands together.

"Me, too," Tana said. "She lets me make cookies too. In the kitchen."

"You're both helpers," Rosie said. "Sit up straight now and finish your sandwiches."

Hank looked toward Bethany, but she'd given them her back and was halfway to the kitchen, her movements hurried, like she couldn't get away fast enough.

"She's modest too." Rosie grinned, but Hank almost didn't notice.

He couldn't remember the last time any woman—any person—had been so unimpressed by his star status, they'd given him their back. Bethany didn't seem impressed with either his looks or the fact he was her landlord.

No, all she seemed to care about was her restaurant. For that, she'd stood in his face and demanded answers. You had to respect a woman like that.

A ringing sound had Hank glancing toward his cell phone on the table. Robert Blackman, his agent. He really, really did not want to talk to Blackie at this moment—he eyed the plate Bethany had set in front of him—not when a gooey grilled cheese sandwich was staring him in the face.

Hank silenced the ringer and bit into the grilled cheese. Once again, he found himself closing his eyes to savor all the flavors on his tongue.

"*Delicioso*, isn't it?" Rosie asked.

"*Sí, señorita*." Hank nodded.

But he was certain he was referring to more than the sandwich.

CHAPTER FIVE

Bethany swiped a hand across her cheek and eyed the lump of sugar cookie dough she'd dumped on the kitchen worktable. Shouts of laughter rang from the other room.

Mister High and Mighty TV Star sat in her front room chatting with Rosie and the children like he was their hired entertainment. Bethany didn't have the heart to tell them they were laughing with the man who might put an end to their free lunches. She raised her shoulders and let them drop but it didn't remove the tension that squeezed her aching muscles like a taut rubber band.

Although he'd said he didn't plan to open a fitness center, Bethany knew his type. She had almost married one. Desmond Mitchell, her lying ex-fiancé, was a handsome, talented, and well-known chef, but he was also without an ounce of compassion for anyone but himself. He had known what the business meant to her and Travis and the entire community, but none of it had mattered. He'd stolen the insurance money she'd been planning to use to pay off the mortgage from their joint savings account. Then he'd used it to rent a fancy apartment in New York and start his own cooking show.

She picked up the rolling pin and attacked the dough as if she could blot out his memory. It had been twelve long months, but his betrayal haunted her thoughts whenever she was tired or lonesome or missing her parents' calm advice.

"Can you believe Apollo is eating lunch in our restaurant?" Travis didn't wait for Bethany to respond. Good thing because she wasn't in the mood. "We should have enough supplies to last the month, and we've got plenty of donations." He paused in the middle of wiping his hands on his shirt. "What's the matter?"

Bethany stopped what she was doing and frowned. "What do you mean?"

"If you roll that dough any thinner, we'll be able to see through it."

Bethany stopped rolling to eye the mangled dough. "Darn it."

Travis held out a hand with a grin. "I'll roll; you watch."

She sighed and gave up the pin.

He pointed to the stool next to the worktable. "Sit there and do nothing. You've been on your feet much longer than me."

"This isn't necessary."

"You don't always have to play the big sister." Travis set down the pin and made a show of washing his hands at the sink and drying them with a dish towel hanging nearby before putting on the plastic gloves they wore to handle food. "You think I don't know what today is? I've been thinking about them too, you know."

That stopped her protests. Because she hadn't been thinking about the anniversary of their parents' deaths. Not entirely. No, half of her mind had been on Hank Haverill and how much he reminded her of her thieving ex-fiancé.

Bethany tossed her gloves in the garbage can, then sat and watched Travis roll the dough. "Don't cut out the cookies. I promised the girls they can help."

Travis nodded. "How's the contest entry coming along?"

Bethany rested her chin on her hands. "The cake I made this morning was good. Close to perfect. And I captured some great photos."

"So you'll submit your entry? In time for the deadline?"

Bethany drew a squiggle in the flour dust on the worktable. "I have 'til next Friday at midnight. Then the voting starts." Next to the squiggle, she added a swirl. "I've already started posting on our social media to ask for votes, and I want to put together a flyer so we can hand them out. The top ten finalists move on to the final round."

"Think we'll win?"

Bethany erased her design and let out a breath. "I know it's a stretch, but I can't stop hoping. Grandma Lou's has a long history, and we're known for our baked goods, so I think people in the community are likely to vote for us. I mean, if we do win, the money will go a long way toward repurchasing this old place." She looked around the kitchen. Even if the restaurant hadn't been a legacy from her grandparents, she would appreciate its rustic charm. Silver pots and pans gleamed from where they hung from the ceiling. Old subway tiles ran across the back wall, and the worktable was made of wood that matched the floor.

Another burst of laughter came from the front room, reminding Bethany of all they stood to lose if Hank opened the fitness center.

"Boy, was I shocked when I walked in and saw Apollo

sitting there chatting with Rosie and the girls like they were old friends."

"Yeah."

"Seems like a nice guy. Once word gets out, it'll be great for business. Camera crews are all over the place—what's wrong?"

Bethany busied her fingers, pleating her apron. "He owns the building."

Travis stopped rolling the dough. "You're kidding?"

"Afraid not."

"Since when?"

"I don't know. His publicist, who was in here earlier, mentioned it."

"He bought it from the bank?"

Bethany nodded and sucked on her lower lip to keep it from trembling. "It's undervalued. His investors advised him to make the purchase. They want him to open a fitness center."

A storm cloud collected on her brother's face. "Here in Tremont? In our building?"

Bethany moved her head up and down, then returned to drawing squiggles. She kept her face low so he couldn't see the tears gathered in the corners of her eyes that threatened to overflow.

"Why? He could open it anywhere."

She pursed her lips. "Beats me." It was a question she had asked herself.

Travis set down the rolling pin and leaned toward her. "Does he need the whole building? Maybe he'll continue to let us rent?"

Bethany sniffed and avoided his gaze. "I don't know, but I'm doubtful." She could feel Travis's penetrating eyes.

"You're crying." He straightened. "Why the heck are we feeding him?"

She rubbed a hand across her brow and shifted her gaze from Travis to the dining room. "I don't know. He said he was hungry. He seemed tired. Rosie and the girls like him." She risked a glance at Travis. His eyes could puncture steel. "I couldn't just kick him out the door—he's our landlord."

Travis's eyes narrowed and his nostrils flared. "What does it matter if he's our landlord if he won't let us rent from him? You're too nice. But I'm not." His expression remained hard as diamonds, and he glowered at her, but Bethany knew his anger was triggered by frustration and caring. For her. Although there were eight years between them, Travis fancied himself her protector after their parents died and Desmond's treachery. He had seen firsthand the devastation and heartache Desmond's betrayal brought her.

Bethany put her hand on his arm and squeezed. "I'm okay, Travis. Please, for my sake, don't do anything rash. We need to stay calm and learn what he's planning."

She hadn't been the only victim when Desmond stole their savings and fled. Her brother had looked up to her ex but had been forced to grow up fast when the rat suddenly disappeared, without explanation. To keep Bethany from falling apart, Travis had taken on the more physically exhausting chores of the business. Against her objections, he'd also reduced his college load to a part-time schedule, so he could help out during the week. If he resented the sacrifices he'd made, he didn't show it. But Bethany suspected it wouldn't take much of a spark to ignite his inner Rambo.

"There's no need to panic," she said—something she'd repeated to herself continually since Hank entered Grandma Lou's. "He hasn't made any decisions, at least not yet. Which is why we should stay on his good side."

"Maybe he'll sell to us if we win the contest?"

"Maybe. It's a stretch to think we'll win, though, so I'm not counting on it. But hopefully he'll let us stay in the building a while longer." She rubbed a hand across the back of her neck. Bethany wished she felt more optimistic, but Desmond had taught her to be wary of handsome, suave men like Hank. If he tried to use his position as landlord to get in her pants, she would boot him out the door, without hesitation. As much as she loved Grandma Lou's, no way would she ever fall for a cheating player again.

The doorbell jangled, indicating an incoming customer. Bethany drummed her fingers against the worktable. "I don't trust him. I know he's not Desmond, but I suspect the minute he sees dollar signs, he won't care about anything else."

Travis stopped staring at the wall long enough to shoot her a frown. The hard look in his eyes softened to worry.

She swallowed the bitterness on her tongue but couldn't prevent some of it from leaking into her voice. "His publicist seemed determined to get him to open the fitness center. That's why news crews are in the neighborhood. They want to interview him about his plans."

Travis gazed at her with growing horror. "And to think I asked for a selfie."

Bethany pressed her lips together. "I know. I'm sorry, Travis." She moved toward the front room. "I'll see who's here and get the girls."

CHAPTER SIX

Hank had finished his soup when the front door opened. A pencil-thin, gray-haired gentleman, pulling a large orange cat on a leash, entered on a small gust of wind that looked like it blew him inside. At first, Hank thought the man was a paying customer because he was dressed in a dark gray suit with a bow tie. But then Bethany came running from the kitchen to help the old geezer to a table with a cup of coffee, and what looked like chicken scraps for the cat. It was clear to Hank the man and the cat were another of her "special" guests.

"It's grilled cheese and tomato soup today, Sam." Her lips softened in a gentle smile. "Hi there." She bent to pet the cat, which purred into her hands, before gobbling up the handout. *Lucky cat.*

Sam coughed and wheezed what sounded like a thank you. His hands shook where he held his cup of coffee.

Instead of going back into the kitchen, Bethany pulled out the chair across from him. "What's the matter, Sam? Did something upset you?"

"Cameramen, Bethany. Outside. Lots of people. The police."

"Oh." Bethany looked up to catch Hank's gaze. She scowled before turning to Sam and patting his hand. "Not to worry. They're here because a famous television star's in town. But I have it on good authority he's *not* sticking around. He'll be gone before you know it, and we can get back to normal. Now you relax, and I'll get your lunch."

Sam nodded and Bethany was off to the kitchen in a blur of movement.

"Can we say hi to Mr. Sam and Gypsy, Mama?" Tia asked, from which Hank surmised Gypsy was the cat.

"Sure, but come right back. Mr. Sam looks like he's having a rough day."

The girls ran over with a chorus of hellos for Mr. Sam and then bent to pet Gypsy.

Rosie leaned in close and whispered, "Sam's been sober for going on five years now. We're all proud of him. He's had a rough time of it."

"Mr. Sam, Mr. Sam." Tia turned to Hank. "We've made a new friend. He's nice."

"Who's this?" Sam glanced toward Hank, his expression blank.

Sam must not own a TV. Hank found himself getting out of his seat and approaching their table to proffer a hand. Sam shot him a gold-toothed smile before giving it a shake.

"Great to meet you," Hank said.

"Here's Gypsy. Isn't she nice?" Tana pointed at the cat lapping the milk that Sam had set down for her like it might vanish before she could get the last of it.

Hank nodded in what he thought was a proper response to meeting a cat. He didn't care for cats. They were far too particular, always fussing with their fur and coughing up hair balls. Dogs were much friendlier—well, except for Woodrow, his current dog. Hank hoped Woodrow wouldn't bite Connor, his brother, who was dog sitting for the weekend.

"We can't pet Gypsy while she's eating," Tia warned him, her face taking on the air of a parent imparting advice the child had heard a time or two. "But when she's done, we can. Right, Mr. Sam?"

"Sure, as long as you're gentle. Gypsy likes it when you pet her."

"Girls," Rosie called. "Let Sam eat in peace. Come finish your lunch; it's getting cold."

"Bye. Gotta go." The girls waved and raced back to their mother.

"Where ya from?" Sam asked before Hank could follow suit.

"Uh . . ." Hank couldn't remember the last time he'd been asked the question from someone who didn't already know the answer. "I live in Los Angeles, but I'm not there much. I travel for my job."

"Is that so?" Sam nodded as if Hank were the Dalai Lama and his words required deep contemplation. He settled back in his chair. "I used to travel quite a bit myself when I was in the Navy. Are you a military man?"

"Uh, no."

"Hank's an actor—the one in town causing all the fuss," Bethany interrupted as if the words tasted like burnt popcorn. She had come up behind him with a golden grilled cheese on a plate in one hand and a steaming bowl of soup in the other. She set them in front of Sam with a sweet smile. "Can I get you anything else?"

"I see you have macarons today. I'll take two of those, if you don't mind."

"Absolutely, I don't mind. Let me get them for you." Bethany turned and left without a word to Hank.

Hank couldn't stop an eye roll. He might as well be wallpaper for all the attention Bethany gave him. He hated to admit it, but he was starting to feel a teensy bit annoyed by her treatment. Even if he weren't a well-known Hollywood figure, he was still a paying customer. He hadn't seen many of those since he'd entered her restaurant.

"She don't much like actors." Sam mumbled the words around a mouthful of grilled cheese.

"Yeah, why is that?"

Sam raised a brow and wiped his face with a napkin. "Doesn't trust 'em. Can't say that I blame her." He took a sip of his coffee. Hank watched fascinated as Sam's Adam's apple moved with each swallow, and then he set down his mug with a clang, almost spilling what was left in the cup. "She got her heart broke by one of them theatrical types. Grab a seat, why don't ya."

Hank couldn't stop himself from pulling out a chair, which screeched against the hardwood floor. One of the legs was shorter than the other. He sat, and the chair lurched to one side with a thump. "Who was it?"

"Huh?" Sam looked up from his plate like he'd forgotten Hank was there.

Hank moved and the chair tilted in the opposite direction with his weight. "The actor who broke her heart. Someone on television?"

"Oh, I don't know." Sam picked up the bowl and drank from it, making loud slurping sounds.

Hank waited for him to finish. Watching Sam eat was a study in characterization and a lesson in patience. When Sam set the bowl down, he wore a tomato soup mustache, which he dabbed at with his napkin.

"Yeah, she don't say much about it. Some fast-talking bum from the Big Apple. He took her money and broke her heart, I guess. I don't ask questions. She's a sweet lady that deserves better, that's all I know. She takes care of everyone." Sam's face lost its friendly expression. He squinted at Hank. "What did you say your last name was?"

Hank sighed. "I didn't—it's Haverill."

"Oh." Sam wrinkled his brow and tapped a shaky finger against his lips. "Sounds familiar. How do you spell that?"

As if his ego hadn't already taken a stomping, Sam was present to finish the job. Hank clung to what was left of his dignity and cleared his throat. "H-A-V-E-R-I-L-L. Haverill."

Sam cocked his head and nodded. Hank grimaced, waiting for the inevitable. *Sam may be old, but unless he lives in a cave . . .*

"Scottish?"

Wow. Sam lives in a cave. Hank was saved from answering by the arrival of Bethany and two large chocolate-cherry macaron cookies, which covered the entire plate she placed in front of Sam. *Nice lady indeed.*

"Here ya go. I made them this morning." She turned to Hank. "I upheld my part of the bargain—you've been fed. I hope you can now see the quality of the food and how special this place is to everyone."

"Sure I can." He suspected Bethany had a lot to do with what made the place special.

"And how devastating it would be to this community if we couldn't continue to operate?"

"I can imagine."

"So you'll continue renting to us?" Bethany turned hopeful gray-green eyes on him.

"Well, I don't know . . . why don't we discuss it over

dinner tonight?" He flashed her a smile women tended to find persuasive.

She hesitated, frowning, and the temperature in the room seemed to drop ten degrees. "Sorry, I can't. The restaurant stays open late." She motioned behind him. "Your bill's on the table."

He looked over to see a yellow piece of paper tucked underneath his empty bowl next to the fifty. Rosie and the girls had vanished, but a few of the other tables were occupied with what looked like regular customers.

"You can pay up front." No warm smiles. No free meals. She wanted him to leave. She hadn't bothered to disguise it. He was being dismissed.

And she was right—he should go. He had only meant to take a small break from his responsibilities—he'd stayed far longer than he'd intended. Elizabeth would be frantic by now. Hank needed to find her and get the interviews over with. Then he would head to his hotel and have a nap. What did he care if Bethany gave him the time of day or not?

He rose to his full height of six foot four. Problem was, he didn't care for the feeling of being brushed aside. It felt like a challenge.

He made a show of walking to his table, pulling out his chair, and settling into it like he had all the time in the world. The chair remained solid and straight on the floor, thank God. He had begun to feel like he was on a ship.

She followed him as he'd expected she would. "You're not finished?"

He kept his expression serene and blinked up at her. "I can't leave without trying one of your amazing whoopie pies. Rosie told me they're quite good. Speaking of Rosie, where did she and the girls disappear to?"

Bethany's eyes narrowed as she gathered his empty plate and bowl. "They're in the kitchen. They help out on Fridays." Her hands brushed by him. The scent of vanilla hung in the air. "There are camera crews outside looking for you."

He groaned. "All the more reason for me to stay inside."

She paused over the dishes. "I thought actors loved the camera?"

He fiddled with his glass. "I do, most of the time."

"Then why are you in hiding?"

He thought about lying. He didn't owe her the truth. She would laugh in his face. She had made it clear that she didn't think much of him.

He glanced up to catch large eyes, framed by long eyelashes. Eyes he could drown in. Their color was somewhere between the sky on a cloudy day and the deep green of the sea.

"I'm exhausted." And feeling sorry for himself after his girlfriend Melanie had left him. They'd fought for most of their relationship, so he wasn't exactly sorry to see her go, but he didn't enjoy being discarded like a piece of trash.

"You can't take a vacation?"

"Not in the middle of the season."

"So take a vacation when the season ends."

"I can't afford it."

Her face lost all expression, and her eyes frosted over like a pond in winter. She picked up the dishes, the spoon rattling in the bowl. "If you want me to feel sorry for you, it's not working. You own this building. You have a place to sleep and food to eat and I'm sure a hefty paycheck. There's plenty of folks around here who have nothing."

He sighed and closed his eyes. He had nowhere to go and no one he cared to spend time with. And even if he had, he needed the money to pay his bills. He'd told the truth. Although he had coughed up the funds to buy the building, he couldn't afford a vacation at the moment. He'd made a series of bad financial decisions when he was younger. He had a slew of staff dependent on him for income. Hell, the taxes for his Los Angeles home alone cost half a million a year. And with Melanie's lawsuit, he had massive legal fees to pay, not to mention the price of his publicist, agent, assistant, stylist, bodyguard . . . to name a few. His show wasn't going to last forever. There were rumors it was on the chopping block. He needed to look for work, not go on vacation.

He opened his eyes. Bethany had paused again, staring at him like he had a pair of devil's horns poking through his scalp. The sight must have been fascinating because she didn't look away. Hank found himself running a hand over his head to verify it was horn free.

He lifted his shoulder in defeat. He hadn't expected her to believe him. She was a stranger. She didn't like actors. And now he owned her building and would put her out of business if he opened that darn fitness center. It wasn't surprising that she didn't trust him. "I'm not looking for sympathy."

The truth is I'm depressed. My girlfriend's gone, my show's going to be canceled, and I don't feel like being in front of a camera right now. "I do want to taste a whoopie pie, though. And I wouldn't mind some company, if you'd like to join me."

Bethany's expressive face fluctuated from suspicion to worry to fear before settling on wary. "Why?"

"I don't like to eat alone."

Hank watched as she took in his statement and weighed it for validity. Though he couldn't help a small grin when he noticed the smudge of flour that dusted her forehead. Her eyes sifted him within their depths, searching for truth maybe—or honesty? Whatever she saw brought another rosy sheen to her cheeks. The hardness in her eyes softened and dissolved, reminding him of frozen grapes. Underneath the frost, there was nothing but sweetness.

"I'll bring you a whoopie pie."

She took off with a rattle of dishes. Minutes later, she returned with a giant whoopie pie on a blue china plate that could have been served at a tea party and a tall glass of milk.

"Take a break and talk to me while I eat?"

His gaze followed hers as she shook her head and glanced toward the clock, whose fork and knife hands were almost at the one. Underneath hung a worn dollar bill inside an old-fashioned frame that looked as ancient as the building.

"I shouldn't. I have snickerdoodles in the oven and need to roll meatballs for soup. And then I need to make quiche for tomorrow's breakfast and reprice products on the shelves."

He put on his best smile—the one *People Magazine* had labeled "most magnetizing." "Please."

Her cheeks flushed like roses in bloom. "Well, I suppose I can spare a minute or two."

Hank found himself grinning like a crazy fool, but he didn't much give a damn.

CHAPTER SEVEN

"This is good."

Bethany fingered her apron and watched as the blond hunk across from her closed his eyes and took another giant bite of whoopie pie. Was she crazy? This was the self-centered jerk who would open a fitness center or sell her building on a whim. She knew it was in her best interest to let him stay and ply him with food, but she shouldn't let herself be mesmerized by the way he enjoyed her cooking. She should stay focused on her business.

"Where did you learn to bake like this?" He took a large gulp of milk and wiped his lips on his napkin.

A warm feeling filled her belly. The feeling she got whenever her cooking brought comfort to another. Despite all the warnings she'd given herself over the last couple of hours, she could not stop a smile from spreading across her face. "My grandmother. The filling is a family secret." She lowered her voice and applied her best gangster accent. "I could tell ya, but then I'd have to kill ya."

He laughed, the sound as strong and rich and attractive as its owner. "I'd die happy. It's delicious. I've never had better. Your grandmother must be quite the cook." He opened his mouth and devoured the rest of the cookie.

Another warm tingle shot through her. "She was. She and my grandpa opened Grandma Lou's and left it to my parents. It was meant to be a restaurant, but Grandma Lou had a soft spot for the hungry. So she began feeding them from her kitchen, and we've continued the tradition. I have a lot of memories in this place. Travis and I grew up working in it."

"Your parents are retired?"

"Oh—no." She looked toward the door as if she'd spotted a customer. She hated this. Her parents had been larger-than-life. It always shook her to say they were gone. As if some part of her thought they were still going to walk through the door, her dad singing the donut song. *Well, I walked around the corner, and I walked around the block, and I walked right into the donut shop . . .*

"What happened?"

Her gaze flew to Hank's. He watched her from under hooded eyes, making her realize his casual questions and laid-back pose were a front. He saw much more than she had given him credit for.

She swallowed, loosening the tightness in her throat. "They passed away in a car accident several years ago. Today's the anniversary of their deaths. Drunk driver."

"I'm sorry." He sounded sincere, as if he understood her pain and sympathized. *Silly. What did Hank Haverill know about loss?*

He stretched his hands and placed them behind his head in a gesture she was beginning to recognize as uniquely his. She yanked her gaze back to the table. To cover the awkwardness of the sudden movement, she asked the question foremost in her mind. "Why do they want you to open a fitness center in Cleveland?"

"I was born here."

"You were? Here?" God, she sounded like one of his rabid fans. "Well, not here but in Cleveland?"

He nodded. "Not far from here. My grandfather always loved this building."

Most people who had been in the building loved it—it was that kind of place. Built more than a hundred years earlier as an inn, it possessed the stately elegance of a bygone era. The outside was weathered red brick and the long windows were set off by charming white fleur-de-lis. Inside, the building possessed high ceilings and wood floors and a sense that time stood still. The old soda fountain counter served as a place to display baked goods and housed the register.

"Where did you grow up?" she asked.

He shrugged as if the answer were trivial. "Not here. Many places. My dad was in the military. We moved to Virginia when I was a baby. I'd lived in ten states by the time I was ten."

"And where do they live now, your parents?"

His lips drooped at the corners, and he hunched forward until his hands rested on the table again. "My dad and I aren't close. I've no idea where he lives right now. My mom died when I was twenty."

"I'm sorry." She couldn't stop a shiver. So he *had* understood her loss. Lived it. "I had no idea. Was it—an auto accident?"

"Nah." He grimaced, and she knew without quite knowing how that whatever had happened to his mother was as bad as a car crash. He didn't elaborate, though, putting Bethany in the strange position of wanting to know more but not wanting to pry. Curiosity warred with courtesy. Curiosity won.

"What was it?"

He moved forward, balling his napkin in one hand. Bethany wasn't certain he would answer, but he did, his voice rough and scratchy and an octave lower.

"Brain aneurysm."

"Oh geez." She shouldn't pry. Even TV stars were entitled to privacy. On impulse, she reached out and patted his arm, touching golden hair. "I'm sorry."

Heat enveloped her. She gazed at her hand in horror, pulling it back as fast as she could without being obvious, then stuffing it under the table and into her apron pocket. What was she doing? She had no business touching him. "That's awful," she finally added.

He offered a lazy shrug again, his gaze still tracking her hand. "It was a long time ago."

"There's no one else—a brother or sister?" She struggled to recall if she'd heard anything about his family.

He laughed, but it was not cheerful, and lifted his gaze from her apron to meet her startled expression. "What are you, a reporter?"

She sucked in a breath at the sting, hating the sarcasm and tone of his voice. Tears threatened, taking her by surprise, and she looked away. It was the emotion of the day. That was all. Why should she care if Hank Haverill thought her a busybody? After he left Grandma Lou's, chances were he would sell the building, and she would never see him again.

Her gaze met his and eyes the color of a perfect summer sky warred with her own. They seemed to suck all the oxygen from the room. Her earlier question still hung in the air, making Bethany wish she could take it back. She pushed her chair out. "I should get back to work."

Hank held out a hand. "Don't go. Please, I didn't mean to snap. It's just, I'm asked a lot of questions. All the time. But this . . . sit, please. I'll explain."

Against her better judgment, Bethany sat—maybe because she believed his apology or maybe because she wanted to know the answer.

He cleared his throat and fingered the etchings in the wood table, his head bowed as if in prayer. "I have two half-sisters and a half-brother. All from different mothers. I've never met my sisters. I only recently met my half-brother, Connor."

He looked up, and his gaze met hers. Sympathy welled inside her like he'd drilled for oil and found her weak spot. Her insides melted, but she did her best not to let pity show on her face. Pity shut down confidences faster than a lightning strike.

"This isn't something I tell reporters." He quirked his lips in a half-hearted smile. "I'd appreciate it if you kept it to yourself. My dad was popular with the ladies. He was also a terrible father."

Bethany placed a hand over her heart. "Look how you've turned out. I bet he's sorry you don't keep in touch."

Instead of answering, Hank leaned back in his chair, ignoring the cell phone next to his plate, which seemed to vibrate every few minutes with an incoming call. "I didn't say we don't keep in touch, just that we're not close. He contacts me every few months or so."

"You don't know where he lives?"

"He's a nomad. Has trouble holding down a job. He never stays in one place for long."

"He wouldn't make the effort to call if he didn't care."

Hank raised his eyebrows and accompanied it with a snort of laughter. "Whatever you say, Pollyanna."

Heat flooded her cheeks, but she kept her voice firm. "A dad doesn't call his child unless he cares."

He slanted a brow. "This one calls because he wants money."

She opened her mouth to argue, then shut it again, causing him to give her a superior smile.

"I told you he's a terrible father."

She puckered her lips. "Well, you have your brother, right?"

Hank shook his head and laughed, raising his glass of milk in a toast, then tossing down its contents like a shot of tequila. She must have looked stumped because he set the glass down with a sigh and continued. "More like he has me. My brother's nineteen. He looked me up because he needs money for college and a place to live. He's bright. Studying business. I couldn't see the sense in making him struggle."

"He lives with you?"

Hank shook his head and stretched his long arms behind his head. "No, he lives on campus. UCLA. Now I've satisfied your curiosity, it's my turn, Beth."

"Oh." She swallowed a bubble in her throat. Her father had been the only one who'd ever called her Beth. She hadn't realized how much she'd missed the simple nickname.

She squinted at him. He looked lazy and relaxed but somehow Bethany knew he wasn't. She dropped her gaze to the table. A perfect rose scarred the wood. The rose had been there all of Bethany's thirty-two years, even longer. Her father had carved it for her mother when they'd been teenagers in love. How could she ever bear to lose this old place? Bethany's eyes burned, but she refused to give in to tears. Instead, she swallowed and raised her head, looking over Hank's shoulder and not at his face. "What could you possibly want to know about me?"

"Who's the actor who broke your heart?"

Bethany gasped, her eyes flicking to his intense gaze before she could prevent it. His question was so unexpected, it felt like he'd dumped a bucket of ice water over her head. She tried to laugh it off and failed. She managed a croak. "He's not an actor."

"Who is he then?"

"Just a chef."

"Someone famous?"

She couldn't help making a face, because Desmond's recent commercial success after he'd stolen her money and broken her heart struck at her pride. "Yes."

He nodded as if that solved some puzzle he'd been working out in his head and leaned forward, folding his hands together. "You're not going to tell me his name?"

She forced herself to stare into his beautiful blue eyes. Strange to think of a man's eyes as beautiful, but they were. Soft as sea foam but deeper than the bottom of the ocean. "Why do you care?"

He smiled, slow and easy, until it reached every corner of his face, revealing his dimples. "I don't know. Do you still love him?"

"Er . . ." For a moment, Bethany's heart stopped before beating a rapid staccato against her ribs and then settling again. Was Hank Haverill flirting? With her? *He's an actor. A celebrity.* Love 'em and leave 'em—that was the secret celebrity code of non-ethics they all followed, wasn't it? And Hank had already admitted he needed money. He wouldn't be sticking around Cleveland for long. He was amusing himself out of boredom or for some other bizarre reason. Well, she refused to be his plaything.

Hank tilted his head and waited. The staccato drumbeat in her chest started up again, louder this time. "Cat got your tongue?"

The cell phone buzzed next to his left hand, causing Hank to glance at it. His lips turned down. "Sorry, it's a text from my agent. I have to make a call. But don't go anywhere. Our conversation is not over."

Bethany was pretty certain her rear end was glued to the chair and her feet to the floor because she couldn't move even if she wanted to.

But Hank was wrong. Their conversation was over. It had to be.

She didn't know what Hank Haverill's motive was, but he must have one. Maybe he wanted her to play nice with the press after he booted her out to launch his fitness center.

Her hands hurt, and she looked at them as if they belonged to someone else until she realized she had a death grip on the table.

She wouldn't be taken in by another con artist, even if he was gorgeous, intelligent, and a TV star. She wouldn't let him destroy her family's legacy. Put her and the other tenants out of business on a whim.

She just had to keep reminding herself of that fact.

CHAPTER EIGHT

"Why haven't you been taking my calls?"

To say Blackie sounded annoyed would be an understatement. Hank moved to an empty table, cupped his hand around the phone, and kept his voice low. "I was eating lunch."

"For over two hours?"

"It was a four-course meal."

"I don't care what it was, I've been trying to reach you because I've got news."

"What news?" The back of Hank's neck tingled, and he straightened in his chair. The last time the back of his neck tingled was two weeks ago when he'd learned he was being sued for $5 million because Melanie claimed his dog, Woodrow, had chomped her leg on a private plane trip, and he did nothing to stop it.

"It's not good. Are you sitting down?"

Hank eyed the wood table. Someone had carved initials into the solid surface: B + D, then scratched over the D so it was almost unrecognizable. He ran a finger over the B. "Yeah, I'm sitting."

"The network is canceling the series."

Hank let out the breath he was holding in a rush and tried to stop the sinking feeling—like he had swallowed a brick—from taking over his stomach. He'd known this day was coming. Had prepared himself. Despite its initial popularity, the show had run its course. Its ratings had been down since December, and the network had put the show on temporary hiatus. In television, that spelled death. It was only a matter of time until the show was canceled. He knew that. Everyone knew that.

Hank cleared his throat. "I'm not surprised."

"Well, have you considered Elizabeth's idea?"

"Yeah."

"Good."

Hank lowered his voice, trying not to let the desperation he felt slip into the conversation. "What about Robin Hood? I thought the studio was in talks to make a film, and I would be considered for the part?"

"They were. You are. There are just no guarantees here, Hank, which is why I think you ought to open Fitaholics. It'll be another source of income. Regardless of the network's decision to cancel the show, people still know and admire you as Apollo—well, they admire your physique. A fitness center will be all the rage. Your name and image will carry a lot of weight. I think it will be a big success. And what better place to open the flagship store than in the town where you were born."

The B on the table, Hank noticed, was carved deeper than the D. Someone wanted to make sure everyone who sat there could see the letter.

"You know what it's like in this business." Blackie continued talking. "There are no guarantees. And there's lots of competition from youngsters. Word on the street is Chambers is up for the role."

Hank cleared his throat and dropped his head in his palm, clutching the cell phone next to his ear. "Why do they want Brent Chambers? He's tall and skinny. No personality either."

"Yeah, well, Mister No Personality was just voted sexiest man alive. He's got that English accent all women love. And now he's with Melanie."

He snorted. "She sure didn't waste any time, did she?"

"It doesn't matter what's in between your ears in this business. You know that. It's all about who you're with and how you look. Women love Chambers. You need to make a change while you've still got it going on. This will be an alternative source of income and that's important to all of us who've stood by your side since the beginning."

"Yeah, about that, I'm not so sure—"

"Jesus Christ, Hank. Are you even listening to me? Your series has been canceled. You are out of a job. I'm looking for another opportunity, but other than the possible movie, there's nothing right now outside of cheesy car commercials, and those aren't going to pay enough to keep the lights on. Not if you want to maintain the lifestyle you're accustomed to."

Hank rubbed his fingers across the table surface. There were plenty of distinguishable letters carved into the wood and dings and scratches all over, but no more Bs. Someone had chiseled a cupcake into the corner.

"Hank, you with me?"

"Yeah, sorry." Hank looked out the window. The sun reflected off the windowpane, making him sweat, despite the old air conditioner cranking in the place. From the kitchen, he could hear the clear sound of a mixer. He raised his head and sniffed. Vanilla and coconut permeated the room. Bethany, he noticed, had left their table.

"As I said, unfortunately, you've been typecast as a superhero. The public isn't clamoring for superheroes right now. The market's oversaturated. They want the more conventional James Bond type."

Hank noticed how the hardware store across the street had an "out to lunch" sign on the door—an extended lunch since it was almost one-thirty. The town was quite quaint if you ignored the iron bars on the lower windows. Not the best location for safety, but Elizabeth believed the gym would attract the young professional crowd that had moved into the area due to special tax incentives Cleveland offered residents.

An audible sigh came through the phone. "I hope you're paying attention. The idea's a good one, and we all stand to make money outta this deal. I'd suggest you jump on it. Have you signed the papers?"

Hank ran his fingers across his chin, feeling stubble. Maybe Bethany had something against unshaven men? "I bought the building. It was a steal. Plus, my grandpa always loved it. But I haven't decided about Fitaholics. It's a big investment of time and money."

"Hank, you know I love you, man. I wouldn't steer you wrong. You got that?"

"Sure." Hank realized Blackie's question had been a rhetorical one, and he had moved on.

"Listen, I want you to spend the weekend thinking about your situation. I mean seriously thinking about it. I get why you broke up with Melanie. I do. But did you give any thought to how that would piss off her hotshot-producer father?"

"No, I—"

"He has a lot of clout, and he ain't happy. LA's a small town. Word spreads fast. The chances of you landing another role in the next few months like the one you had are slim. Hollywood has been better to you than to most. But let's not push our luck, eh? Promise me you'll at least *consider* the fitness center idea."

Hank rubbed his burning eye sockets. The mixer had stopped, and a woman's voice sang what he thought might be a Christmas song—ironic since it was the height of summer. He strained to listen and caught the word baby—"Santa Baby" or maybe "Baby, It's Cold Outside"? Definitely something baby. The voice was warm and sultry, like the hot summer day.

"Yeah, sure."

"Great. From the pics I've seen of that old building, you'll be doing everyone in town a favor."

Unbidden, Bethany's panicked face appeared in Hank's mind. "I didn't say I'd open a fitness center. I said I'd consider it."

"Yeah, well, don't wait too long. We have a window of opportunity here. You need to strike while the iron's hot. 'Forged in Fire,' right, Apollo?"

Blackie's gruff laugh rang through the phone until Hank had to pull it from his ear to prevent deafness. One bright spot about the show being canceled? He wouldn't have to hear its annoying theme song at least once a day. What did it even mean?

"I'm looking out for your best interests, you know. We all are."

"Sure."

"Okay, kid. Call me when you've made your decision,

got it? But don't take too long. This situation calls for decisive action. We're all counting on you."

Hank remained there a moment, grimacing at his phone after he'd ended the call. Then he texted Elizabeth. He'd played hooky long enough.

CHAPTER NINE

Bethany stopped singing Christmas songs and cracked another egg to add to the beef and breadcrumb mixture. There was only one way to mix meatballs and that was with your hands.

Who's the actor who broke your heart?

The melody hadn't blotted out the memory of Hank's deep voice, which echoed in her mind like a tolling bell. She put on rubber gloves, trying to stop a shiver from running down her spine. Travis was out front, waiting on customers and wiping down tables. They'd had an influx as word spread of their famous visitor. Rosie stood next to her, helping the girls make cookies.

Do you still love him?

Bethany put her hands in the bowl and squeezed the mixture, but her mind was not on the task. She couldn't stop the sound of Hank's voice in her thoughts. And the look in his eyes. Like he wouldn't rest until he had dragged her heartbreak from her.

Our conversation is not over.

Another shiver. It was over. He must have left the

premises by now. The phone call he'd made had been serious. She could tell by the way his voice had lowered, and he'd hunched over his phone to guard it from prying eyes. Her eyes.

"Are you cold, honey?" Rosie asked.

"What?"

"You're shivering like you're cold. And you're singing about it being cold outside. You're not getting sick, are you?"

Cat got your tongue. "Oh, no. Just thinking about—stuff."

"I know what you're thinking about—your hot customer. Wowza, did the temperature in this place just go up or what? No wonder you're singing winter songs."

"Don't be silly." Bethany refused to crack a smile.

"Did you get your picture with him? The girls and I did."

"Didn't even think about it."

"You should have. It's not every day a TV star joins us for lunch. I can't wait to post it on my Instagram. Is he still out there?"

Bethany frowned and rolled a meatball. "I don't know."

Rosie's eyes widened. "You're a better woman than I am, that's for sure."

"Hi, Mr. Hank," Tana said. "We're making heart cookies. Aren't they nice?"

"Speak of the devil." Rosie's voice dipped, and she moved her lips like a ventriloquist. Her normal bright smile remained in place, a trick Bethany wished she could master.

Hank lounged in the doorway, blinding as the sun. Heat shot through her body, forcing a gasp. Her lungs and throat froze. His warm gaze zeroed in on Bethany before taking in the cookies the girls were painting with red icing. "Sure are, sweetheart." He winked. "You two master chefs need any taste testers?"

"You can try one of the broken ones." Tia pointed to a crumbled cookie.

Hank pulled himself away from the wall and moved toward them, his gait smooth and confident. "Don't mind if I do." He scooped up the partial cookie and popped it into his mouth. His eyes closed in mock excitement before he opened them again. "Wow. You girls sure are some bakers. These are delicious. Are you positive you made these?"

"We did," Tia said. "We're not lying."

"I don't know if I believe you. Better try another one." He nabbed another broken cookie and shoved it in his mouth, to the girl's delighted laughter.

Bethany refused to be swayed by his adorable antics. "You're still here," she observed dryly as she forced her hands to continue making meatballs.

"Disappointed?" He smiled, and his eyes shone with some unnamed emotion.

Rosie chuckled and clicked her tongue. "She's not."

Hank leaned his long arms against the worktable. "I told you our conversation wasn't over."

Oh, but it was. At least for her. Bethany lowered her eyes to the bowl and continued shaping meatballs, one after the other. "Did you need something?" Her skin tingled. Despite her brain's warnings, her hormones bowed to his god-like presence.

"I have to head out, but I promised you dinner. What time does the restaurant close?"

"Not until seven. Then there's cleanup after. I won't get home until nine. I'm afraid it's impossible."

"I can help Travis close as long as you're okay with the girls being here," Rosie offered.

Bethany frowned. "Sure, I'm okay with the girls being here, but that's not necessary. I don't need dinner." She managed a quick glance at Hank. "You're off the hook."

His lips slowly tilted upward. "But I'd like to, Beth."

She kept her voice firm. "I can't. And don't call me that." She pulled a large plastic bag from under the work-table and began filling it with meatballs.

Rosie let out an exaggerated cough, causing Bethany to glare at her. She didn't need any interference.

Hank persisted. "What if we have dinner inside the restaurant? After you've closed. I'll do the cooking."

Bethany was certain her mouth hung open.

He laughed, the sound low and attractive. "What, you think I don't know how?"

"No." Bethany removed her gloves, tossed them in the trash, and sealed the bag of meatballs. "I figured you have your own personal chef."

Hank grinned, and Bethany couldn't miss how his eyes crinkled at the corners and his dimples flashed.

"I do. But only on set. The rest of the time, I fend for myself. So how about it?" He batted his eyelashes. "Wouldn't you like to tell your friends Apollo cooked for you?" His smile morphed from charming to wicked and the heat in the room rose another notch. "We can even take a picture for your Instagram." He turned his head and winked at Rosie.

Now Bethany did laugh. The man could charm a rattlesnake. Why should she say no? She wanted to save her business and those of the other tenants, and it was only an evening. She would use the opportunity to convince him to let her repurchase the building. She tipped a shoulder. "All right."

Hank grinned. "I'll see you at seven." He turned to

leave as Travis rushed into the room, making a beeline for them, looking like he had to take an exam and had forgotten to study.

"There's a roomful of customers in there." He pointed at Hank. "Fans wanting your autograph. And a lady. She says you're needed for an interview." Travis turned to Bethany. "She wants to bring cameras inside Grandma Lou's. What should I tell her?"

"Tell her no." Hank responded before Bethany could. "I'll do the interview outside." He touched Bethany's arm and warm heat traveled to her heart. "I'm not looking to cause problems."

He nodded and left before Bethany could ask the most important question: Was he planning on putting her out of business?

HANK FOUND himself whistling on the way out the door, and there was a bounce in his step that hadn't been there before. He told himself it was because of all the sugar he'd eaten, but he knew no amount of sugar had ever given him this particular jolt of happiness.

"You'll stand here, Hank." Elizabeth pointed to a spot on the sidewalk marked with a piece of yellow tape. A crowd of at least a couple hundred had gathered to watch the proceedings.

He stepped on the spot, smiling widely for the camera operator who snapped a photo and then peered through the lens to study it before snapping another one. Hank kept his smile fixed in place until the photographer gave him a thumbs up sign.

Then Elizabeth pointed to a female reporter in a

lavender top and white skirt who stood a few steps away. She had short, straight blonde hair and a thin face. Smiling, she thrust out her hand to shake his.

"Nice to meet you, Apollo. I'm Susan Winchester from *Channel Ten News*."

The cameraman moved into position. Hank eyed the green flashing light, making sure to keep his expression friendly.

Susan Winchester spoke to the camera. "Television star Hank Haverill, who is best known for his portrayal of the Greek god Apollo, is in Cleveland this weekend to purchase the historic Parker building in Tremont. The building was built in 1892 and used as a hotel before it was purchased by the Parker family in 1952 to operate a kitchen, and later, a pantry to help feed the neighborhood. In addition to Grandma Lou's, which is still operated by the family's descendants, the building houses a number of specialty stores, including a popular antique bazaar, jewelry warehouse, and a barbershop."

She turned to Hank and tipped the microphone his way. "Hank, can you tell us why you decided to purchase the historic Parker building?"

"Sure. My grandparents used to live nearby. I visited the building from time to time as a small boy. When I heard it was on the market, I couldn't pass it up."

"I've heard you're in talks with the city to open a fitness center. Is that correct?"

"It is. Fitness has always been important to me, and I've learned a lot over the years, which I would enjoy sharing with others." He recited what Elizabeth had coached him to say, doing his best to sound sincere.

"What about the local businesses in this building? Won't they be displaced when you renovate?"

Hank's palms grew sweaty, but he resisted the urge to wipe them on his shirt. He kept his smile fixed in place. Thankfully, Elizabeth had prepared him for this question. "No decisions have been made at this point, but if we do open a fitness center, we'll work with the current renters to secure another location, if desired. Our goal is to blend in with the local community and make a positive addition to the city of Cleveland."

"I read somewhere you work out four hours every day. How do you manage that with such a busy schedule?"

"It's not easy. But I think staying healthy is important. I try to stick to a daily routine of exercise and eating well." Except today, when he'd devoured more bakery items than he'd eaten in the past five years.

"Well, I think our viewers would agree, you sure manage to make exercise look good. I'll be anxious to try the new fitness center once it's built. Any idea when that might be?"

Hank kept his smile in place. "As I said, nothing's decided at this point."

They finished the interview, which Susan assured him would be on the evening news. Then he signed autographs for a few minutes until his driver showed up to escort him and Elizabeth to their hotel. Hank sighed as he settled into the limo for the drive to their hotel. He closed his eyes for a moment, remembering the delicious cookies and the sound of Bethany's laugh when he'd left her kitchen.

"Now that we've got that out of the way," Elizabeth said, looking at her phone, "you can catch some sleep, and we can have dinner tonight."

Hank rubbed his whiskers. "Sleep sounds good, but I've already made dinner plans."

"Who with? We're supposed to fly out tomorrow, remember?"

"Yeah, let's cancel that. We can fly out Monday. I want to stick around for a bit."

Elizabeth's eyes widened, and she tilted her head. "What's this about?"

"This is where I was born." He hoped Elizabeth would let it go at that, but of course, she didn't.

"Hank, who are you taking to dinner?"

He fumbled in the center bar for a glass and the bottle of Irish whiskey. "Bethany Parker."

She crinkled her nose as if a decomposed body was hidden underneath the leather seat. "The owner of the restaurant? You must be kidding me. Whatever for?"

He poured the golden liquid into the glass and added ice chips. "I promised her I would."

"Let's get this straight. You're staying in town to take out the restaurant owner you're putting out of business? Not the wisest idea, Hank."

He downed the whiskey, enjoying the familiar burn. "I never said it was wise. Just that I was doing it."

Elizabeth made her I-can't-believe-you'd-be-so-foolish face and pulled a glass from the bar along with a bottle of Shiraz. "You're asking for trouble. I'm sure she's been throwing herself at you ever since you entered her restaurant. You're threatening her livelihood. Stands to reason that she'll do anything to convince you *not* to open Fitaholics. Besides, you should know better than to get involved with someone who clearly needs money."

"She's not after my money. She barely acknowledged me today."

Elizabeth rolled her eyes toward the roof of the limo and

took a sip from her glass. "I've seen that act before. Women play hard to get all the time. It's the surest trick in the book to get a guy interested. You should have seen her face today when I told her you owned the building. You would have thought she'd lost a child. Take it from me, the woman's manipulating you."

Hank pictured Bethany as she'd sat across from him in the restaurant, her eyes lighting up while she talked about her parents and grandparents. And the flicker of sympathy he'd caught when he'd told her about his parents. There had been nothing artificial in either expression. "I don't believe she's putting on an act. But does it matter? It's one dinner."

Elizabeth looked like she wanted to say more, but thankfully their driver pulled up to the hotel entrance, putting an end to the conversation.

"Get some rest, Hank," Elizabeth said as she left him to enter her hotel room. "I'll call you later to see how your evening went."

He passed his security card across the lock as his phone buzzed. His assistant Pamela's face flashed on the screen.

"Hi, Hank. You asked me to call you if I heard from the realtor about the house on West 10th Street. Well, he called today. The house you want is on the market. What do you want me to do? Should I make an offer on your behalf?"

Hank stilled in the doorway of the suite. The plushness of the room could rival the best hotels in New York, but he paid little attention to the interior or his black suitcase, which the hotel staff had brought up earlier. Adrenaline moved through his veins, causing his heartbeat to thrum a wild rhythm. After all this time, the house would be his. The house where he'd spent some of the happiest days of his childhood. The house he associated with his grandparents and comfort and love. "Give them whatever they're asking."

"Got it."

"Oh, and have my financial officer call me."

Hank ended the call, kicked off his sandals, and settled himself on the bed. He should set an alarm, but he would only close his eyes for a second . . .

HANK BLINKED and peered around the dark room. Something had awakened him. A buzzing vibrated against his leg—his cell phone. He fiddled with the down comforter until he found it.

"Hello." He cleared his voice in a futile effort to dispel the sleepiness.

"Hank, sorry if I woke you. It's Dave Atkins from Sunrise Financial. Your assistant asked me to give you a call. She said you're interested in purchasing a house in Cleveland?"

"That's right." Hank propped himself against the pillows, put the phone on speaker, and rubbed his groggy head. "Though that's not why I asked you to call me. Listen, I took your advice and purchased the deed on the Parker building."

"That's an excellent move, Hank. Are we to go forward with the plans for the fitness center, then?"

Hank stretched his legs out in front of him. "Not yet. I'd like to continue to rent for the moment."

"I wouldn't advise that. According to the inspector, the building is in need of some immediate repairs. There are safety issues. It will take a considerable investment in the building to continue renting. Otherwise, you run the risk of lawsuits."

Hank swung his legs over the side of the bed. "What kind of repairs?"

"Some items are simple. Lights that need to be replaced, cracks in the walls that need to be patched—that sort of thing. Others, such as water leaks and a parking lot with potholes are more extensive."

Hank stood and flexed his arms. "I have a wild idea. I'm rather handy. Why don't I take first stab at the repairs?"

"You, Hank?" His advisor sounded surprised. And who could blame him? Hank was a celebrity, not a handyman. "Don't you have more important things to do?"

"Not for at least a month." Hank crossed to the window and pulled the drapes open to view the city below. His city, now that he owned a piece of it. "My show's been canceled. I don't have another job lined up. This would be a productive use of my time."

"But you can probably make more money doing appearances—commercials, speaking events, that sort of thing."

"Maybe, but I don't have anything lined up right now. I'll spend some time in Cleveland."

"Well . . . if you say so." His advisor didn't sound at all sure. In fact, he sounded a lot like Hank had just told him he wanted to join a monastery in Tibet.

"Do me a favor. Email me a list of the repairs the inspector identified, and I'll take a look."

"Very good. I'm on it."

Hank ended the call. That's when he noticed the time. His stomach sank like he'd swallowed one of the hand-weights he'd lifted almost every day of his life. It was eight-thirty. He was late for his dinner date with Bethany. He searched the Internet for Grandma Lou's number, tapped it into his phone, listened to Travis's recorded voice telling him they were busy in the kitchen, and left a hurried message. Since he had no idea where she lived, he would have Louis, his driver, drop him off at the restaurant.

He just hoped she'd get his message and wait for him.

CHAPTER TEN

Bethany eyed the hands of the kitchen clock. *Eight-thirty. No Hank.* He hadn't returned like he'd promised. The energy drained from her body, and with it, her normal optimism.

She pressed a hand against the dull ache in her lower back and tossed the kitchen sponge into the sink. They'd had so many sit-down customers due to his unexpected visit and all the media attention and fans who'd shown up that she'd been on her feet all day.

Bethany put a stack of dishes away in the cupboard, eyeing the familiar blue pattern that had once belonged to her grandmother and mother.

On an ordinary day, the legacy would have filled her with satisfaction, but not today. The evening ahead stretched dull and endless like a laundry line of old clothes. She shook her head as if the movement might shake some sense into her. Had dinner with Hank meant so much?

Bethany selected another dish to put away as the old dishwasher churned next to her. It didn't get the dishes as clean as she liked, but it worked. They'd used every plate, bowl, and glass available, including the prized china, so she'd hand-washed, then dried the more delicate pieces.

She untied her apron, her movements sharp and efficient. She should have expected he would change his mind. Should have learned from experience. He was a celebrity after all. Weren't they all fickle and unreliable?

She stuck her head into the dining room where Travis and Rosie wiped tables and the girls colored pictures of cupcakes in a coloring book she kept on hand for such an occasion.

". . . doesn't need to know," Travis was saying. When he saw her, he held up a giant black bag of trash, as if that was the reason for his comment.

"Who doesn't need to know what?" Bethany asked, entering the room. "You have a dead body stashed in there?" She pointed at the trash bag but didn't wait for an answer. Instead, she grabbed a dishcloth from the nearest table and began wiping it.

Travis sighed and dropped the bag. "You're not gonna like it."

Bethany raised an eyebrow in the best imitation of their mom she could muster and pretended indifference. "If it's about Hank Haverill not showing up for dinner tonight, that's not unexpected. He's a busy man. I'm sure jet lag caught up with him."

Travis scratched the back of his neck. "I suppose I should just tell you. You're gonna see it sooner or later."

"Uh-oh." Bethany's stomach sank further, and she stopped mid-wipe. "See what?"

Travis held up his cell phone, then moved toward her and turned it so she could read the heading on the page he'd pulled up: *Apollo Actor to Open Fitaholics in Historic Tremont.* She grabbed the phone and scrolled.

Underneath was a picture of Hank in front of their restaurant, smiling.

Darn it. Hadn't she known he would give in to pressure and open the stupid fitness center anyway? She returned the phone to Travis and collapsed into the nearest chair. No wonder the jerk had ditched his plans to make her dinner. Afraid to face her wrath. Probably lied about knowing how to cook too.

She clutched the sides of the chair and managed a shallow breath. Then another. She dropped her head in her hands. If she ever saw him again, she would give him a piece of her mind. But not now. Now she wanted to crawl into a hole and cry.

"I'm sorry, Bethany. You were right to suspect him of lying. What are we gonna do?"

"It's a lousy shame, that's what it is." Rosie pushed in a chair. She had stuck around to help with cleanup because they'd had so many customers, and the place was a mess. "He was so kind to the girls. Seemed like such a nice man." She shook her head. "And to think I posted his photo on Instagram. I'll delete it. I promise."

Despite the weakness in her limbs, Bethany forced her body to move. To stand. To pick up the dishrag again and function as normal. "No need to do that on my account. I knew him for a stud rooster the moment I set eyes on him. After every feathery hen in the hen house."

She resumed wiping tables, ignoring the looks of sympathy that Rosie and Travis were shooting her way in turns. "The good news is, since he's not coming, you two can head on out." She motioned to the front. "I'll clear out the register and follow. I don't think any of us will have a problem sleeping after the day we've had. And chances are, tomorrow's going to be busy too."

"Are you sure you'll be okay?" Travis asked. "I don't like you walking to the car by yourself at night. I'll stay and help."

Bethany shook her head and patted his shoulder. "Thanks, Travis, but I need to be alone right now. I've got my pepper spray. Besides, you've got the early shift tomorrow. I can sleep in."

She turned to Rosie. "The girls must be tired, and you have to work tomorrow, so you all need to get home and into bed too."

It was a measure of their exhaustion that neither Travis nor Rosie argued with her plan.

Bethany stayed another half hour to tally the day's earnings—three times the amount of a normal day. She should count her blessings. She'd made money, and now she knew Hank Haverill for the lying, scheming actor he was.

She filled a small plate with tuna, grabbed her keys and purse, placed her hand on the pepper spray, and opened the creaky back door. A single harsh light lit one side of the small, dark parking lot where her car was parked. The other light had burned out long ago. She kept meaning to have Travis replace it.

She gripped her keys and stared into the inky blackness. Bethany glanced toward the bushes. A tree branch snapped, and she smothered a shriek, pointing her pepper spray toward the sound. Nothing appeared after a full minute spent staring down the bushes. She let out a large sigh of relief. At least a couple of times a year, there were stories of people held at gunpoint and robbed in the area.

She darted a quick glance toward the full moon, which cast an aura of romance over the night sky. The irony wasn't lost on her. She bit her cheek and swallowed the feeling of disappointment churning in her stomach like waves on jagged rocks as she set down the plate.

"Here, Walter. Here, kitty." She searched the parking lot for the hungry tabby cat who haunted the place.

A soft breeze caressed her cheek before a flash of something in the sky caught her attention—a falling star. Bethany sucked in her breath as she watched the fading glow. Tears pricked her eyes as she made a wish, more out of habit than with any hope it would come true. But she needed all the luck she could get. Bethany's heart raced as a clunk sounded, and something rustled in the bushes. She gasped, then laughed nervously at herself when Walter appeared, meowing and running toward the dish. She let out her breath and bent to pet the cat.

"Hi, baby. Had a feeling you'd be hungry tonight."

She stood and watched Walter eat, listening to the sound of a car engine approaching, stereo thumping. The vibration passed through her, reminding Bethany it wasn't wise to be alone in the dark, even with an eight-foot fence in place. She held out her car keys and depressed the unlock button until her Toyota let out a reassuring beep and flashed its lights.

A dark figure moved to her right. Blood pounded through her veins. She gasped and, in her haste to get her finger on the button of her pepper spray, dropped her keys.

"It's okay. It's me," a familiar voice said.

"God, Hank." She held her hand over her heart and sucked in air to try and stop it from beating out of her chest. She narrowed her eyes. "What the heck do you think you're doing sneaking up on me like that? You almost got an eye full of pepper spray."

Hank held his hands in the air, as if he expected at any moment to get hit with the lethal stuff. His tall form loomed large, and Bethany caught a whiff of his clean, masculine scent. "What are you doing here?"

"I knocked at the front door, but no one answered. I heard you calling someone. So I climbed the fence." He shrugged his broad shoulders like it was nothing.

Bethany tore her gaze from the fence to Hank to the fence and back to Hank again. Maybe he was part god.

"I work out." Hank grinned. "A lot."

She clenched her jaw. She was not impressed. He could go climb some other girl's fence.

He moved toward her. "Who were you talking to?"

"I was calling Walter." She pointed at the cat, who had not looked up from his plate once to check on her.

"I came to apologize." He reached out a long arm to snag her hand like it was an everyday occurrence, but she dodged it by stepping backward.

"I'm sorry I scared you. I tried to call the restaurant earlier and got voicemail. I'm guessing you didn't check your messages. I know I'm late, but are you still hungry?"

She shook her head and glared, although she knew it was wasted on him in the dark. "The kitchen's closed."

"I could take you to a restaurant. There must be a good one nearby." He moved his head, and she caught a flash of his face in the moonlight. He looked earnest . . . young even.

"I ate already."

"Ice cream?"

"I'm not hungry." She picked up her keys and began walking to her car. He followed, as expected. If there was one thing she'd learned about Hank over the course of the day, it was that persistence was his middle name.

"Coffee?"

"I don't drink coffee at night."

"Then breakfast in the morning."

Bethany stopped at her trunk and placed her hands on her hips. "Stop trying to manipulate me. I read the interview you did today. You're going to open the fitness center and put me and the rest of the tenants out of business. You can forget the whole meal thing. I don't care if you are my landlord. We have nothing to talk about."

She turned and walked to the driver's door. She didn't trust herself to say another word. She was angry and disappointed enough to burst into tears, and she refused to give him the satisfaction of knowing she'd fallen for his line about wanting to cook for her. She'd believed there was more to Hank than what she'd seen on television. She was a fool. Maybe he would take her silence as a hint and go away.

He did not.

"Beth, wait. Let me explain. Please."

She turned, catching another whiff of his musky scent. At some point this evening, he'd changed his clothes because with the parking lot light over their heads, she could see he had on a white V-neck and a pair of dark shorts that showed off his athletic build to perfection. She was eye level with his chest and his lovely golden chest hair. She raised her gaze to his. "I don't like liars."

He flinched, and his lips slanted down. "I didn't lie to you. I was on the phone talking to my financial advisor. I called the restaurant to tell you I was running late. You didn't answer and, apparently, didn't check your messages." He reached out a hand, but she backed away from it. "Please, I'd like to make it up to you."

She narrowed her gaze. He dropped his hand by his side. "That's not what I'm referring to."

"What then?" He looked perplexed, but it was dark, and he was an actor.

"Oh, come off it, Hank. You did the interview, right? Or do you actors have body doubles who talk to the press for you?"

He cocked his head to the side and frowned. "Yes, and I told the reporter nothing had been decided yet. Let me guess, the gossip rags said I'm opening a fitness center, and you believed them."

She crossed her arms. "Yes, they did. So that's how we're going to play this? You're going to tell me you're *not* putting me out of business? Oh, and it wasn't a rag, it was our local news station."

He shook his head. "I'm not surprised. They're always looking for news, and I'm sure Elizabeth set the stage. That's her job. And yeah, that's right, I didn't promise anyone anything. And I wasn't talking over my finances to screw you over."

She scoffed. "The local news lied on purpose, then? Why would they do that?"

"They only aired parts of the interview. I told them the same thing I told you: Nothing's been decided yet. I didn't say that I was going ahead with it. There's a big difference."

She shook her head. "Not where I come from. You told me you weren't feeling the fitness center. Now you're in talks with the city to make it happen? Sounds like lying to me." She turned to open her door.

"Now hold on."

The desperation in Hank's voice stopped her.

"That call I got while we were having lunch was from my agent. My . . ." He shifted from one foot to the other. "My series has been canceled."

She wanted to get in the car and speed off, leaving him in her dust. She wanted to indulge in a good cry followed by a large container of peanut butter ice cream. She wanted to forget she had ever met Hank Haverill. But something stopped her. Some tiny bit of empathy. Acting was Hank's life just as Grandma Lou's was hers. Her hand stilled on the door. She glanced at him over her shoulder. "So you decided maybe you'd better open the fitness center anyway, right?"

"Look, nothing's decided. But the last thing I want to do is put you out of business. I said I'd rent to you and the other tenants until I figure out what I'm doing. I meant it. Can't we just ignore the press for one night?"

She turned to face him, releasing all the pain, frustration, and heartache of the last few years in a single moment like she'd lifted the lid on a sealed pressure cooker. Tears stung her eyes. "No, Hank, *we* can't. This place" —she flung a hand toward the building—"is my livelihood. Travis's too. It's all we have left. It's all that's left of our parents and grandparents too. I can't just *pretend* everything's fine. If you mean what you say, then put it in writing."

She would not cry in front of him. She would not. Bethany opened her car door. She needed to get home and put this sorry mess of a day behind her.

"Beth, wait."

She made the mistake of sparing him a glance. He stood next to her, his hands in his pockets again. He looked lonely and . . . lost.

She let out her breath in a huff. "What?"

"I meant what I said. I'll have my lawyers draw up a lease agreement, which I'll sign, but in return, you have to do something for me."

She settled her hands on her hips and curled her lip. "Like what?"

"Give me a lift home."

She frowned and looked toward the street as if a vehicle might appear. "You don't have a car?"

"No, my driver dropped me off. I'd hoped to catch a ride home with you after."

Bethany tightened her hands into fists. Had he thought he could charm his way into a sleepover? Enjoy a late dinner and then get her into bed? In that case, he wouldn't have needed a ride home. She understood. A TV star like Hank was used to getting what he wanted—including adoring fans throwing themselves into his arms every day.

He must have caught a glimpse of anger on her face because he waved a hand. "Never mind. Forget it. I'll call my driver. My hotel's not far."

She hesitated. He said he would sign a lease agreement, which would guarantee she would be able to rent for the next few months. Long enough for her to learn if she'd won the contest and had the money to repurchase the building. All she had to do was give him a short ride to his hotel. Seemed like an easy enough trade. "You'll sign a two-month lease agreement?"

"Yeah." He nodded his handsome head and seemed almost embarrassed. "I'll have my attorney draw up the agreement and get it to you to sign tomorrow."

She hooked her thumb toward the passenger seat and sighed. "Hop in."

CHAPTER ELEVEN

Hank's stomach twisted like a wrung-out washrag, but he ignored the unusual sensation, putting it down to indigestion. He'd eaten quite a few cookies today. It couldn't be because Bethany thought he was a liar. Up until this morning, she'd been a stranger. Why should he care what she thought?

"Where are you staying?" she said, her voice clipped. She stared at the road ahead, her profile severe.

"The Ritz-Carlton." He settled his head against the cloth headrest and watched her small hands on the wheel. Capable hands. She kept her nails short and unpainted.

"That's what I thought. It's not far. I'll drop you off at the front."

He turned to look at her. "Why did you think I'd stay at the Ritz?"

Now she did flick a glance his way before giving him her profile again. "It's the most expensive hotel in the city."

Like staying in a nice hotel was a sin. He sighed. Her bad opinion of him was worse than the critics in his last review. Like he was all fluff and no substance. What did she want from him? Did she expect him to beg? He tugged on his seat belt, which tightened around his neck like a noose. Fine, he would beg.

"Beth, let's call a truce. Please."

She turned onto Huron Avenue. The Ritz was just ahead. He didn't have much time to convince her to let him make it up to her. Thank God there was a traffic light, and it had just turned red.

"Look." She stopped at the light and turned toward him. Her eyes appeared dark and mysterious in the glare. "I don't know what game you're playing, but I'm not part of your team, okay."

She put her pixie nose in the air. He supposed she was trying to look off-limits, but it served to emphasize her cuteness—like an annoyed little angel. He fought an incredible urge to break through the wall she'd erected . . . to touch her.

Instead, he clasped his hands together and did his best to sound contrite. He wanted to get to know Bethany better. Hank couldn't remember the last time he'd wanted anything more. And this was more than mere physical attraction. He wanted to know what she thought about—her dreams and heartbreaks and loves. He cleared his throat. "This is no game."

She snorted. "Sure it is. You're not used to a woman saying no. I represent a challenge or something, don't I? Be honest. After this weekend is over, you'll be back in Los Angeles. You'll start panicking because you're out of work. You'll start thinking maybe a fitness center isn't such a bad idea after all."

"Well . . ." Hank tapped a finger on his knee.

The light turned green, and Bethany stepped on the

gas. Her lips thinned. "That's what I thought." She pulled up to the hotel. "Here you are, safe and sound."

Her tone could freeze water. She glanced his way, giving him the kind of look a bus driver might give her passengers at the end of the night. A get-off-my-bus-so-I-can-head-home sort of look. Impersonal, tired, cynical.

"Good night, Hank. Good luck with your career. I'll look for your lease agreement in the morning, and I'll make sure you get your rent check on time."

The crazy idea he'd mentioned to his financial advisor earlier surfaced like a fan waving a poster to get his attention. Hank stayed put. "What if I do?"

Bethany turned to frown at him. Now he had her full attention.

"Do what—open a fitness center in my building? Force us out of business?"

"No, stick around." He unbuckled his seat belt. His heart raced as he leaned toward her. "I mentioned that my series was canceled. I have no job, nowhere to be at the moment. And I'm interested in diversifying. What if I invest in your business? I'll start by checking out the building—determine what repairs need to be made." The more he talked, the more the idea took on a life of its own.

Her eyes widened but she remained unmoving—except for her lips, which turned down in a frown. "You can't be serious."

He kept his expression businesslike, looked into her magical eyes, and did his best to persuade her. "Oh, but I am. If I'm going to allow you and the other tenants to stay in the building, I should make sure the structure and businesses are sound. I'll start with yours. Unless"—he raised a brow—"you have an issue with me checking out your place? Is there something you're not telling me?"

She narrowed her eyes. "How long are you talking?"

Hank lifted a shoulder. "It's a historic building. Might be a while. Let's say a month?"

"Where will you stay? At the Ritz?"

"With you," Hank could not resist saying, smiling at Bethany's outraged expression. "Relax, I'm kidding. I have options. It's not a big deal."

She put the car in park, but her hands still gripped the steering wheel. "Don't you have people to inspect the building? What do you know about old structures and repairs?" Her lips parted as if she couldn't quite believe she was considering his idea.

He shot her a superior grin. "A lot. I grew up in old buildings. My mom wasn't much good at fixing things, and as I told you earlier, my father wasn't around. I'm a decent handyman. Don't look so surprised."

He sat on his hands when all he wanted was to touch her—to wipe the surprise off her face. "I noticed the temperature is hot in some places and cold in others—must be due to the way the place is insulated and the age of the air conditioner. And a light is out near the back door. That's a safety issue."

She licked her lips like a nervous cat. The scent of lemons and vanilla permeated the air. Heat flared between them like someone lit a match.

"I know the light's out," she muttered. "Travis will put in a new bulb."

"And there's a drip," he breathed. He couldn't stop himself from eyeing her lips. "From the faucet in your kitchen."

She blinked as he leaned a little closer. "And your dishwasher's on its last leg."

"I know. I'll buy a new one when I have the money."

"What do you say?"

"Say?"

He smiled. She wasn't as impervious to him as she would have him believe. "About me sticking around. To make repairs to your building and . . ."

Just a few inches more and their lips would meet. He could anticipate the velvety softness of hers, taste their sweetness. Hank swallowed, sucked in air, and forced his wayward thoughts back to the matter at hand. "To see if I might want to rent to you long-term."

If he kissed her, she might kiss him back and it could lead to more. *Tonight. Now.* His body got the message loud and clear.

He leaned back and struggled to curb his enthusiasm. He was her landlord. He did not want her thinking a night with him was an even exchange of goods and services. No matter how enjoyable it would be in the moment. They would regret it later. Hank did not want that. No, he was pretty certain he wanted a lot more than sex and regret. He had traveled down that particular highway plenty of times. This time . . . He unfastened his seat belt. This time he wanted so much more.

He smiled and winked. "I'll take that as a yes." Before she could protest, he opened the door and scrambled out with a jaunty wave. "See ya tomorrow, Beth."

BETHANY WATCHED Hank's long-legged stride eat up the distance from her car to the entrance of the Ritz. The door attendant greeted him, all smiles. Hotel staff rushed to offer their assistance, along with a security guard and someone who looked like a bouncer. Two young ladies approached with pen and paper, pleading for autographs. How long had they been waiting?

Bethany forced herself to draw breath.

Hank ran a hand through his hair and tossed a glance Bethany's way, catching her stare. He reacted by presenting her with a wide smile—and those darn dimples. Then he turned to the girls, signed their papers with a slash, and went inside. He didn't look back. Bethany watched the entire scene until Hank and his entourage vanished from sight.

Her hands shook on the wheel. She took deeper breaths, but still her heart beat an unsteady rhythm. Her head felt like an egg had cracked inside it and was about to spill. What was wrong with her? Hadn't she learned anything from her time with Desmond? Weren't all celebrities lazy, lying cheats? And this one—she gripped the steering wheel until her hands were white—could tempt a nun.

She forced her hands to loosen, find the gear shift and put the car in drive, while her heart beat a *rat-a-tat-tat* on the walls of her chest. Hank Haverill played her like a set of drums. Her insides were jumpy, as if she were offbeat because of their latest interaction. Trouble was, Bethany felt somehow like the way to get back on track was to be played again. And she would not let that happen. *Never again.*

She stepped on the gas and headed toward her house—the house she'd grown up in and where she and Travis still lived. A cute yellow bungalow that welcomed her at the end of the day like a sunny smile.

Bethany drew in another sharp breath in a desperate attempt to slow her beating heart. It was one thing to feed and talk to a television star who looked and acted like a Greek god. It was fantastical to think said television star might find her attractive . . . might want to stick around and be with her. He claimed it was to act as a repairman for all the things wrong with the building, but Bethany didn't buy his story for a moment.

She bit her lip. Maybe she was wrong. *Maybe it's my cooking.* But if Hank Haverill wanted her, he wasn't the type of man to show restraint. She had a feeling that whatever Hank desired, Hank got.

She turned onto her street and pulled into the driveway. Travis had left the porch light on, but the inside lights were off, which meant he was in bed. *Thank God.* She wasn't up to talking to her brother tonight.

The blood in her veins churned like water, and her stomach quivered. She sat in the driveway, tilted her head back on the headrest, squeezed her eyes shut, and shivered. She wasn't at all sure she was strong enough to fight her attraction to Hank Haverill.

And that scared the stuffing out of her.

HANK ENTERED his hotel room feeling good, but it didn't take long for his mood to sour. It came in the form of a phone call from dear old dad. The old man possessed a sixth sense capable of zeroing in on Hank's happiness and then blasting the emotion to smithereens.

"Hank, it's your father. Sorry to call so late, but I have something important to talk to you about."

"Does it begin with an M and end with a Y?" Hank put his phone on speaker and closed the blinds on the view of the city and twinkling lights outside. You never knew when a crazed photographer or fan would decide to climb the building just so they could peer inside his window and snap a few pictures. He did not relish the thought of being caught in his boxers.

"No, it begins with a C."

"Coins?" He set the phone on the bed and sank down next to it, eyeing the clean lines of the plush ivory comforter.

"You always did have an odd sense of humor."

"How would you know? You weren't around for the majority of my childhood."

"Are we back to that old song again? How many times have I explained that I visited when I could? I had a lot going on back then."

Hank's blood sizzled like water on a hot pan. Sweat dotted his forehead. He pulled his shirt over his head and shivered as the cool air from the air-conditioning hit his skin. He removed one shoe, then the other and stretched his legs across the bed. "I didn't need a visitor. I needed a dad."

"You have a dad."

"Now who's joking? All right, I'll play along. What do you want . . . *Dad*?" Hank slipped off his shorts until he was sitting in his boxers.

"Connor mentioned you're in Cleveland this weekend, investing in some kind of fitness center. What's that about?"

"Yeah, my advisors and staff seem to think it's a good investment. I'm not sure I'll do it, though. There are four mom-and-pop businesses in the building. If I open a center, I'll force them to move, which would probably make them close. I'm going to be here a while longer, while I figure it out."

"It's not your job to keep a bunch of little mom-and-pop stores alive, is it?"

"Well, no, but—"

"This could be real promising for your brother."

"Opening the center?"

"Yeah. It could be a great career opportunity. You know, I'm real proud of how he's pursuing his education. He's got street smarts, but he's always struggled in school. His grades aren't real good. He'll probably have a tough time landing a job when he graduates."

"What Connor's lacking is stability. It's hard to get good grades when your dad's never around and can't keep a job and take care of his family. His grades will get better now he doesn't need to worry about funding his education."

"Well, he'd never ask you, but I hope you'll consider him as a possible manager after he graduates, when you open the center."

Hank rubbed a hand back and forth across his head to ease the ache behind his sinuses. "Sure, *if* I open a fitness center, Connor's welcome to be a part of it." That would have to satisfy his father.

"I'm not surprised you're staying on in Cleveland. You always did like that city. Remember the old house your mom's folks used to live in?"

"You mean the one you sold out from under me?" He couldn't keep the bitterness from his tone. "Of course I remember. All of my favorite childhood memories were spent in that house. I used to stay a month every summer."

"Now don't get all mad at me. I thought I was doing you a favor at the time. Never understood what you and your mother loved so much about the old place. Just a bunch of crumbling bricks if you ask me. We didn't get much for it when it sold."

Hank rubbed his burning eye sockets and flopped back on the bed. The house was a sore spot. It had been a legacy from his mother's family. It never should have been sold, but somehow his dad had managed it while Hank was half out of his mind with grief.

He put his hands behind his head and studied the curves in the ceiling so he wouldn't lose his temper. A chandelier hung in the middle of an oval medallion above his bed. "Is that all? 'Cause I'm beat. It's been a long day."

"Son, I wish you'd give me a chance. I'm proud of you, ya know. You've done well for yourself. You shouldn't get mad because I'm asking you to send a few opportunities your brother's way. Family first and all that. Speaking of which, I hesitate to ask but . . . I could use a little loan. Just enough to cover the rent and truck payment for the next couple of months. I promise this will be the last time."

"What did you do with the money I gave you six months ago?"

"It's gone."

Gone? "That was ten thousand dollars. What did you do with it? You were supposed to use the money to get settled." He couldn't afford to keep giving money away. Especially now that his series was canceled.

"I did. But we had debts to pay—car loans, your sister's braces. And then . . ."

His father's voice trailed off. Hank leaned closer to the phone. "I can't hear you."

"I lost my job."

Hank stifled a groan. "What was it this time? Fight with a coworker? Showing up late?"

"Guess they thought I called off one too many times."

"I'm not always the most punctual, but even I know you need to show up for work and behave to hold down a job."

"I was sick. Bad case of bronchitis. I've been having trouble keeping up. I can't put your sisters and stepmom through moving again. We just got settled in this apartment in Nashville. It's expensive. Plus, we have to pay utilities. We barely have any money left over for food each month."

A muscle twitched in Hank's jaw. So they had landed in Nashville. "Will five thousand cover it?"

"Yes, yes it will . . . well . . . thanks, son . . . it's getting late, so . . ."

"Goodbye." Hank did not wait for a reply but ended the call. He got up in one fluid movement and prowled the room until he ended up in the bathroom, where he eyed his reflection with distaste. His eyes looked like they could burn a hole through the mirror.

Why had he answered his father's call? He had known as soon as he'd seen the number that the old man wanted money. He always did. It shouldn't have come as a surprise. Yet, somehow, he always took the call, hoping his father wanted something more. Something like a real relationship. Something like the warm affection he'd glimpsed in Bethany's eyes when she'd talked about her family over lunch.

Would he ever know what it felt like to be loved for something other than his money?

CHAPTER TWELVE

Although he was forced to get up with the roosters to exercise during the week, Hank had never been a morning person on the weekends. Until now.

Somehow, he managed to show up at Grandma Lou's, freshly showered and dressed, by nine the next day, which he considered a minor miracle. Bethany wasn't present to notice and be impressed by his early arrival. Travis was behind the counter. The pleasant young man from the day before had morphed into an unhappy proprietor.

"Why are you here?" He greeted Hank with a grunt, wiping his hands on a towel as if he were a boxer anticipating a fight.

"For a donut. I'll take one of those chocolate ones with the sprinkles." Hank pointed at a display of pastries. "And a cup of coffee, black."

Travis glared at him, and Hank thought he might refuse, but he turned and grabbed a coffee cup. He must have decided to keep silent in favor of a sale. *Smart kid.*

Travis pulled a donut off the paper, put it into a brown paper bag, and shoved it at Hank, along with the cup of coffee. "One donut and coffee to go. That'll be four-fifty." He curled his lip. "What's with the shiny new toolbox?"

Hank gave him an easy smile. "You like it? Bought it across the street just now."

Travis's expression did not change. Hank continued. "I had some downtime, so I thought I'd check the place out this morning. Make a few repairs."

Travis narrowed his eyes, his displeasure filling his entire face, all the way to his hairline.

Hank kept his tone casual. "I'm the landlord and the building needs attention. Where's your sister?"

"Not here."

Obviously. Hank smothered a sigh. "When do you expect her?"

Travis stiffened, jutting his chin. "Not sure. She didn't say." He thrust a hand out to Hank with his change.

Hank didn't move. "You keep it."

Travis did the staring act again before pulling his hand back with the generous tip. The kid showed promise . . . reminded him of Connor.

Hank's phone buzzed in his pants pocket. He turned and found a booth to unload his stuff before checking the number. *Elizabeth.* He had forgotten. She'd arranged some publicity stunt for the day. He breathed deeply and tried to dispel the feeling of doom that hung over him like a dark cloud. He had promised her he would pump iron at the local gym to attract a crowd, so she could plug some pics of him on Instagram . . . or maybe it was TikTok. He had trouble keeping track.

Hank sent Elizabeth a text to reschedule and set the phone down to devour the donut. *Pastries two days in a row and no workout.* He would need to redouble his efforts on Monday. *Not today, though.* Today he'd reserved for himself and Bethany Parker. If she ever showed. Last night, he'd ordered New York City cheesecake to be delivered after Rosie told him it was Bethany's favorite. Now he only needed to convince her to have dinner with him. He watched the door like a hawk in between checking his texts. Then he remembered the wobbly chair and that he was supposed to be fixing things. So he crawled under the table to give it a look and that's how he overheard the women.

"No dogs allowed in the place, Daphne. Remember, the owner doesn't like them."

From his vantage point under the table, Hank noticed two pairs of women's feet some distance away. One of them wore stilettos. His gaze rose a little higher to take in a pair of long and shapely legs.

"How could I forget after the scene she made the last time. Not to worry. I left poor Gulliver in the car and cracked the windows. What's she got against dogs, anyway? She lets that old man in here with his awful cat all the time. It's not fair."

The door jangled, but before Hank could crawl out from under the table to see who'd entered, the other woman's next words stopped him.

"I knew her in high school. Straight-A student. She's one of those business sorts, you know. Never married, no kids . . . a *cat* lady . . ."

This last was said as if liking cats was the worst thing in the world, which was not far off from Hank's general feeling about cats, but still . . .

". . . surprised her restaurant is failing."

"I heard from a friend she *did* have a fiancé, but the guy stole money from her and took off. That's why the business is doing so badly. They can barely keep the lights on. A shame 'cause the food is good."

"Yeah, she dated the guy on that cooking show . . . what's the name . . . Chef Master or something."

The woman who knew Bethany in high school let out a high-pitched cackle, which made all the hairs on the back of Hank's neck stand on end.

"No, silly, the Chef King. He lives in New York and has his own cooking show. But he's back in town. I ran into him at the grocery store yesterday. Said he was working on an idea for the next episode."

"That's cool. Well, I heard she's entering some baking contest to try and save the place. The winning restaurant gets a pretty hefty sum of money."

"Hey, we'd better grab a table. This place is filling up fast. Imagine Apollo turning up in our little neck of the woods. If you see him, holler. I wanna get his autograph."

The voices faded as the women crossed to the opposite corner of the café, and Hank let out his breath. Not surprising some of his die-hard fans would show up on the chance he would be here. He should have thought of that. But now he had something more to think about. *Bethany and the Chef King.* A dark feeling settled in his stomach like a bad dream.

Hank wedged a folded napkin beneath the chair leg to keep it from wobbling and dragged himself out from under it to sit at the table, doing his best to remain hidden. If he were going to make Grandma Lou's a hangout, he'd need to come up with some sort of disguise.

He whipped out his cell phone and did a quick search for Chef King. An image popped up of a clean-shaven man, thirtyish, with spiked brown hair. Hank scanned the caption—*Man Candy: Desmond Mitchell talks about life as the Chef King.* He was dressed in a blazer and a collared shirt, open at the neckline. The crossed arms and expression on his face smacked of confidence and ego and a certain weakness—like he would throw a temper tantrum if he didn't get his way.

The doorbell chimed and Hank glanced toward the entrance. A dozen people, give or take, came through the doorway. *No Bethany*. He stifled his disappointment.

Someone tapped his arm. Hank turned to see a teenager with purple hair and a spike through her lip. She held out a black Sharpie. "Oh, wow, Apollo. My friends are never gonna believe this. Can I get your autograph?"

Jingle-jingle. The door was on a continuous ringer. Still no sign of Bethany in the crowd.

"Uh, sure." Hank took the pen and stood. "You have something to write on?"

"Yeah." She drew her pants partway down, exposing white skin beneath a deep tan line, and pointed at her bottom.

Hank chuckled. This wasn't the first time he'd been asked to sign a body part. He'd signed hands, arms, backs, knees, legs, and even foreheads. He drew the line at teenage asses, though. "I don't think so."

"Worth a shot." The girl grinned.

Hank couldn't help but laugh. "How 'bout I sign your arm. What's your name?"

The girl held out her arm. "Name's Angie but everyone around here calls me Angel."

"You come here often, Angel?" Hank signed his name with a flourish and handed her the marker.

"Yeah, my parents own the antique bazaar next door. I wait tables on weekends when this place is busy. Like today. The whole city's here to see you."

Hank glanced up and groaned. A line had formed behind Angel, winding around chairs and tables toward the front. The woman with the long legs stood near the exit. He should have given more thought to his role . . . dressed the part. He was supposed to be a maintenance man, not a TV star. "Angel, have you seen Bethany?"

"She's not in early on Saturdays. Hey, is it true you now own this building? My dad says you're going to make us all leave."

Hank frowned. "No one's leaving." He pointed at his toolbox. "I'm here to help. Tell your folks I'll be stopping by to make repairs."

Angel eyed her arm, tracing her finger over his signature. "Really? That's so cool. Hey, will you take a selfie with me?"

"Sure." Hank put his arm around her shoulders and flashed a smile as Angel held up her phone.

He might as well spend the morning signing autographs. As long as he was in the building, the crowd wasn't going away, and it would make Elizabeth happy. He would go back to being the dang maintenance guy when Bethany showed up.

BETHANY BREEZED through Grandma Lou's creaky back door and hung her purse and jacket in the small locker where she kept her things. Although she'd come in the back, it seemed more cars than usual had been parked on the side streets.

She dug the copy of her grandmother's prized chocolate cake recipe from the cookbook and smoothed the worn paper on the worktable. For what must have been the hundredth time, she studied the ingredients with her penciled-in notes. She had memorized the recipe long ago, but looking at her grandmother's familiar scrawl and the cluster of food stains on the paper bolstered her confidence. Time was running out to tweak the recipe. Her entry was due online in six days.

Loud chatter came from the dining room, indicating an influx of customers. Bethany left the recipe on the work-table, washed her hands, and put on her apron. The cupcakes would have to wait. The menu was simple on Saturdays—soup, quiche, and various salads and sand-wiches—but Travis and Angel wouldn't be able to handle a large crowd alone.

She collided with her brother as she headed out of the kitchen. "Is everything okay?"

"Bethany, you're here. I just sent you a text. Apollo's back."

"Now?"

"Yes. He's signing autographs. I thought you said he'd get bored and return to LA?"

Bethany clutched the sides of her apron. "Well, he will. I'm sure he'll be heading back just as soon . . . my God." Panic shot through her system like a bullet. A line of people snaked out the front door and onto the sidewalk.

"See what I mean? The line keeps getting longer. The news is here filming, and that woman Elizabeth showed up. Angel and I can't keep up with all the orders. What should we do?"

Bethany took a deep breath to flush the panic from her brain. "He'll have to leave. I'll tell him. You keep the real customers happy, and call Rosie to see if she can help."

The first thing Bethany noticed when she rounded the corner was the almost empty display case that should have housed dozens of donuts but now held only a few and some crumbs. The second thing was Hank in his element, surrounded by excited fans, all wanting his autograph. She cupped her hands around her mouth and yelled, "Hank. Hank Haverill. Yoo-hoo. Apollo."

Hank didn't glance her way. Neither did anyone else. No one could hear her.

"Hey, can I get some service?" A middle-aged man in a Cleveland Browns jacket leaned on the counter, his lips turned down.

"Yes, I'll be right with you. I just need to get Hank Haverill's attention."

The man scratched his balding head and looked from her to where Hank was surrounded by adoring fans. "He's never gonna hear you. Can't you see he's busy?"

Bethany ignored the man and looked for something to stand on, but every chair was filled. She thought about standing on the counter, but she could picture the news reporter turning his camera on her and the headline the next day: *Grandma Lou's Owner Distressed Over Sale of Building.* She squeezed herself past the counter. That was as far as she got.

"Hey, get in line, lady. I was here first."

Bethany turned to see a skinny teenage boy in cutoffs and a tank. His greasy blond hair covered his eyes. His voice went up and down an octave as teenage boys' voices tended to do. Next to him stood two similarly scrawny friends. Did they have enough to eat? They looked too thin to Bethany. Their clothes were dirty and torn in spots.

Bethany gave them her sternest look, the one her mother always used when she whined once too often. "I'm sorry, but this is important. I own this restaurant, and I need to talk to Hank Haverill. Move aside."

"We all want to, lady." Sarcasm dripped from his voice.

"Look how long the line is. We've been waiting over an hour. It's not fair we have to give up our spot."

Bethany followed his pointed finger out the front door and narrowed her eyes. This was her business. She would not wait in a long line to talk to Hank, and she did *not* have time to argue with a mouthy adolescent. She drew a breath. "Listen."

Her mother used to recite a proverb whenever dealing with difficult customers. Bethany could almost hear her voice. *You can catch more flies, Bethany sweetie, with honey rather than vinegar.* Like the sun poking between dark clouds, an idea shimmered in her mind, building in intensity. She forced her lips into a semblance of what she hoped was a smile. "How would you three like free donuts while you wait?"

The teens looked at the remaining chocolate donuts with sprinkles in the display case, then to Hank, and back to Bethany. Their eyes widened. "Really?" the first boy asked.

Bethany fixed her smile in place. "Yep. Let me line jump, and you and your friends can have the last three."

The boy licked his lips. "These are my younger brothers. You got yourself a deal. We'll take 'em."

She smiled and nabbed the donuts, but paused before handing them to the boys. "How would you like to earn donuts and breakfast or lunch every day for the rest of the week?"

"What do you mean?" The first boy tilted his head, his expression wary.

Bethany kept her voice professional. "I'm offering you a job in exchange for food."

The boy's surly expression vanished, but suspicion flared from his brown eyes. "What job?"

"I could use some extra hands to wash dishes this week. As you can see, we've had a rush of customers."

"Seriously?" The suspicion was replaced by cautious enthusiasm.

"Yes. See that man over there? That's my brother, Travis. He can show you what to do. Give me two hours of your time each morning, and you'll each earn donuts and a meal. Interested?"

"Yes, ma'am," the first boy responded for the group.

"What are your names?"

"I'm Sean, that's Liam, and he's Declan." The boy pointed at each brother in turn.

Bethany firmed her lips. "Okay, Sean, Liam, and Declan. I do have a few rules. No swearing, and you'll wash your hands before you get started and any time you use the restroom."

The boys passed each other a look before the oldest boy spoke again. "Yes, ma'am."

She grimaced. "And everyone around here calls me Bethany."

The boys nodded and the spokesperson responded. "Okay, Bethany."

Bethany proffered a donut to each of them in turn, along with a smile, and moved in front of them in line.

"You," Elizabeth said, when Bethany had made it near the front fifteen minutes later.

"Me." Bethany kept her smile firmly in place. "I run this place, remember? I need to talk to Hank. Get me to the front of the line."

Elizabeth looked at her like she had an orange for a head. "I'm sorry. It wouldn't be fair. There's someone ahead of you. How do you spell your name?"

Bethany wrinkled her nose. "B-E-T-H-A-N-Y."

"Spell your last name."

"P-A-R-K-E-R. What's this for?"

Elizabeth wrote her name on a sticky note and gave it to Bethany. "Give it to Hank. Here's paper."

Bethany clenched her jaw. "I don't want his autograph. I need to talk to him."

"Well, now's your chance."

The couple in front of her moved to the side, and like the parting of the Red Sea, there stood Hank in all his god-like glory.

"There you are." He smiled as if he'd been waiting for her the whole time and not the other way around. "I've been hoping to talk to you." He took the piece of paper, his eyes lighting up like twin sparklers. "You want my autograph?"

"No, I don't want your autograph." She snatched the paper from his hand. "What I want is for you to leave the premises. Now."

His smile dissolved. "And here I thought you'd be happy to see me." He waved a hand at the crowd. "I know this is a little wild, but it's got to be good for business."

"Hank, a crowd of people this size is gonna want to be fed."

His smile reappeared, triumphant. "Right."

"Our restaurant isn't equipped to feed a crowd this large."

"Oh." His face fell. "Sorry, I didn't think about that."

"You need to get out. Fast. Take your fan base elsewhere or tell them you're done, and they should go home."

"Elizabeth's not going to like this."

"Tough."

"Smile." Elizabeth pointed a cell phone in their faces.

"No." Bethany shook her head. "Absolutely not."

"Don't be a spoilsport. Hank's Instagram account gets millions of hits every day. Think about how good all this is for your business."

Hank put an arm around her. Bethany opened her mouth to argue, and Elizabeth snapped the picture.

"Next," she said.

Bethany did not move. "You need to end this now."

"Yes." Hank's eyes glittered, and Bethany realized she had underestimated him again. "If you have dinner with me tonight. We can talk about the repairs I'm making to the building, and I'll give you the lease agreement I promised."

"Next!" Elizabeth shouted.

"Move, woman, you're holding up the line," someone behind her shouted.

"Well?" Hank asked with a grin. "Shall we end the chaos in exchange for one measly meal?"

"I'll have dinner with you, Apollo honey."

Bethany turned to see Daphne Miller in a set of four-inch-high electric-blue heels, skimpy shorts, and a bikini top that showed off her recent boob job.

"My turn, Bethany sweetie." She smirked, cutting in front of the teens, who were too busy downing the donuts and wiping sticky fingers on their clothes to protest. "How do you feel about dogs?" she asked Hank.

Bethany had seen and heard enough. She turned to Hank. "Get rid of this crowd, and I'll have dinner with you."

Hank grinned. "You said the magic words."

CHAPTER THIRTEEN

Bethany eyed her figure in the full-length mirror in her bedroom, fighting a feeling of déjà vu. What were the chances Hank would bother to show up this time? And what did one wear to dinner with a television star anyway?

She stripped off the offensive yellow dress. The plunging neckline was a bit too revealing. Besides, yellow was a happy color, and it looked like lemons, and she sorta smelled like them after spending a good portion of the day baking lemon cookies. She didn't want to smell like food or seem too nice. She wanted to appear businesslike. That's what this was about. Collecting the lease agreement and maintaining her business. Getting Hank Haverill to agree to let her and Travis repurchase the building from him once they had the money.

She yanked a purple dress from the closet and pulled it over her head.

The dress fit her curvy figure without being too snug. No boobs in sight. Plus, purple was the color of royalty, which ought to count for something. She smoothed a hand through her hair. Now to tackle her mop of dark curls.

A knock sounded on the door. "Are you decent?"

Bethany grabbed a hairbrush from the vanity and hollered, "Yeah, c'mon in."

Travis entered, moved a small pile of discarded clothes on her bed, and sat. "You don't need to go out with him. I don't care if he *is* our landlord. I'll tell him where to go."

Bethany ran the brush through her hair. "He's not a bad person, Travis. He plans to fix up the building and rent to us for at least a few months. Why not humor him—it'll cost a couple hours of time?" She squinted at her reflection in the mirror. "And I get a free meal."

"It's cool he's Apollo and all, but why's he hanging around, bothering us?"

She shrugged and found a lightweight sweater. "I suspect he's bored. He broke up with his girlfriend. His show's been canceled. He doesn't have anything better to do. Does it matter? One dinner and we're done."

Travis flopped back onto the bed and stared at the ceiling. "Where's he taking you?"

Bethany frowned at her reflection and pulled a headband that matched her dress over her hair. "I don't know. He didn't say, and I forgot to ask. Somewhere posh, I suspect. Do you think this is professional enough?"

Travis propped himself on his arms. "Sure. How do you know where to go?"

"He's picking me up."

"You think that's smart?"

Bethany raised her eyebrows. "It's not like he's going to kidnap me."

Travis sat up, his brows drawing together. "You don't know what he's capable of. He's unpredictable like that scumbag, Desmond. This morning, he tried to pass himself off as a maintenance guy. Bought a toolbox from Doug's Hardware. Who knows what he's got in there?"

"A famous television star is unlikely to be a serial killer."

A car pulled up in the driveway, causing goosebumps to travel down Bethany's spine. Her eyes met Travis's in the mirror. Regardless of the bravado she pretended, the truth was Hank Haverill was about the scariest thing she'd dealt with since she had discovered their empty bank account after Desmond left town. And not because she thought he was a serial killer. But she had promised dinner in exchange for his cooperation, and Bethany planned to keep her end of the bargain.

She turned with a quick smile. "He's here. Listen, I'll text you my location as soon as I know what it is."

Travis stood and gave her a quick hug. "If you want to come home early, I'll come get you."

Bethany thought about it for a moment. If the evening went south, she would be dependent on Hank for a lift. "That's not a bad idea."

"Text me. Even if you're just uncomfortable, I'll be right there."

Bethany blinked away tears. She and Travis only had one another and their restaurant, which was why they looked out for each other. "Thanks, Travis. You're the best brother ever."

The doorbell rang, and Travis followed her to the front door, which she opened. She blinked at the short, balding man standing in the entrance. He was dressed in black pants and a blue dress shirt. A long black limo took up half the driveway.

"Oh, hi."

"Hello, ma'am. I'm Louis, Mr. Haverill's driver. I'm here to collect you."

Bethany peered around him, but there was no one else outside. "Hank's not here?"

The man smiled with a shake of his head. "No, he asked me to take you to your destination."

"And where is that?"

"I believe he preferred it to be a surprise."

"I'm not fond of surprises." She shot the driver a cool look.

Louis did not hesitate. *Used to Hank's shenunigans, most likely.*

"Understandable, ma'am. Mr. Haverill did say you might object to not having an address. Here it is."

He handed a piece of paper to her.

"Edgewater Drive," Bethany read.

Travis peered over her shoulder. "Looks like a private residence."

"That it is, sir."

"He must have rented a house," Bethany said. "He didn't mention that."

"I believe he rented it today. As you might imagine, there is no guarantee of privacy in a public restaurant, so Hank thought dinner at home would be best." Louis smiled and gestured toward the limo. "Are you ready, ma'am? I have instructions to get you there by seven."

Bethany nodded. "Call me Bethany, please." She turned to Travis with a smile she hoped looked reassuring and handed him the slip of paper. "Pick me up by midnight, unless you hear from me sooner . . . Cinderella and all that."

"I'll be there." Travis's gray-green eyes—so much like their dad's—darkened with concern.

She gave him a swift hug. "Love you. I'll be fine."

Louis opened the door to the limo and waited for her to enter before shutting it. Bethany settled inside, air bubbles flitting around her stomach. She plastered on a smile to make sure Travis knew she was okay.

And then they were pulling out of the drive, and she was waving goodbye, and Bethany was certain she had just strapped herself into a roller coaster, and the first hill would be a doozie.

~

HANK LIFTED the lid on the shiny copper frying pan and took a whiff. The smell of carrots and chicken cooking in soy sauce mixed with garlic and sweet and sour hit his nostrils in a pungent burst. His stomach rumbled in anticipation. Other than the donut this morning, he had eaten little.

He picked up a big wooden spoon and stirred the concoction with one hand, then turned the burner off under a pot of rice with the other. He glanced at the time on the microwave at the same moment he heard the car in the drive.

Hank wiped his hands on a dish towel and went to open the door. A flicker of excitement darted through his veins. When was the last time he'd had this feeling of anticipation? He searched his memories, but nothing came to him.

He checked his appearance in the giant hall mirror to make sure nothing was stuck in his teeth. His hair was a bit messy, but his light blue shirt and white shorts weren't stained.

He grabbed the door handle. Crap, he was losing it. Why the heck did the thought of Bethany spying a bit of carrot in his mouth or dirty clothes cause his heart to beat out of his chest?

He shook his head at his foolishness and turned the

handle. He'd entertained plenty of women before. This shouldn't be any different. *But it is.*

Hank plastered on his best Apollo smile and opened the door. There she stood, stunning in a purple number that contrasted dramatically with her dark curly hair. The evening sun cast a golden shadow across her face, and that, in combination with the dress, gave her a magical air. Her large eyes, more gray than green at the moment, looked at him as if she'd never seen him before.

He stood a little taller in his loafers. His Apollo smile faded, and his heart thumped fast, reminding him of the first time he'd stood in front of a camera. Beads of moisture formed on his forehead. The words of welcome on the tip of his tongue disappeared in a mountain of mush.

"Umm, can I come in?"

The scent of lemons and sugar surrounding her stunned his senses. The humidity this close to the lake caused her hair to look curlier than it did when he'd seen her at the restaurant. A strand of it blew across her cheek, and without thinking, he reached out to brush it from her eyes. She flinched as if he had struck her, and her cheeks turned pink.

He dropped his hand. "Yeah, sorry. I was . . . uh . . ." *Pull yourself together, man.* "In the kitchen."

Never had he wanted to impress a girl as much as he wanted to at that moment. "C'mon in."

Bethany hesitated, then crossed the threshold, and Hank fought an urge to scoop her up caveman style and carry her away. He would beat his chest and yell *mine all mine* to any who tried to take her from his arms.

He smiled at his foolishness and shut the door. His wild attraction to Bethany was the mood of a moment—here today and gone the next. How else to explain why rational thought deserted him in her presence?

"Something smells good. You're cooking?" She stood there looking sweet and innocent and as tempting as any of his leading ladies. Except this was not the effect of makeup, costume, and millions of dollars in plastic surgery. She was as real as it got.

"I told you I'd make you dinner." He presented her with a casual smile, which he hoped hid his thoughts. "Why do you persist in your disbelief, woman?"

He didn't wait for her answer. Instead, he led her into the kitchen. "Follow me."

CHAPTER FOURTEEN

Bethany followed Hank's tall form into a massive kitchen and tried not to check out his butt. Did it have to be so . . . sculpted?

He turned and caught her gawking before she could look away.

He raised his eyebrows and laughed, and she moved her gaze to the bubbling frying pan on the stove. She swallowed. "Smells good. What is it?"

"Wait and be surprised." Hank gestured toward the rustic wood table set for two. "Have a seat."

Bethany dragged her gaze from the stove to the table and took a moment to appreciate its artistic splendor. Three perfect pink peonies nestled in a small glass vase in the center of the table and a gold runner ran down its center. The plates were white, but the utensils were gold to match the runner. A wine glass sat in front of each plate, and in front of them sat a gold bucket filled with ice and a bottle of Riesling.

Hank pulled out a plush gray chair and waited.

Not a date.

Bethany sat, glad to sink into the chair's velvety soft-ness. She shifted her gaze to Hank, who had collected the wine bottle but remained hovering over her, his shirt open at the neckline so she caught a tantalizing glimpse of his golden chest and some sort of medal on a silver chain. He smelled like soy sauce and temptation. *Just business.* "Did you do all this yourself?"

He laughed and the sound sank into her bones. "I'd like to take the credit, but I only had the good taste to rent an already decorated place and hire a maid service."

Hank took the wine to the counter and opened it. His long fingers were deft on the bottle, and Bethany imagined what it would feel like to have his hands on her. *Ridiculous.*

"Wine?"

She nodded and shifted in her chair to watch him cross to her and fill both wine glasses. Hank presented one of the glasses to her, then he sat across the table and raised the other.

He smiled, slow and easy, like they had all the time in the world. His blue eyes met hers across the rim, grabbed a hold of her heart and squeezed. "To Grandma Lou's."

Her heartbeat lurched along, but she managed to lean forward far enough to clink her glass with his and take a sip. Wine had never tasted so good.

She cleared her throat and struggled to think of some-thing casual to say. Hank refilled their glasses. She had drained her glass, which was not the wisest decision, but it soothed her nerves. He returned to the stove to serve them both a plate of stir-fry.

He set a steaming dish in front of her and then sat on the opposite side of the table.

She took a bite of carrot to avoid looking at him. If she

kept her eyes off his gorgeous physique, maybe she could keep her mind on her reasons for being there.

An awkward silence stretched between them. Bethany swallowed. "How'd you get into acting?"

He set down his fork. "It started with a modeling contract. I was discovered by an agent while walking down the street with a friend. I didn't have anything better to do, so I agreed."

She waited for him to continue, and when he didn't, she risked a glance his way. Candlelight cast a warm glow on his face as he watched her, eyes hooded.

"So then you were offered an acting role?"

He shook his head and downed the rest of his wine. "No. My agent encouraged me to try out for a small role on a soap opera. I did and got that part and, soon after, bigger roles. The rest, as they say, is history. You can Google all this, you know."

"Oh, I . . ." Why hadn't she thought to Google Hank? She wiped her face with her napkin. "There hasn't been time."

Hank shook his head and stabbed a piece of chicken with his fork. "Have you even watched my show?"

"Well, maybe an episode . . ."

He placed a hand over his heart. "You've stomped on my ego and crushed it."

"I don't watch a lot of TV."

He shot her a look of pure mischief. "No making excuses for your bad behavior. You'll have to be punished. I think putting you on dish duty ought to do it."

He laughed, and her skin tingled. Life had been so serious up to this point, she'd forgotten what it felt like to be teased by a man as virile and confident as Hank.

Desmond had never teased her. He'd been too busy

telling lies and emptying her bank account to further his career.

She pushed her food around her plate but couldn't stop a smile from sliding across her lips. "I suppose that's a fair trade."

"Beth."

She glanced up to find him studying her, all traces of laughter gone from his expression. "Ask me something you wouldn't find on the Internet."

She couldn't look away. She took a sip of wine and set down her glass before clearing her throat. But when she spoke, her voice came out hoarse—the effects of the wine. "What was your grandpa like?"

Hank nodded and leaned back in his chair. "Tall and broad-shouldered. He worked in a factory making keys. Had a kind heart. I used to spend a month with him and my grandma in the summers."

"You must miss him."

"When I was a kid, I thought he was invincible. He believed in working hard. But he knew how to have fun. When I stayed with him, he took me to see the Cleveland Indians—now the Guardians."

"You like baseball?"

Hank put his hands behind his head. "Yeah. Haven't been to a game in a while, though."

"How come?"

"Busy. On the road traveling a lot. Baseball wasn't high on my ex-girlfriend's fun list." He rubbed the back of his neck. "What about you? How do you spend your free time?"

Bethany sipped more wine and thought about telling a lie because the truth was depressing. But the atmosphere was warm and intimate and ripe for honesty. Besides, Hank would forget her when he returned to Hollywood. There wasn't much danger of his remembering her sad life or having it end up in a magazine. "Baking, cooking. I don't have free time. All my energy goes to the business."

"Ah yes, the business."

She arched her brows. "Why do you say it like that?"

Instead of answering, he shrugged. "I knew our conversation would end up there."

"Why not? You told me we would talk about it. Grandma Lou's is my life."

"So I gathered." He got up from the table, selected a manila folder from a nearby drawer, and handed it to her. "Here's the lease agreement. I'd suggest you have your attorney look it over in the morning before you sign it."

Bethany flipped through the contents, relief creating a gentle swell in her chest at the official-looking documents. "Thank you."

Hank nodded, crossed the kitchen, and pulled a crystal plate filled with different wedges of cheesecake from the fridge. "Dessert?"

Bethany's eyes widened. "Wow, I love cheesecake." She raised her gaze to his. "How'd you know?"

He grinned. "A little birdie named Rosie told me. This is from a place called Eileen's in New York City. You're gonna love it."

"You had it shipped?"

"Yeah." He shrugged as if it were no big deal. "Eileen's is known as the best cheesecake in the world. What flavor do you want?"

"How did you get it so fast?"

He waggled his brows. "Well, ma'am, it's a little-known service called overnight shipping."

She couldn't stop a laugh at his ridiculous customer service voice.

"After I heard you liked it yesterday, I ordered it as an apology for missing our earlier dinner. Figured it might help get me in your good graces. What kind do you want, Beth?"

"Blueberry." She licked her lips. "Why are you doing this?"

Hank lifted a shoulder. "Giving you cheesecake? Well, I needed a dessert to go with dinner, and—"

Bethany pushed her chair out, the sound loud in the large room, and stood. "No, Hank. I mean why are you doing all of this?" She pointed at the dinner table. "Making me dinner. Fixing up the building? Why do you need to get on my good side? What do you want from me?"

Hank sighed and slid a piece of blueberry cheesecake onto a small plate. "Your company? I'm not your ex-fiancé. I don't need or want your money."

Bethany sucked in a breath. "You've been listening to gossip, haven't you?"

"Not intentionally." He made a face that she could almost interpret as apologetic. "I overheard people talking about your ex-fiancé in the restaurant this morning."

"Well, that's not surprising. People around here love to talk." A dull ache settled in her stomach. She sat back down. "I wasn't accusing you of wanting money. But all this energy you're expending . . . it must be for something."

Hank crossed to the table and set the cheesecake in front of her but didn't move away. Instead, he crouched next to her, so they were eye level. "I'd like to get to know you better. That's all. No ulterior motives. No evil intentions. I thought we could be friends."

"Friends." Bethany tested the word on her tongue and found it disappointing. Why would a TV star and the landlord of her building want to be her friend? She looked at her lap. Had she secretly been hoping Hank wanted more than friendship from her? Was she crazy? She'd only met him yesterday morning.

"Yeah." Hank tucked a stray curl behind her ear.

Bethany raised her head and frowned. She would have brushed his hand away, but the motion was so quick, she couldn't react in time. Plus, she wasn't sure that he knew he'd done it, and she didn't want to make a scene. And . . . she'd kind of liked it.

"I could use a friend right now. And I have this feeling you could use one too. Will you be my friend, Beth?"

Put like that, it seemed ridiculous to say no. But Bethany wasn't taking chances. "What does it mean to be your friend, Hank? What are you expecting from me?"

"A slice of cheesecake? A stroll after dinner to see the stars?" Hank pointed to the window in the other room, where Bethany caught a glimpse of Lake Erie. "It's a beautiful night, and there's a lake outside. What do you say? Friends?"

Bethany looked into Hank's clear eyes and caught the same vulnerability she'd glimpsed there yesterday. What was more, she understood it—the loneliness. She could use a friend too.

Instead of answering, though, she sank her fork into the thick cheesecake and took a bite. She closed her eyes around the creamy concoction. Hank was right. This might be the best she had ever tasted.

She opened her eyes to see him watching her. "Tell you what. You let me take a slice of this home for Travis, and we'll be friends."

Hank laughed and the worry disappeared from his expression. "You can have the whole darn plate."

CHAPTER FIFTEEN

"This is a great rental. How'd you find it?" Bethany held her sandals in one hand while they strolled along the beach. She tried to remember the last time she'd squished sand between her toes.

Hank shined a flashlight ahead of them. "My assistant, Pamela, tracked it down."

"She's traveling with you?"

"No, she's in LA. But she takes care of stuff like this for me."

"You're lucky to have her."

"Yeah, I suppose. Most celebrities do use assistants—we have crazy schedules."

"Is she upset with you for staying in Cleveland?"

Hank picked up a stone and tossed it into the lake. The breeze ruffled his hair. "She's used to my travel schedule. I'm not at home much. It won't be my first trip here or the last. She's paid well to organize my life."

"I bet Elizabeth's not happy you're sticking around."

"Why do you say that?"

"I don't know. She seemed anxious to get things settled."

"She is. I haven't made it easy on her by hiding in your kitchen. She works hard to make sure I get the right publicity. One wrong story could damage my career and tank hers along with it."

Bethany stopped to dip her toes in the lake. Although it was a warm night, the water was cold, and that and Hank's concerns sent a chill through her body. The threat of his career ending reminded her of his plans to open the fitness center. "Is your career in trouble?"

"Maybe. I don't know. My agent calls it a dry spell. I try not to think about it. If I did, I'd drive myself nuts."

"Is that why you're planning to renovate our building and start your new business venture, so you'll have another source of income?"

Hank turned and grabbed her hands, catching her off-guard. She gasped at the feeling, so warm and solid against her skin. "I'm not putting you out of business. I don't screw over my friends."

She kept her hands in his, but it was too dark to see the expression on his face. Surprise carved a hollow in her gut. "So you'll fix the building and let me rent?"

He squeezed her fingers. "I'd like to."

Hope rose like a fragile bubble in her throat.

"But it won't last forever."

The bubble burst, sending a surge of fear through her body. She pulled her hands from his and wrapped them around her middle.

"Listen, if I don't open Fitaholics, I'll need to sell the building at a profit. My financial advisor says I've got too many expenses at the moment to hang onto it forever. If you have the money, I'm more than willing to sell the building to you first. If not, I'll need to look for another buyer. I'll try to find one who will rent to you and the others."

Bethany drew a shaky breath. "How long do I have?"

Hank toed the sand. "I need to make a decision in the next couple of months. I heard you're entering a baking contest with a large cash reward for the winner?"

"Boy, news sure travels fast. That's right. I'm entering my Grandma Lou's chocolate cake with buttercream frosting in a baking contest sponsored by Fresh & Easy, one of the largest cake manufacturers. Deadline is Friday. Finalists will be notified in two weeks, and the winning restaurant will be announced a few days later."

"How much could you win?"

Five hundred thousand. How much are you looking for?"

Hank sighed and shined the flashlight at the lake. "At least $1 million. But I'll tell you what. You win the contest, I'll figure out a way for you to make payments until you own it."

"You will?" Bethany walked to where he stood waving the flashlight beam back and forth on the water, her heart pounding.

He flicked a glance her way. "Sure."

Was there a catch? She waited for him to elaborate, but instead he pointed the beam at the night sky. "Do you believe in wishing on stars?"

He turned the flashlight off, and dozens of twinkling lights could be seen in the inky darkness, reminding her of an old poem her grandma used to recite: *Night let its sable curtains down and pinned them with a star.* Looking at the vast universe, she could almost believe in wishes. "I'd like to. Do you?"

"Well, that depends."

She turned to look at him, but she couldn't see anything in the dark, and his deep voice held secrets. "What do you mean?"

"It depends on your answer to what I wished for just now."

Her throat tightened. Had he wished for a roll in the sack? Somehow, she suspected Hank's offer of friendship came with a price. She steeled her heart for whatever he was about to say. "What is it?"

"I wished you'd come back in the house and watch TV with me for a little while."

"Wh-What?"

"I can't have you as a friend if we don't spend time together. That's what friends do."

He was teasing her again. Bethany smiled, but a surge of shyness hit her like the waves crashing against the shore. She was beginning to like Hank Haverill. And that emotion was dangerous. Last time she'd liked a man enough to value his friendship, he'd fooled her into believing he loved her, then broke her heart and stole her life savings.

"What do you say, Miss Parker? Can you stomach watching TV with Apollo?"

Bethany took a deep breath and allowed a tentative smile, although she knew he couldn't see her face. She crossed her arms. "Okay, but only if we watch your TV show."

Hank paused. "Nah."

"C'mon, think what a thrill it will be for me to watch *Apollo* with Apollo." She laughed again and drew a curvy line with her big toe in the sand. "I'll post it on Facebook tomorrow. Impress all my friends."

Hank turned the flashlight on, blinding her, before tipping it again toward the sky. "You're making fun of me.

My massive ego can't take it. Next, you'll be offering acting advice."

Bethany raised a brow. "So you won't do it?"

"I didn't say that." His tone grew serious. "I don't watch my shows."

She drew closer; close enough to tap him on the arm. "Why not?"

He turned toward her, and the flashlight illuminated his entire face, revealing the vulnerability she'd glimpsed the previous day when he'd told her about his dad. And then he was looking back toward the lake, taking the light with him. The beam revealed little whitecaps that broke the water. "It's hard to see yourself playing a role. Everyone's a critic. Even me."

"Hank." This time she touched his arm and kept her hand there. A tingle of nervous energy traveled from her hand to her stomach, but she brushed it aside.

The first hill on this roller coaster had been a drop. And there had been lots of twists and turns on the ride. Now she was coming in for the landing.

Her voice had not been much above a whisper, but still he turned toward her. She took another breath and tightened her seat belt. "I won't critique your acting."

His breath was warm on her cheek. "Promise?"

His hand settled on hers where she touched his arm, and it felt like he'd stroked a thousand nerve endings. Her breath hitched, and her voice when it came out sounded breathless to her ears. "Yes. I'm sorry I haven't watched much of your show before now."

"Okay. Let's do it."

"It'll be fun."

"Fun," he echoed. He dropped his hand, and Bethany was shocked at how much she felt its loss.

He pointed the flashlight toward the house. She imagined he smiled, but she couldn't tell. "Let's go have some fun."

She should thank him for the dinner. She should say it's time to go. Instead, Bethany let him lead her up the steps and into the house. After all, what was a little fun between friends?

THE EVENING WAS GOING BETTER than Hank had dreamed. Bethany seemed relaxed and happy and willing to get to know him—both as Hank the actor and the man. Not as her landlord. *A friend.*

He ushered her into the house and led her into the family room, where a giant flat-screen TV faced a pair of oversized white sofas. Okay, he was not a huge fan of the white sofas; they were a little too stark for his tastes. But they were comfortable and complemented the liquor tray on the sideboard. Besides, they made a great backdrop for Bethany in her stunning purple dress.

"Make yourself comfortable." He waved a hand in their general direction and watched as she settled her small frame among the cushions, looking like a vibrant jungle flower.

Hank searched until he found the remote on the sleek coffee table and flicked through the menu until he located his TV series. He cocked his head in Bethany's direction. She sat straight and tall, not even leaning against the back of the couch.

"You go ahead and get started," he said. "I'll bring you another glass of wine."

"Okay." Her lips tilted up. This time she showed some teeth.

Every time Bethany smiled or laughed at something he said, Hank felt like he'd won a prize. He was starting to understand her moods and adjust his actions to suit. Her smile now meant she was nervous—would he take the seat next to her or would he go for the recliner? He wasn't sure which she wanted, but he knew what he wanted. To sit as close to Bethany as she would let him. To occupy her personal space until she craved his touch as much as he craved hers. But neither of them needed complications. So friends they would stay.

He pressed play on the remote and then made his way to the kitchen where he poured the last of the Riesling into her glass. He opened another bottle, then took it and the glass back to the family room. He returned in time to hear the end of the show's theme song. As usual, he cringed inwardly at the lyrics. "Who battles darkness with a bright desire? Who employs a sword forged in fire?"

And there he was garbed in an outfit that made the most of his pecs, though he knew every woman who watched was looking at more than his muscles. This particular episode was the one where he wrestled a python.

He was in top physical form when they'd filmed the show last year, and the camera angles made the most of his muscular physique. For months after it had aired, men wrote asking for his personal exercise regimen. Women had asked if he needed a partner. One crazed fan showed up at his home in LA claiming to be his wife, and he'd filed a restraining order.

Hank gave the glass of wine to Bethany and then sat next to her, leaving a comfortable distance between them. Despite his efforts, she tensed like a mouse who'd been discovered by a cat. She took a large swallow of wine and then another, before setting it on the coffee table.

Hank refilled her glass. He wasn't trying to get her drunk—he wanted her to relax. He yawned and stretched and placed his arm on the back of the couch. Bethany leaned forward and stared at the television. On screen, Apollo raised the golden python above his shoulders and threw it in the air. She sank against the cushions, and Hank held his breath, realizing how close his fingers were to tangling in her hair.

Her gaze remained on the television screen. Hank spared it a glance in time to see the rescued woman throw her arms around the god's neck, while the crowd cheered. The camera zoomed in on their kiss. Hank grimaced, remembering how cold the actress's lips had been. They'd tasted like wax.

He slid his gaze back to Bethany. From the corner of one eye, he could see she was intent on the TV. She didn't even flinch when she leaned farther back, and his fingers brushed her hair. Hank settled them there and bit his tongue. He wasn't putting the moves on her. Friends could touch a little, couldn't they?

Bethany blinked and closed her eyes.

What would happen if he pulled her into his arms? For some reason, watching her watching him kiss his costar cranked up his desire. He was a man, after all. And the smell of her next to him, as good as a lemon cream puff, didn't help. She dropped her head on his shoulder like it was the most natural thing in the world. Hank forgot to breathe.

She didn't move, so he stroked her scalp, running his fingers through her soft waves. He moved his hand back and forth, first in small motions and then covering more territory.

Hank didn't know how long they stayed like that, him

rubbing her head. Did she enjoy his touch? The way his body reacted to her closeness, you would think he'd never held a woman before. If he kissed her, would it change the budding friendship between them? Maybe she wanted more from him?

Hank turned his head to the left so his lips landed in her hair. That was when he heard a soft grunt. Had he frightened her?

Hank tilted his head to check her face and stilled. Bethany hadn't been coming on to him; she had passed out on his shoulder.

CHAPTER SIXTEEN

Hank didn't know how long he remained there with Bethany sleeping on his shoulder. Thirty minutes? An hour? He stayed until his arm fell asleep. Then he managed to rest her head against the cushions and shake his arm until the pins and needles disappeared.

Even then, he stayed where he was, watching her sleep. Some magic he couldn't name shimmered in the air around them until his cell phone buzzed, breaking the spell.

Elizabeth. She'd been worried about him. He owed her some attention. Hank grabbed the phone and went into the kitchen to take the call so he wouldn't disturb Bethany.

"I think you should shelve Fitaholics for now. Head back to LA."

He frowned but kept his voice low. "Not even a hello, first? I thought you wanted the fitness center?"

"Sorry, it's late. I do want the fitness center. Scout's honor. But Blackie has some movie roles he wants you to audition for. We're done here for a while."

"Since when? Yesterday, he told me all he could find were cheesy car commercials."

"Since today. He told me you're up for a major award for *Apollo*. He wants you back in LA."

"I'm not going back there yet." His voice came out sharper than he'd intended, although it was exciting to learn he was up for an award. He ran a hand through his hair.

There was a pause. "Why? What's keeping you in Cleveland?"

Hank sighed. "I need a little downtime. I'm not flying out on Monday. I'm staying here a few weeks."

Elizabeth paused. Hank could picture her running through all the arguments in her head. She settled on one. "If you need downtime, we'll go to Barbados. At least there we'll have sunny skies every day and beautiful beaches."

"I don't need sunny skies and beaches. This is the city where I was born. I want to visit a few places while I'm here."

"It's the girl, isn't it?"

Hank paused, flicking a glance toward Bethany.

"What girl?"

"Don't play dumb. You know who I mean. The restaurant owner you invited to dinner. Have you slept with her yet?"

A groan sounded from the couch. Hank waited to see if Bethany was waking up, but she stilled.

"That's none of your business. I just got out of one relationship. The last thing I need or want is another."

"You've got to be kidding."

Hank could picture Elizabeth rolling her eyes and filing her nails. "What's there to kid about? I'm serious."

"Oh yeah? That's what you said about Melanie, remember? You and she were just gonna be friends. Next thing I know, you're moving in together, and look how long that lasted. Now we gotta deal with the fallout from her pissed-off father and a lawsuit."

"That was different. Melanie's Hollywood. Bethany is" —Hank turned back to the family room—"a real friend. She takes my mind off everything."

"You may think of her as a friend, but she's female and she's human."

Hank leaned against the wall. "What's that supposed to mean?"

Elizabeth managed to sound sharp and bored at the same time. This personality trait of cutting through the bull-shit was one of the reasons he liked having her around. But for some reason, he found himself clenching his jaw.

"It means, you'll break her heart. You always do."

Hank straightened. "That's ridiculous. Melanie's not heartbroken, she's mad."

"Take it from me, Hank. She was heartbroken first. Hell hath no fury like a woman scorned and all that. The best thing you can do is to stay far, far away from this poor girl. You're vulnerable—and on the rebound."

"She's not a rebound." His voice came out louder than he wanted. Hank glanced again at Bethany. She lay in the same spot, unmoving. He turned away and lowered his voice. "I won't break her heart. I'm not looking for a serious relationship. Besides, she doesn't even like me. I'm threatening her livelihood."

Elizabeth scoffed. "Oh, she likes you all right. You're worth millions."

"She's not after my money."

"What do you mean?" Elizabeth's tone sharpened. In Hollywood, people were catty and selfish and generally full of themselves.

"I mean she cares about people, Elizabeth. She's feeding the hungry out of her restaurant."

Elizabeth huffed. "Okay, point taken."

"Great, you see where I'm coming from?"

"No, I see she doesn't have much business sense." Hank pictured Elizabeth grinding her teeth. "Which is all the more reason why you should stay away from the girl. Hank, I'm not trying to rain on your parade. But this is your career we're talking about. Bethany Parker will be yet another drain on your finances. You're already having second thoughts about opening Fitaholics. Next, you'll be giving her back the building."

Hank opened the fridge and found the cheesecake. He scooped a slice on a plate and nabbed a fork from the drawer.

"Hank Haverill, you have not agreed to give away the building, have you?"

"No," he mumbled around a bite of cheesecake. He would up his workout tomorrow.

Elizabeth snorted. "Hank . . ."

"Listen, she's entering her grandma's restaurant in a baking contest that could earn five hundred grand in prize money. I told her *if* she wins the contest and *if* I sell the building, I'd sell to her. She's aware I need to make a profit whatever I do. What's the big deal?"

"The deal is you're supposed to be shelving this project and returning to LA, not giving the building away to charity."

Now it was Hank's turn to roll his eyes. "This is not charity, Elizabeth. For God's sake, I'm not gifting her the building. If I decide to sell it to her, she'll pay for it just like any other buyer. If she can't purchase it, I'll find someone who can."

Hank finished the cheesecake and put his dish in the sink. Despite what he'd threatened Bethany with earlier, the service he hired would do the dishes in the morning.

"Ah, Hank." Elizabeth sounded disappointed.

He sighed and leaned against the sink. He didn't know what he felt for Bethany. He hardly knew her. He tried again to provide some rational explanation Elizabeth might believe—or maybe he was trying to convince himself. "She amuses me, that's all. A distraction. I've had too much stress."

"Okay. Have it your way. Sleep with her and get it out of your system. It wouldn't be the first time."

Hank clenched his jaw until it ached and injected as much sarcasm as he could into his voice. "I don't need your advice on who to sleep with. You're my publicist, not a counselor, remember?"

A sound from the couch told him Bethany was awake.

Elizabeth didn't seem fazed by his bitterness. "Yeah, and as your publicist, I'm advising you to let the woman alone and get back to your career in LA. This attraction you feel is the thrill of the chase. It will only last until you find the next challenge. You know it as well as I do. You'll break her heart."

"Hey, I gotta run."

"Wait, where will you be tomorrow?"

"I don't know. I'll text you in the morning." Before Elizabeth could press him for details, he ended the call.

He turned to see Bethany standing in the kitchen, sandals in one hand, hair tousled, and eyes wide.

"Why didn't you wake me up? It's midnight."

He strolled toward her with a grin. "You didn't turn into a pumpkin."

She did not return his smile. Instead, she dropped her

sandals and slid her feet into them. "I gotta go. Thanks for dinner."

"Beth, wait. I'll take you home."

A car horn beeped outside, and they both turned toward the sound. She shook her head and hurried toward the door. "No, Travis is here. Bye, Hank."

Before he could stop her, she opened the door and dashed from the house.

What had she overheard?

Hank scooped up the white sweater that had slipped from her hands when she'd run. He brought it to his face and let the scent of lemons surround him.

CHAPTER SEVENTEEN

"We've got more orders than normal," Travis announced. He entered the kitchen with a stack of dirty dishes, which he set on the worktable, and slips of paper he'd scratched the orders on, which he handed to Bethany.

Bethany glanced at the papers. Her stomach roiled and twisted like a pot of boiling acid. "Angel here yet?"

Travis shook his head. "She's sick. So's her mom. Mitch Williams is by himself in the store next door. But the three boys from yesterday are here."

"Oh, great. Send them in, would you?"

"I will, but they look like they haven't eaten in months. I came in to get them breakfast."

"Okay. Did you call Rosie?"

Travis loaded plates with heaping piles of scrambled eggs, hash browns, and sausages before carrying them toward the door.

He called over his shoulder, "Yeah. She's got a job cleaning this morning. It's a big house and the owner's letting her bring the girls. She can't help us this morning, but they'll come once they're done." He slipped through the swinging doors, and Bethany closed her eyes for a moment. Her head throbbed as if angry gremlins with hammers were pounding on her temples. Served her right. What an idiot she'd been last night, drinking too much wine, falling asleep on Hank's couch, and then waking up to that *horrible* conversation.

She opened her eyes to see Travis was back with another stack of dirty dishes and more yellow slips of paper.

"Are you okay?"

Bethany nodded and said a silent prayer to get through the rest of the day without tossing her cookies. "Yeah. Just tired."

"The table closest to the front window wants two breakfast specials as takeout and a dozen donuts. Oh, and Sam's here with Gypsy. He's asking for you."

Bethany came from behind the worktable and wiped her hands on a blue-striped towel. "Okay. Why do you look like you're ready to tell someone off?"

"He's here again. Dressed funny this time. I almost didn't recognize him."

Bethany stilled. She didn't bother to ask Travis who *he* meant. "How's he dressed?"

Travis shrugged. "I think he's supposed to be a handyman. He's got on overalls and a matching blue hat. You want me to kick him out?"

Yes. She shook her head and sighed. "No, I'll handle him."

"That lady's here, too—Elizabeth. I heard them arguing in the corner. At least they aren't attracting a crowd this time."

Hank's voice from last night echoed in her head. *I don't need your advice on who to sleep with.* Bethany bit her lip. He didn't know it, but she'd heard a good part of his conversation with Elizabeth. If she hadn't been so humiliated and hurt, she would have called him out on it right then and there. Thank goodness she'd thought to have Travis pick her up. "What are they talking about?"

"Who knows? He's got his toolbox. I don't think she likes it. I heard her tell him he's wasting his time here."

Bethany grabbed a pitcher of orange juice. "Well, on that point, we agree. Work on filling the orders. I'll take care of Sam and . . . them."

Travis looked like he wanted to say more, but Bethany didn't stick around to hear it. Instead, she breezed into the dining area, trying to keep her gaze from Hank and Elizabeth and failing. They were in the middle of a heated conversation and didn't notice her. Bethany kept moving. She nodded at the boys, who looked like they'd eaten half their breakfasts already, and spotted Sam. She made a beeline for his table.

"Hi, Sam. Orange juice?"

Sam removed his hat. "Morning, Bethany. That'd be fine. Looks like another sunny day."

Bethany filled his cup. "That it is. Your usual for breakfast?"

"Yes, indeed. I'm looking forward to eggs and hash browns." Sam squinted at something over her shoulder. "Did you hire a maintenance man?"

"Oh." Bethany turned, sloshing the orange juice.

Hank stood behind her in a white shirt and blue jean overalls, as Travis had warned. The overalls had pockets. In one, Bethany spied a tape measure. She raised her gaze to Hank's, who in turn arched a brow at her inspection from under a blue baseball cap—as if there was nothing odd about the way he had dressed, as if Bethany were the odd one.

"Good morning." He grinned and held up his toolbox. "I thought I'd get started with the kitchen today." He tilted his thumb over his shoulder.

Now it was Bethany's turn to raise a brow. "The kitchen?"

Hank smiled wider, if that were possible. "I plan to look at that cranky dishwasher."

She made a face. "It's not cranky—just old."

"She's not the only old and cranky thing in this café." Sam cackled, bringing Bethany back to her surroundings with a jerk. Orange juice splashed up the sides of the pitcher and she placed it on the table. Sam wasn't wrong— Bethany certainly felt old and cranky worrying about what would happen to the family business—but she cringed inwardly, wondering what Hank was thinking.

Hank laughed, and Bethany felt her cheeks warm. He obviously thought the description was amusing. She ignored him and turned to Sam, wiping her hands on her apron. "Sam, I'm not that old and cranky, am I?"

Sam's smile faded. "Oh, I didn't mean you." He pointed at his chest and sighed. "I was talking about *myself*. At least, that's what my wife always called me—old and cranky."

Bethany sniffed. "She didn't deserve you."

"They don't make 'em like this one," Sam said to Hank. "Prettiest and kindest girl around to an old fellow like me. You treat her right now, ya hear?"

Hank tipped his hat. "That's my plan."

"Uh, Sam, Hank and my relationship—it's business. He's here to make improvements to the building."

Sam didn't look convinced. He straightened his bow tie. "I thought he was an actor?"

Bethany wiped the handle of the pitcher with her apron. She didn't look at Hank. "Well, he also happens to own this building. He's agreed to let me rent for a couple of months and to fix up the place. That's why he's dressed like"—she flung a hand in Hank's direction—"this."

"That right?" Sam squinted at Hank and then shook his head, like he couldn't make sense of the outfit. His gaze flitted from Bethany to Hank and back to Bethany. "He owns this building?"

She kept her voice cool. "Yes, for the time being." A meowing sounded at her feet and Bethany used the opportunity to reach down and pet Gypsy. "He plans to sell for a profit."

Gypsy purred and Bethany kept her gaze on the cat and far away from Hank. "To Travis and me, if we can come up with a down payment."

Sam clapped his hands. "That's wonderful news. We know how worried ya been. Ain't that right, Gypsy, my dear?"

Gypsy meowed in answer. Bethany straightened and grabbed the orange juice. Let Hank worm himself out of that one. *Mister-I-Can't-Afford-Distractions.* She flashed a hard smile at Hank, who didn't look as fazed as she'd imagined he would be. Then she turned to Sam. "I'll be right back with your breakfast and something special for Gypsy."

"I'll be here, waitin'," Sam said.

Bethany took off toward the kitchen, not looking to see if Hank followed. Of course, he caught up to her with an easy stride.

"What's the matter?"

"I don't know what you mean." She tried to speed up, but when she entered the kitchen, he was still by her side. She pointed to the right. "Dishwasher's over there."

Travis shot her a concerned look when he saw Hank, but when she shook her head to show she had the situation under control, he left the kitchen carrying several plates of food. Bethany moved to the cupboard, where she kept her prettiest china, and found a plate. Turning back to the worktable, she began scooping scrambled eggs onto the plate, while Hank remained standing in the same spot. Bethany flitted him a glance. He had taken off his hat and was twirling it in his hand. Somehow, he made a pair of handyman overalls look impressive.

"I thought you were here to fix things?" Bethany huffed.

"That's all I get? Not even a good morning and thank you for the dinner last night?"

Bethany stopped what she was doing and plastered on a polite smile. "Good morning, Hank. Dinner last night was delicious. Thank you. I'm sorry, but I've got customers to feed." She held up the plate. "I need to get this to Sam while it's hot."

Hank ignored her, standing in the way like a cement giant.

Bethany tried to get by but couldn't squeeze past. She gave a sigh and tipped her head to the side. "What is it?"

"I thought we agreed to be friends," he said, his voice mild. "What happened between last night and this morning to change your mind?"

"Nothing." She kept her gaze on the plate of food to keep it from spilling and to avoid Hank's penetrating eyes.

"Last night you fell asleep on my shoulder."

She had? Her gaze caught his, and she couldn't look away. She raised the plate a little. "Food's getting cold."

He didn't budge. "Was it something I said?"

He was not going to move until she gave him an answer. Fine, she would give him one. "Elizabeth . . . nice to know I'm an amusing distraction."

"Ah." His tone was thoughtful. "You overheard our phone call."

"Yes, now will you let me by?"

"So this means we can no longer be friends? And here I thought we'd made progress last night."

Bethany looked around. Although she knew the kitchen was empty except for the two of them, she dropped her voice. "Hank, you were talking to Elizabeth about sleeping with me. That doesn't sound like a friend."

"I just said that to get her off my back. I've known her a long time. She tends to interfere in my personal life. I'm sorry you had to overhear that."

Silence reigned between them for a moment. A silence fraught with accusations and anger and hurt. At least on her part. "Apology accepted. Now, can I get by?"

Hank's expression was guarded as he lifted his toolbox. "I'd better take a look at that dishwasher."

He stepped aside, leaving her free to deliver Sam's breakfast.

CHAPTER EIGHTEEN

Bethany slipped through the swinging doors and wound her way through the noisy dining room to Sam's table. All the while, she fought the sick feeling creeping through her veins like poison, like she'd done something wrong. Like she'd made a horrible mistake. Like she'd rushed to a decision and destroyed something precious before it even had a chance to take root. *Crazy.* All she'd destroyed was the chance for Hank to take advantage of her.

"Here ya go, Sam. And scraps for Gypsy."

The orange cat lifted her head and meowed as if she understood—which she would, given the fact that Bethany brought her leftovers whenever she fed Sam. Bethany placed Sam's dish on the table in front of him and crouched to give Gypsy her bowl. The cat devoured the scraps.

"He's not what he seems, is he?"

Bethany tilted her head toward Sam, whose hands rested by his silverware, unmoving. "If you mean he's not a handyman, you're right. I told you before, he's an actor. Aren't you going to try the scrambled eggs?"

Sam didn't move. Was he ill?

Bethany stood. "What's the matter?"

He shrugged and grabbed his napkin.

"Sam, whatever it is, spit it out."

Sam made a show of opening the napkin and tucking it into his shirt. Bethany tapped her foot on the floor. "Sam . . ."

"I like him."

Bethany bit her lip. "You don't know him."

"I know enough. I know he's as taken by you as the rest of us."

Heat flamed Bethany's cheeks and spread to her heart. "Don't be silly. I just met him on Friday."

Sam smiled and nodded and shoved a forkful of scrambled eggs in the vicinity of his mouth. "And now he's fixing your dishwasher. If that's not love, I don't know what is."

Something sharp poked Bethany's shoulder. She turned to see Elizabeth, her slim figure in a yellow sundress and clogs. The outfit's carefree style contrasted with the determined expression on her face. "May I speak to you somewhere private?"

"I'm sorry, it's a busy morning. Maybe later."

"My apologies, but what I have to say concerns the welfare of you and your business. It cannot wait until later."

Bethany considered Elizabeth's condescending face. Why did she feel like she would regret this conversation?

She looked around. Where could they go to be private? Hank was playing handyman in the kitchen, Travis worked the counter, and most of the tables were filled with regulars.

From the corner of her eye, Bethany spied an open table in the far corner where the boys had been sitting, which was now empty. Travis must have them busy washing dishes. "Over there."

Elizabeth followed where she pointed. "Excellent." She

took off toward the table. By the time Bethany arrived, she was seated, looking cool and smug.

Bethany nabbed the seat across from her, smoothed her clammy hands across her apron and held them together on her lap underneath the table. She studied Elizabeth, who had the look of a disgruntled Persian cat about to bite.

Bethany spoke in her most soothing voice. "What can I do for you?"

Elizabeth snorted and brushed her hair behind her ear, like women who are attractive and know it do. "It's more about what I can do for you. Listen, I know you think you've got Hank wrapped around your little finger and all, but I'm here to tell you it's a pleasant illusion."

Bethany pleated her apron underneath the table. "I assure you, I don't have Hank wrapped around my little finger."

Elizabeth continued as if Bethany hadn't spoken. "Hank's going through a bit of a rough patch right now, and he doesn't need complications. I've been working hard to keep him focused on his career. He's lonely and vulnerable and likely to make promises he can't keep. The man leaves a trail of broken hearts behind him wherever he goes. I don't want you to be his next victim."

"I've no intention of being a victim."

Elizabeth tilted her thin lips in the semblance of a smile. "Good, because if it stays that way, I might be able to pull some strings to help you win the baking contest."

Bethany raised her eyebrows.

"Don't look so surprised. Hank told me you're entering a family recipe. I've been with Hank since the beginning. He knows how hard I work to ensure his success. That's why he tells me *everything*."

She shouldn't have bothered emphasizing the word.

Bethany had heard last night how Hank revealed details of his personal life to Elizabeth. She swallowed a sharp stab of jealousy and trained her gaze on Elizabeth's inscrutable one. "How would you help me win?"

Elizebeth smiled like she'd cast a net and caught the biggest fish in the sea. "I've read the rules of the contest. Finalists are selected based on social media votes, correct? I'm *very* good at my job, Bethany. I'll get you the votes you need to be a finalist."

Bethany took a deep breath and tightened a hold on her temper. "That would be cheating, wouldn't it?"

"Oh, pah." Elizabeth flung a hand in the air. "How can it be cheating if those are the rules? I'm not breaking any laws by getting others to vote for your restaurant, am I? Besides, I'm only ensuring you final. The win depends on you and your recipe."

Bethany wrinkled her brow. Elizabeth was right. Bethany had planned to encourage the entire neighborhood to vote for Grandma Lou's. "What do you expect from me in return?"

Elizabeth leaned forward and lowered her voice. "Stay away from Hank—let him concentrate on his career. Don't respond to any invitations. Maintain a professional business relationship. That's all I ask."

Bethany clenched her hands in her lap and struggled to think. What Elizabeth proposed made sense, didn't it? With Elizabeth's help, she and Travis would be closer to winning the contest and keeping Grandma Lou's solvent and in the family. She forced her hands to relax. "What about the fitness center?"

Instead of answering, Elizabeth reached into her Chanel purse and pulled out a tin of mints. She selected one white mint from the case and offered the entire box to Bethany.

Bethany shook her head.

Elizabeth tossed her hair over her shoulders and smiled, but it didn't reach her cool silver eyes. "It's Hank's decision whether he sells or opens Fitaholics. I couldn't in good conscience sway him one way or another."

"So there's still a chance he'll turn our building into a fitness center?"

Elizabeth laughed low and confident and fierce. "Frankly, I'm more concerned with getting Hank back to Hollywood than in opening a store. But as I've said, I've known Hank a long time. Chances are he'll sell the building. And if you have the money, I won't do anything to discourage him from selling to you. Fair enough?"

Bethany understood now why Elizabeth was good at her job. She hadn't denied that they might still open the center, but she'd left room for Bethany to achieve her goal. Staying away from Hank Haverill made smart business sense. She would accept Elizabeth's offer. Hank would return to Hollywood, Bethany would win the contest and buy the building, and all would return to how it had been before Desmond's betrayal and Hank's arrival on her doorstep.

"Yes," she said.

"Wonderful. Shall we shake on it?" Elizabeth held out a long pale hand.

Bethany watched trance-like as she moved her arm from under the table and clasped Elizabeth's palm with her darker one.

"I'm glad we understand each other." Elizabeth stood. "When does voting start?"

"After midnight on Friday."

"Remember, stay away from Hank, and I'll get started on garnering the votes you need." She nodded, queen-like, slipping in a small, satisfied smile, and turned with a flip of her hair.

Bethany's stomach gurgled and her temple throbbed. She hugged her arms. Maybe she should have kept her hand in her apron pocket and showed Elizabeth the exit? But it was too late. The deal was made.

And Bethany meant to uphold her end of the bargain.

CHAPTER NINETEEN

If Bethany thought the deal she'd made with Elizabeth would be hard to keep, she soon learned otherwise. After Hank fiddled with her dishwasher, he left the kitchen without another word or glance her way.

Bethany continued cooking and filling food orders until Rosie came from her cleaning job to help them serve the lunch crowd. She did her best to ignore the sinking feeling in the pit of her stomach. It felt somewhat like the dry, hot center of a fiery volcano.

Bethany told herself that her stomachache was the direct result of too much alcohol. She told herself that Hank's departure was a good outcome. She told herself that she didn't care. Still, she couldn't quit glancing out the window, nor stop her heart from racing whenever the door chimed.

Which it did, nonstop, for the rest of the day.

"Business is booming." Travis found her emptying the dishwasher for the twentieth time since the boys had left. "If this keeps up, we'll more than break even this month."

He paused and peered at Bethany like he feared she would puke.

Bethany continued stacking plates on the worktable. A piece of hair landed in her mouth, and she blew it out.

"You must admit he's good for business. Everyone who comes in is asking for him."

Bethany tried to keep from rolling her eyes and failed. "Speaking of which, where did he go? I haven't seen him in a while."

"I think he's over at Mitch's. I saw Daphne heading there a few minutes ago, and you know she doesn't like antiques. How's the dishwasher running?"

Bethany gazed at the sparkling dishes and tried not to think about Daphne chasing after Hank. Since high school, Daphne had become a notorious flirt who wasn't bashful about using her considerable charms to seduce men she viewed as rich and powerful. If Hank was looking for a night of fun, Daphne would be sure to give it to him. "Hank didn't lie about his fix-it-up capabilities. Whatever he did seems to have increased the power of the spray."

"He also fixed the creak in the back door."

"Really?"

"Yes, and the uneven floorboard and the broken shelf in the pantry."

"Well, he's ensuring his investment is in good shape, that's all. Listen, it's almost quitting time. After I finish unloading these dishes, I'm going to make a batch of chocolate cupcakes with buttercream frosting. Can you check on the girls? If Rosie needs a break, I can keep them busy in the kitchen."

Travis shuffled his feet. "I don't think you need to worry about the girls."

Bethany glanced up from where she leaned over the dishwasher. "What do you mean?"

"They've been trailing our maintenance god all afternoon. I was finally able to bribe them away with the promise of tacos." He held up two small plates filled with a taco, apple slices, and a snickerdoodle. "I'll deliver their meals, then help Rosie with cleanup."

Bethany stared after Travis as he left the kitchen. A self-centered actor would not put up with two little girls hanging on his tail for long. Sooner or later, he would grow bored with his pint-sized audience and drop the maintenance man act. And when he understood Bethany was not putting out, he would return to the city of angels, and she could get back to normal.

She finished unloading the dishwasher, washed her hands at the sink, then pulled out ingredients. Her entry was due by midnight Friday night, and she wanted to make certain the recipe was as tasty as she remembered.

She boiled water and then whisked the dry ingredients together in the mixer. Then she added the wet ingredients and the boiling water to the cake batter. She poured the chocolate batter into the cupcake tins, popped them into the oven, then moved on to tackle the vanilla buttercream frosting.

"Wow, smells great in here." Rosie came through the kitchen door, carrying a tray of dirty dishes.

"Cupcakes are in the oven. If you and the girls want to stick around, I'll let you try one."

"We'd never pass up your chocolate cupcakes." She put the dishes in the dishwasher. "You're planning on joining us for princess movie night, right? *Beauty and the Beast* is on the menu."

"You know I never miss it. Tell you what, why don't you

take the girls home and get them into their PJs. I'll follow with the cupcakes. It'll be a fun surprise."

"Perfect. Um, there's something I ought to mention first."

"What's that?"

"Well . . ." Rosie wiped her hands on the towel. "Well, the thing is . . ."

Bethany stopped whipping the frosting. "What?"

"I invited Hank along."

A tingle swept through Bethany's body. "You didn't."

"I did, and I'm sorry. I know this is our tradition, and he might sell Grandma Lou's out from under us. But he's been so kind to the girls, and despite being famous, I think he's lonely. We don't have much to offer someone like him. I thought it would be a simple thing the girls and I could do to repay his kindness today. He let them pound nails into boards and screw in light bulbs. They can't stop talking about it."

Bethany added more powdered sugar to the mix and resumed stirring, but her mind was far from the task. "He actually said yes?"

"He did. I was as surprised as you, but the girls begged him to come along. I think he misses having family around."

"Does he know I'm going to be there?"

"Sure. I told him it was a weekly thing for us. He said he didn't want to intrude, but I told him he wouldn't be. Are you mad?"

She should refuse the invitation. She'd promised Elizabeth she would stay away from Hank. Would Elizabeth consider Bethany's acceptance a breach of their bargain?

Tia and Tana came flying into the kitchen with Travis not far behind them. "Miss Bethany. Miss Bethany. You comin' to our princess party?"

Bethany wiped her hands on her apron. "Um, I don't think—"

The girls' faces dropped, taking Bethany's heart with them. She couldn't bear their disappointment. It wasn't their fault she'd made a deal with Elizabeth. Besides, she'd only promised to decline invitations from Hank. She couldn't stop other people from extending invitations, and Hank from accepting. Could she? And if *she* happened to be at the same party, that wasn't her fault, was it? Of course not.

She met Travis's eyes over the girls' heads and they exchanged a silent message. Hers asked: Will you come? His replied: If I must.

Bethany shifted her gaze to the girls, who held back tears. She granted them her warmest smile. "I wouldn't miss it."

"Yay!"

Travis crouched next to the girls. "Am I invited, too?"

"Yes," Tia and Tana chorused, rushing into Travis's arms.

"You want to watch a princess movie?" Rosie asked.

"Sure." Travis tipped his head toward Bethany. "It's high on my bucket list right now."

"Okay, I'll make popcorn. It will be fun. We'll look for you both around eight." Rosie shifted her attention to her children. "*Vamos*, girls. Get your things."

"Bye, Mr. Travis. Bye, Miss Bethany." The girls ran into the dining area, and Rosie followed them with a wave to Bethany.

"Good luck with the contest entry—I'm sure it will be a winner."

"Thanks, Rosie. Don't forget to cast your vote for Grandma Lou's any time after midnight on Friday."

"Got it. See you later, Travis."

The minute Rosie was out the back door, Travis was on Bethany like sprinkles on cupcakes. "Why would a television star come to a little girl's princess party?"

Bethany finished pouring the second batch of cupcakes. "You're asking me? Guess he likes kids and Disney movies."

Travis's frown could have stretched all the way to downtown Cleveland. "I thought after last night you were through with him. You two have something going on I don't know about?"

"Of course not. I don't know why he agreed to come to the princess party. It's probably because he's lonely, like Rosie said. Why are you looking at me that way?"

"Don't be naïve, Bethany. He's after you. Maybe you should pretend to be sick. The girls will understand, and I can have a little talk with Hank."

Bethany opened the oven door and placed the pan of cupcakes on the top shelf. "There's no need for a talk. I'm a big girl. I know how to tell a guy no. Besides, you'll be there. What could go wrong?"

CHAPTER TWENTY

Bethany eyed Daphne Miller who sat next to Hank on Rosie's worn brown couch. When she'd imagined what could go wrong, she hadn't imagined Daphne as part of the equation.

"I hope you don't mind me tagging along with Hank," Daphne said, presenting Bethany and Travis with a smile as fake as her boob job. Bright pink hoops dangled from her ears. She proceeded to squeeze Hank's arm as if it were her personal possession.

"Not at all." Bethany scratched the back of her leg with her free hand—the other held her cupcakes in a plastic container. The woman gave Bethany a serious case of hives. She forced her lips into what she hoped was an upward tilt and tried not to look like she cared. "Rosie in the kitchen?"

Daphne shrugged. "I think she's helping the little angels with their PJs. Hi, Travis. Aren't you the handsome one? Ooh, is that your winning recipe?" Daphne moved her palm to Hank's leg and smirked. "Hank mentioned you were entering a contest."

"He did, did he?" Bethany's gaze traveled from

Daphne's hand to Hank's face. He removed Daphne's hand, stretched his long legs in front of him, and offered her a sleepy smile.

"That was mighty sharing of him," Bethany said. "Travis, why don't you grab a seat. I'm going to put these cupcakes on a plate."

"Hi, Miss Bethany. Hi, Mr. Travis. We've got popcorn," Tia said, racing into the family room in pink princess pajamas. Tana and Rosie were not far behind her.

Bethany held up the plastic container. "And we brought dessert."

"Yay!" Tia and Tana cheered. "Can we have one?"

"Sure, if it's okay with your mother."

"Girls, tee up the movie and sit next to Travis," Rosie said. "Bethany and I will get some plates and napkins." She motioned for Bethany to follow her into the kitchen.

The minute they were behind closed doors, Rosie turned to her and lowered her voice. "What's Hank doing with Daphne Miller?"

Bethany frowned. "That's what I was going to ask you. You didn't invite her?"

"Are you loco?" Rosie's brown eyes flared with annoyance. "Of course, I didn't invite her. Why would I do a horrible thing like that? Hank just asked if a friend could come with him. I didn't think to ask who it was. She did bring a fancy pistachio dessert, though." She pointed to a cake with a light green cream filling, then rummaged around in the cupboard, bringing out a white plate, which she handed to Bethany.

"So Hank invited her."

"I'm seriously disappointed in his taste."

Bethany popped the cupcake holder open and began

adding the cupcakes to the plate. "First impressions can be deceiving. Still feeling sorry for him?"

"Actually, yes. He has to be desperately lonely to invite that man-eater along."

"Or he craves attention from women. According to Elizabeth, he breaks hearts wherever he goes."

"I can believe it. But maybe he felt sorry for her. Daphne can be persuasive, as you well know. What should we do about it?" Rosie picked up a tray with a pitcher of water, cups, and a big bowl of popcorn. "This was supposed to be a cozy family night."

Bethany grabbed the plate of cupcakes and the pistachio cake. "What can we do? It's not like we can kick her out. Let's make the best of it. But I hope you won't be offended if Travis and I leave as soon as the movie is over."

HANK KEPT his eyes on the television screen, but his thoughts were far from *Beauty and the Beast*. They kept returning to the woman who sat on the opposite side of the room, the girls cuddled on either side of her. Travis lay on the recliner next to them, his head tipped back, snoring. It wasn't surprising he had fallen asleep—the kid worked harder than anyone Hank knew, including himself.

He shifted on what had to be the pokiest couch he'd ever had the misfortune to sit on, and dodged Daphne's groping hands for at least the twentieth time. He'd worked himself into quite a stew this morning after Bethany had made it clear just how little she thought of him. Then he'd spent the afternoon tinkering with machinery and pounding nails. He had about convinced himself that she wasn't worth his attention, when the girls had invited him to their princess party. Daphne had begged him to let her tag along, and he'd felt sorry for her. And he figured it wouldn't hurt for Bethany to see that other women found him attractive.

Hank slanted a glance at Bethany. She and the girls made a pretty picture with their dark heads pressed together, their eyes glued to the television, and their lips parted. On screen, the narrator announced the curse: The Beast must learn to love another and earn Belle's love in return by the time the last petal fell, then the spell would be broken. But who could ever learn to love a beast?

Why did Hank feel like the hourglass had been turned? That he needed to find a way to convince Bethany he was worthy of her attention, or he would be lost forever like the darn beast.

She raised her head and her eyes caught his—dreamy, puzzled, soft. Something moved inside him—almost a physical pain—and he couldn't look away. A hunger burned. But it was not sexual . . . not really. No, he hungered for her warmth and kindness. He longed for her to look at him the way she seemed to look at every other stray who wandered into her inner circle. He yearned for her to find him worthy. He was caught in her spell—a spell woven from loneliness and need and desire.

"I'll get more water," she said, scrunching her face in what Hank called her keep-your-distance frown and grabbing the pitcher. The dreaminess in her eyes hardened into ice chips. She turned and marched into the kitchen. Daphne moved her roaming hands into his hair, bringing Hank back to reality with a sudden hard tug. This was what he'd wanted, wasn't it? For Bethany to see him as desirable. But the victory felt shallow in the moment.

Hank removed himself from Daphne's clutches, stood,

and collected their dirty napkins and plates. "Don't get up," he told Daphne when she rose to follow him. "I'm just getting rid of the dishes. I'll be right back." He followed Bethany into the kitchen.

The minute he opened the door, she turned from filling the pitcher with water. When she spotted him, her eyes widened. "Did you need something?"

"Yes." *A douse of ice-cold water.* What was he doing? His gaze caught hers and he moved forward on autopilot. He'd tried being her friend and that hadn't worked.

Like a mouse who's spied a cat, she froze.

"You're spilling." He motioned to the overflowing pitcher.

She cocked her head and then her eyes widened further, and she twisted in a hurry to shut the water off and empty the excess. When she turned back, he was there. In her space.

"What do you want?" She lifted her chin. Her breath was warm on his face. Chocolate and vanilla filled the space between them.

"I think we need to talk."

Her eyes narrowed and dropped to his lips. "About what?"

"About this."

He bent his head, giving her plenty of time to duck.

She didn't.

Maybe the beast could be saved after all?

His lips met hers; brushed once, twice. His pulse throbbed. He didn't rush the kiss, nor did he linger. He waited for her to give him a sign that she craved his touch as much as he did hers—that the attraction he felt for her wasn't all one-sided.

She let out a sigh, and her small hands reached around

his neck and pulled him closer. That was all the sign he needed.

HOW LONG DID they stand in the kitchen, swaying back and forth like a jukebox was cranking out love songs? One minute? Ten? Bethany could almost hear the strains of a violin or a softly strumming guitar, almost feel the touch of a magic wand and fairy dust.

His lips pressed against her mouth—as firm and full and hot as she'd dreamed they would be. His tongue swept the edges of her mouth and then plunged inside. She breathed in what smelled like a forest of evergreens. She wanted the kiss to go on and on forever. To lose herself in the feel of his soft lips and perfect physique.

Bethany wrapped her hands around his broad shoulders and tucked herself into his hard chest like she'd imagined doing since they'd walked on the beach and he'd told her that he wanted to be friends. But he wanted to be more than friends, didn't he? And God help her, so did she.

He groaned and framed her face with his large hands, deepening the kiss. She heard herself mew like a kitten. Her hands tangled in his golden hair like she'd seen his female costar do on the television screen. After seeing the on-screen kiss, she'd imagined what it would feel like to be his costar. Now she knew. Her blood heated into a roaring inferno.

She kissed her landlord. She kissed a celebrity. She kissed Apollo.

The first strains of sanity floated in her brain. What was she doing? Desmond was also a celebrity. Hadn't she been down this path before? This passion blossoming between her and Hank—it wasn't real. It was the thrill of the chase for Hank—the challenge of a moment; a victory claimed. He would take what she offered and, like any summer fling, would end it when Hollywood beckoned. Her life was here, in Cleveland, with Travis and her friends and Grandma Lou's. Not in some jet-setting lifestyle in Los Angeles with an actor who looked like a Greek god. And if Elizabeth found out . . .

She pushed against his chest until he raised his head from his assault on her lips. Bethany had no doubt her deal with Elizabeth would be over. She would never gain the votes she needed in the contest to save Grandma Lou's. Besides, she'd made a bargain. "Hank, I can't. I'm sorry."

His eyes were dark with desire, and for a moment, they didn't seem to register her words. He tilted his head. "You're right. This isn't the time or place. Later?"

She pulled herself from his arms. "No, Hank. I can't do this with you."

He didn't move, but his forehead creased, and his eyes squinted at the corners. "Why?"

"*Dios mío!*" A scream erupted from the other room.

Rosie.

Bethany tore herself from his arms and dashed into the family room, Hank hard on her heels. Her heart worked double-time in her chest. The scene that confronted her was as dramatic as any movie. Rosie and Daphne were crouched over Tia, while Tana stood to the side sobbing, and Travis worked his cell phone.

"What is it? What's happened?" Bethany reached the huddled group at the same time as Hank.

"I don't know," Rosie said, out of breath. "She's having some sort of reaction. What should I do?"

Tia's face and throat were swollen, and her skin was red and blotchy. She struggled to breathe.

"An ambulance is on the way," Travis said, his cell phone pressed to his ear. "They say they'll be here in less than five minutes. If you have an EpiPen, use it. Is she breathing? If she's not, we need to perform chest compressions."

Hank peered over Rosie's shoulder. "She's breathing, but it's a struggle."

"Hang on, *niña*," Rosie said, squeezing Tia's hand. "Hang on. An ambulance is coming."

Hank leaned toward Rosie. "Do you have an EpiPen?"

Rosie shook her head, eyes wide. "No."

Bethany gazed in horror as Tia gasped for air.

"Turn her on her back," Hank told Bethany and Rosie. "Daphne, find a blanket."

Daphne hesitated and then took off down the hall, her high heels clunking, while Bethany and Rosie turned Tia on her back, and Hank checked her pulse.

"She's stopped breathing." Hank's voice remained steady, but Bethany could hear the urgency in his tone. "I'm going to do chest compressions. Travis, how much longer?"

Hank began pressing Tia's chest and counting.

"Three minutes," Travis said.

Three minutes seemed endless. How Hank managed to stay calm and know what to do, Bethany couldn't fathom. Daphne brought the blanket, and Bethany covered Tia's lower half, while Hank worked on her chest, and Rosie spilled a steady stream of terrified words in Spanish. The only comfort Bethany could provide was to Tana, who clung to her side.

"They're here." Travis rushed to the door.

Then the ambulance crew swarmed inside, taking over

for Hank who wiped the sweat from his forehead with the back of his hand.

"*Mi Tia, mi niña.*"

Hank turned to Bethany. "I'll go with Rosie and Tia in the ambulance so Tana can stay with you."

Rosie raised grateful eyes to him. "Gracias, Hank."

Bethany hugged Rosie. "Travis and I will take care of Tana. Go. We'll follow you to the hospital in my car."

Then Rosie and Hank were out the door, and Bethany rushed around like one of those robotic vacuum cleaners that bounce off walls, gathering a change of clothes for Rosie and Tia, their personal items, Tia's favorite stuffed dog, and anything else that came to mind.

CHAPTER TWENTY-ONE

"Mama?"

Hank took off his hat and let out a breath he hadn't known he was holding.

Rosie sobbed and smoothed a hand across Tia's forehead where she lay in the hospital bed, hooked up to countless machines. "*Gracias a Dios.* You're awake. How do you feel?"

"Good. Is that Mr. Hank?"

"Yes, *pequeña.* He saved your life."

"You almost died," Tana said, crowding in next to her mother. "I was scared. So was Miss Bethany."

Hank noticed Tana still clutched Bethany's hand, her pale face streaked with tears. Now that the crisis had passed, his brain began to function again.

"What do you think caused it?" Rosie asked the doctor, a middle-aged woman in scrubs.

"We won't know for sure until we've completed all of our tests, but nuts are a common allergen, and you mentioned there was a pistachio dessert?"

Daphne gasped, and Hank's eyes met hers. "I brought a pistachio dessert. I had no idea the child was allergic."

"Has your daughter ever eaten them before?"

Rosie looked at Tia. "Tia, did you eat the pistachio cake?"

Tia's face dropped like she'd done something wrong.

"It's okay if you did," Bethany said. "Your mom isn't mad. She just needs to give the doctor the right information."

The child fingered the sheets. "Yes. It made my tongue feel weird."

"That's most likely the cause, but we'll confirm," the doctor said to Rosie. "In the meantime, you and your daughter must be extremely vigilant to make sure she never comes in contact with pistachios again or ingests them. You'll also need to have an EpiPen on hand. Tonight's emergency could have been fatal. She was lucky this gentleman reacted so quickly to her distress." She squinted at Hank. "Don't I know you from somewhere?"

Hank wiped his hands on his jeans and suppressed a sigh. Of all the times for him to be recognized.

Hank was grateful when Travis jumped in to explain. "Television. This is Hank Haverill. You know—Apollo."

The doctor's eyes lit up like it was the Fourth of July. "That's it. I knew I recognized you from somewhere. So you're a hero on screen and off now, aren't you?"

"Well, I don't know about that," Hank said.

"He is our hero." Rosie gave Hank a tremulous smile. "I don't know what we would have done without you. Thank you, Hank." She held her hand out to him.

Hank took it and squeezed. Warmth flooded his chest. "It was nothing."

"It was not nothing, Hank," Bethany said, her eyes like

shining twin stars. "What you did tonight was truly amazing. You saved Tia's life. We—I thank you."

Bethany's words from the kitchen floated in his mind: *I can't do this with you.*

Hank's gaze met hers. For a moment, the room disappeared. He hadn't done what he'd done to earn Bethany's approval. His reactions had been instinctive—a summer of first-aid training in Boy Scouts brought to life. He hadn't thought beyond that. And he would not wish the last hour over again. But the way Bethany looked at him now—it made him feel like he could scale a mountain or leap tall buildings in a single bound.

"I'm so sorry I brought that dessert. You were wonderful." Daphne hooked her arm through his. "A real superstar. Everyone needs to know what a hero you are."

Hank blinked. He'd forgotten she was in the room. "I wasn't alone. All of you helped."

"But you're the man of the hour, aren't you?" She gave him a smooch.

His female costars and rabid fans were easy with their affections, kissing his face and draping their arms around him all the time. He'd never enjoyed it, but even less now with Bethany's eyes on him. Daphne's flirting seemed outrageous and wrong. He removed his arm from hers, ignoring her pout.

"Let's allow Tia some rest now," the doctor said. "We'll keep her here overnight for observation. However, if all is well, she should be able to go home tomorrow." She looked at Rosie. "You're welcome to stay in the room if you'd like."

Rosie nodded.

"We brought you an overnight bag," Bethany said. "You should have everything you need. Tana can stay with me tonight. I'll bring her by in the morning."

Travis spoke up. "You and Daphne need a lift home?"

And that's how Hank ended the night squashed between Daphne and Tana in the back of Bethany's tiny Toyota.

~

BETHANY TOLD herself Hank was off-limits. He was too theatrical, too larger-than-life. Too used to being doted on by the opposite sex and getting whatever he wanted.

But seeing him in the backseat of her Toyota—this large man, used to roomy, expensive vehicles with a driver, scrunched between a yawning five-year-old and a woman who wanted nothing more than to strip him naked—made him seem vulnerable. Her eyes kept meeting his in the rearview mirror before he caught her at it, and she shifted her gaze back to the road.

"I'll take Tana home first," she said to Travis. "It's after one, and she's falling asleep. I'll get her to bed, and you can drop off Daphne and Hank at Rosie's so they can get their cars."

"Oh, I didn't bring a car," Hank said. "There's only one at Rosie's, and it's Daphne's, not mine."

"I can give you a ride, Hank honey."

Bethany tried to stop herself from glancing into the back seat and failed. Daphne had her chest pressed against Hank's shoulder. Hank's eyes met hers, and he had the audacity to grin before turning to Daphne.

"Kind of you, but my ride is already on its way. Beth can drop me off at her house, and I'll be picked up there. Travis can take you along to fetch your car. As long as that's okay with you all?" He directed the last bit toward the front.

"Sure," Bethany said. Did her voice sound a little breathless?

Daphne persisted. "Couldn't your driver give me a ride to my car?"

"Afraid not. I need my beauty sleep. I have to be in the gym tomorrow by 7 a.m."

"What gym do you go to? Maybe I could tag along?"

Bethany couldn't imagine how Hank would untangle himself from Daphne's suggestion without being rude.

"Sorry, my workouts are intense, and I can't afford distractions. I always work out alone."

She should have realized a woman like Daphne would prove no match for Hank. He appeared to have plenty of practice in dealing with clingy females.

Ten minutes later, she swung into her driveway and put the car in park. "Home sweet home."

Travis stretched and opened his door. "I'll carry Tana into the house."

But Hank was halfway out of the car with the sleeping child in his arms. "I've got her. You okay to drop off Daphne?"

Travis raised his brows at Bethany until she gave a slight nod, indicating she would be fine. "Sure," he told Hank.

Moments later, she and Hank had Tana in the house and tucked away in Bethany's bed for the night. She left a nightlight on in case the child woke and was afraid or needed to use the bathroom.

She gestured for Hank to precede her, and then she followed him into her family room. His presence dominated the small space. The room seemed to shrink and take all the oxygen with it. She rubbed her neck and struggled to think. "How much longer until your ride gets here?"

He checked his cell phone. "Fifteen minutes."

Bethany pointed to the couch. "Why don't you grab a seat. Thirsty?"

"Don't wait on me. You're exhausted. Sit and rest." He patted the spot next to him.

She shouldn't sit that close to him, but she was too worn out to remember why. "Thank you again for saving Tia's life. I'm so grateful you were there. You were amazing."

"Grateful enough to tell me what you meant in the kitchen earlier tonight?"

His deep voice sent a chill through her body. Her cheeks warmed, so she bowed her head to hide from his sharp eyes. "I'm not sure."

The soapy smell of Hank's aftershave hit her senses like a cool breeze.

"You said you can't be with me? Why?"

Several thoughts flashed through her mind in quick succession, starting with: *I'm too busy with the business*, moving to: *You're my landlord*, and ending on: *I promised Elizabeth*. All were valid excuses, but gazing into his ocean-blue eyes turned those ideas to mush. She finally managed, "I'm not interested in a one-night stand."

Something glittered in his eyes. Disappointment? Hurt? Anger? Whatever it was, he shook his head. "If that's all I wanted, don't you think we'd have done the deed by now?"

Irritation swept through her bloodstream. Did he think her such an easy target? She straightened her spine. "That's just like an egotistical actor. What makes you think you'd get that far with me? Not every woman would take their top off at the thought of spending the night with the glorious god Apollo."

As soon as she flung the words at him, she regretted them. He'd saved Tia's life tonight, and all she could do was hurl accusations.

"That's not what I meant, and you know it. I know you think all celebrities are slime-buckets, but if all I wanted was sex, don't you think I would have moved on long ago?" He spoke as if his words took him by surprise. "I've stayed in Cleveland when my agent and publicist want me to return to LA."

"Hank—"

"I've asked for your friendship—even watched my TV show with you."

"Hank—"

"Do you really think I'd spend time getting to know you if all I wanted was a one-night stand?"

"Hank, it's late, I'm tired. I didn't mean to be hurtful."

"Then be honest. Why can't we spend time together? What are you afraid of?" His eyes held hers, demanding answers. And really, what would be the point in keeping secrets? Hank said he wasn't looking for a long-term relationship.

Bethany wished she could invent a lie and make it sound convincing. But lies deserted her, so she resorted to the ugly truth.

Blood rushed to her face, and her cheeks burned, but she didn't flinch from his hard gaze. "I promised Elizabeth I'd stay away from you."

CHAPTER TWENTY-TWO

Hank stood, the tiredness in his bones vanishing in an adrenaline flow of pure frustration. "What the . . .? Why would you do that? And don't give me any bull, I deserve the truth."

To Bethany's credit, she didn't cower from his anger even though he towered over her. Her oval face looked pale but calm in the lamplight. "Elizabeth promised to get Grandma Lou's the votes it needs to final in the contest. She said she has a pretty active following on social media. In return, I'm to keep my distance from you. I had every intention of doing so until Rosie invited you to princess night."

Her voice sounded almost accusatory, like he was the one at fault, which fueled his annoyance. He clenched his jaw and injected plenty of sarcasm into his voice. "Ah, yes, let's not forget the contest and your never-ending quest to save the restaurant. It appears you'll do most anything to accomplish that feat, even make bargains behind my back. Well, I have news for you: Despite her bossiness, last time I checked the payroll, Elizabeth works for me."

She didn't flinch, although her face grew paler, if that were possible. Or maybe it was his imagination.

She lifted her chin. "Why do you allow her to tell you what to do?"

"She's good at her job, that's why. And she tells it like it is."

"Does she know you're here?"

Her pride, calm demeanor, and worry over Elizabeth triggered the full force of his anger.

"You mean, does she know I spent the evening with you? Don't worry, your little secret pact with Elizabeth is safe for now."

"You really didn't tell her?" She seemed to shrink a little, as if she'd been holding her breath.

He studied her clenched hands. "If I'd told her I was going to a kid's princess party, I'd have gotten an earful. She thinks I'm getting a good night's sleep. I'm supposed to work out early tomorrow, remember?"

"But I thought—" She covered her mouth.

He raised an eyebrow. "What? That I'd spend the night with Daphne?"

Her cheeks took on a pinkish sheen, and she lowered her gaze.

"According to you, that's my MO, isn't it? Hollywood player that I am. What then? C'mon now. Spill."

She frowned. "I thought you and Elizabeth told each other everything?"

Was she joking? But no, her expression was serious. He took a step backward. "Where'd you get that idea?" Even as he asked, he knew. "Is that what Elizabeth said?"

Bethany nodded.

Her gullibility sparked his anger. "And you believed

her?" Was it his imagination or did she look surprised by his reaction?

She nodded again and blinked, before dropping her gaze to her lap. "Why wouldn't I, after hearing what you said to her about me?"

Hank sighed. His irritation fizzled like a dead sparkler. He couldn't judge Bethany's reactions by every other person he knew in Hollywood, who seemed to only want to take advantage of him. She was straightforward and expected those around her to be too. Elizabeth would see her little white lie as stretching the truth for his own good. But Bethany would not. Not after she'd overheard him talking about her to Elizabeth.

His phone buzzed with an incoming text, but he ignored it. He sat down on the couch next to her. "Beth, look at me." His voice sounded like he'd swallowed gravel.

She raised her head until their eyes met.

He cleared his throat. "Elizabeth lied. It's true we've known each other a long time. But I don't tell her intimate details of my relationships. She confronted me about the amount of time I'm spending with you. She's concerned you're a threat to my career because I haven't returned to California. But what you overheard was a one-sided conversation. She told me to sleep with you and get it out of my system. I told her to lay off."

Bethany wrinkled her pert nose, igniting in him an insane desire to kiss it. "Why would she think I'm threatening your career? We're not even dating. And I've never asked you to stick around. That was your idea."

He found her hand and threaded his fingers through hers. The contact had his skin tingling and his heart lurching. "I know that, and you know that, but Elizabeth doesn't. It's her job to make me look good. And I haven't made it easy on her by spending all my time eating cookies, dodging her events, and fixing up the building. She blames my lack of focus on you." Which was close to the truth, but Hank didn't think now was a good time to mention it.

"But you *are* planning to return to Hollywood, right? Once you've made all the repairs?"

His breath hitched. "Eventually. I live there." He couldn't stay in Cleveland forever, even though he'd purchased his grandparents' house. His career—or what was left of it—was in LA. He would have to return to the city if he wanted to work, and that meant any contact he had with Bethany would need to be long-distance. Unless he could convince her to sell the shop and move or let Travis run it. But of course, he was getting ahead of himself, wasn't he?

Bethany wriggled her fingers from his and stood, pointing at the front door. "Your driver's here."

He stayed where he was. The ache in his chest from earlier in the evening started up again. "We're not finished here."

"Hank, you should leave."

Why did he feel like she was ejecting him from her life forever? And why did it hurt? They'd only known each other for three whole days. He looked at his watch. Four if he counted today. Not long enough for him to get this attached. Maybe Elizabeth was right? Maybe this was all about the challenge?

He shook off the disturbing thoughts and stood. It shouldn't bother him if Bethany never wanted to see him again. There were loads of women who did—plenty who were far more glamorous and far less prickly. He would never have to work this hard for their attention. Most would spread their legs at a smile from him. They wrote their numbers on napkins and mailed him letters with nude photos. They hung on his every word and praised his physique.

He moved toward her, not stopping until they stood facing each other. Trouble was, none of those women had his heart racing like Bethany. None of them made him feel like she did—like he could gain weight and develop a paunch or lose his hair, and it wouldn't matter as long as he was loyal and kind and cared about others.

She held herself tall and steady, not flinching from his gaze. The humidity had curled her hair into tight ringlets. Not a flaw marred her perfect skin. Her stormy eyes seemed to peer into his soul, wresting his demons from him, one by one. He fought an incredible urge to kiss her again. To make her want him as much as he wanted her.

He swallowed and resisted the desire to run his finger down her petal-soft cheek. All those other women paled in significance next to her honesty. She was a rare and precious gift, and she would slip through his fingers unless he found a way to gain a foothold and hang on tight. She was a prize worth fighting for, and he was a fighter. He would not give up. He could not. "Look me in the eyes and tell me you don't feel this connection between us."

His heart pounded so hard he was certain she could hear it. Her pupils dilated, making her eyes look dark gray. A pulse beat in her neck, but she didn't move away. When she looked at him the way she was, as if she saw him for who he was—not Hank the actor but Hank the man—all reasonable thought deserted him.

"I do feel it."

Relief surged through his veins. He released the breath he'd been holding. He bent his head—close, closer—giving her plenty of time to reject him. Her lips parted. He could feel a little puff of breath. He took his time, filling his lungs with her unique smell until their lips touched. He liked the shape and softness of her lips, he liked her warm vanilla sugar scent, he liked the way she made a small sound in the back of her throat before opening her mouth under his. He liked *her*.

His body tightened, and he deepened the kiss, slipping his hands behind her shoulders and angling his mouth over hers. Long minutes crept by as he lost himself in the incredible taste of her—like a tall glass of lemonade—not too tart, not too sweet. *Perfect.*

Outside, a car honked, reminding him of where he was, reminding him that this was not the way he wanted to win her over—with chemistry. She should want him for all the reasons he wanted her: because she liked him as a person, because the bond between them was undeniable, because she thought a relationship with him was worth the risk.

He broke the kiss and rested his head against her forehead, breathing hard. "Forget about your bargain with Elizabeth. Forget about all the things you might have heard or read about me or what the gossip rags say. Give us a chance, Beth."

He drew far enough away to watch the play of emotion in her expressive eyes: desire, worry, fear. "I can't, Hank." Her voice trembled. "Your life's in Hollywood. Mine's with my brother in our restaurant—with my neighbors and friends in Tremont. I could never survive in your world. I wouldn't know how."

She was right. Hank knew she was right, but it wasn't what he wanted to hear. He stalled for time. "I'm not asking you to marry me."

He wanted her to say it didn't matter. That she wanted to be with him as much as he wanted to be with her. That she trusted him enough to override her cautious nature.

"I'm not good with casual dating, Hank." Lights flashed through the window, and she glanced toward the door. "Your ride's here."

He studied the stubborn line of her lips. "Please tell me you'll see me tomorrow."

"I will see you tomorrow. You're fixing our building." She smirked, and he couldn't help but laugh, relieving the tension between them.

"Smart aleck."

He would not give up. Tomorrow was another day. He would sleep on it and resume his campaign in the morning. She was worth every bit of anxiety and longing and pain she kindled in him. She was worth the wait. "Have it your way, princess." He tweaked her nose. She swiped at his hand but was too slow.

"I'll be by tomorrow. There's a drip in the bathroom sink, and I promised Sam a game of checkers. You can ply me with whoopie pies." He winked. "It will be just like old times."

Now it was her turn to laugh. "Old times. It's only been three days."

He moved to the door, yanking it open. "Four days. And look how much progress we've made."

CHAPTER TWENTY-THREE

Bethany released her breath in a rush and rested her head against the closed door. How she'd had the strength of mind to resist Hank's advances she would never know. The man had serious persuasive ability. And he smelled and tasted good enough to nibble on.

She pressed her fingers against the flat surface. *My God.* It was well after one in the morning, and she needed to get to bed. But how would she ever fall asleep with her blood zipping through her veins and her stomach vibrating with fear and excitement and her entire being longing for his touch?

She forced her legs to move—to go through her night-time routine—put on PJs, wipe off makeup, brush teeth. All the while her mind relived their latest encounter. *I'm not asking you to marry me.*

She pulled a pillow and a light blanket from the hall closet and settled on the couch. Of course Hank was not in it for keeps. He made no secret that he planned to return to California. Their relationship would be brief. She would be foolish to think otherwise.

Yet, with his mouth on hers and their bodies pressed close, she had almost been willing to shove caution aside for a night of shared passion. She shivered and drew the blanket around her shoulders. She was not a short-term relationship kind of girl. When she gave herself, it was for keeps. After Desmond left, she had sworn she would never go down this path again with a man only to have him leave her. She would not risk everything she knew and everyone she cared about for a momentary pleasure.

Please tell me you'll see me tomorrow.

Her heart had leaped at those words. Of course she wanted to see him tomorrow, and the day after, and the day after next. He was a toxic drug that her mind and body craved but could never have. Because with one kiss, she was lost. How much worse would it be if she slept with him, and he broke it off, which he would inevitably do when he returned to Hollywood? She would be a mess—worse than when Desmond left.

The key sounded in the lock, and Bethany knew Travis was home. She closed her eyes and pretended to be sleeping.

BETHANY WOKE to the sound of the doorbell. She glanced at the clock—it was six in the morning. Who would be at her doorstep so early? Had something happened at the hospital?

She tossed the blanket aside, ran her hands through her hair, and hurried to check the peephole. A delivery man stood on the front steps, a large vase of flowers in his hands. She opened the door and gazed in astonishment. Purples, oranges, yellows, reds, and greens dominated the bouquet.

"Here you are, ma'am." He thrust the flowers in her direction and handed her a pen. "Can you sign here?"

"Of course." She peeked around the bouquet to sign her name and took the gift inside, her nose thrust into the fragrant grouping. A small square envelope rested among the stems.

She set the vase on the coffee table, opened the envelope, and stared at the two words scratched in black ink.

Say yes.

Her hands trembled, and she dropped the card.

Hank's words from the night before floated in her brain. *Please tell me you'll see me tomorrow.* And her response: *I will see you tomorrow. You're fixing our building.*

If she needed proof Hank wouldn't give up until he'd won her over, she had it. And she had to admit, the flowers were gorgeous, the man was charismatic, and the weaker half of her wondered why the heck she resisted his advances. Why not forget the bargain she'd made with Elizabeth and enjoy the time she and Hank had together, fleeting as it would be? What woman wouldn't want to date a television star? Imagine the tales she could tell her grandchildren one day.

She picked up the card and set it among the flowers. She had to remain firm because the saner part of her understood that any kind of relationship with Hank would turn her ordinary life into something entirely different. Something that could only lead to heartbreak.

No sense dwelling on it. She was a working girl and needed to get her butt in gear or she would never get to Grandma Lou's on time. Hank was pumping iron this morning, so she wouldn't see him anyway. And she had to send the lease agreement to her lawyer, put out an e-news-letter, update their website, post on their social media accounts, and pass out flyers encouraging customers to vote for their recipe, starting Saturday.

She went up the steps and hurried to her bedroom to get dressed, then knocked on Travis's door until she heard his sleepy mumble.

"What?"

She cracked the door open and spoke to the mound underneath the blankets. "I'm heading out to open Grandma Lou's. You'll need to take care of Tana and bring her to Rosie when she's up."

"I will," he mumbled, turning over and burying his head in his pillow.

An hour later, Bethany donned an apron, whipped up some batter, and placed a batch of apple-cinnamon muffins in the oven. While she waited for the muffins to bake, she put the lease agreement in an envelope and addressed it to her lawyer. She glanced toward the door when the first customers entered, half expecting Hank in his mainte-nance-man garb. She told herself she was relieved when it was only a few regulars, wanting their donuts before work.

She stocked shelves and made broccoli cheese soup, turkey club sandwiches, two gallons of sweet tea, and a strawberry Jell-O salad for the lunch crowd, but when she served her first plate, Hank still hadn't put in an appearance.

At three, she paused on the way to the kitchen with an armful of dirty dishes and glanced out the window. Sunshine beat against the glass. A few cars moved up and down the street. A typical late afternoon summer weekday in Tremont, Ohio. *No Hank.* Maybe he'd already grown bored with her—succumbed to Daphne's charms, or those of some other crazed fan of his?

She made her way to the kitchen and piled the dirty dishes in the sink so she could unload the dishwasher. She opened the door and clutched a handful of silverware. From the other room, the jangle of the doorbell sounded. Her heartbeat tripped into high gear, but when she set the silverware down and walked into the dining room to see who'd entered, it was not Hank. She tried to ignore the heavy feeling settling in her stomach like a bad batch of brownies.

She wiped her hands on her apron. "Hi, Patty. Everything okay next door?"

"Oh sure, everything's fine." Patty's family had owned the antique bazaar for as long as Bethany could remember. She was a large woman who laughed a lot and often braided her long dark hair, although today she wore it down. She also made pasta sauce that could rival that of the best chefs in Cleveland's Little Italy. Desmond, the thief, had nagged her for the recipe before he'd left town. Later, they'd discovered that he'd used it on his show, claiming he'd tweaked the recipe, making it his own.

Patty twirled a strand of hair with one hand and gestured with her other hand toward the large black kettle plugged in behind the counter. "I came over to see if you had any soup left. Mitch and I didn't have time for lunch."

"Sure. I'll get it for you."

Bethany grabbed two to-go containers and ladled hot soup into them. "Busy day?"

"I'll say. Our Hollywood hunk was in—replaced the rotted wood step out front. Attracted a few onlookers, so he took off a while ago. For a television star, he's mighty handy with a hammer. Heard he saved Tia's life last night too."

Bethany placed the bowls of soup in a brown paper bag. Patty handed her a ten-dollar bill and rambled on.

"Mitch and I are thrilled with him as our new landlord. He's done so much for this old place already." Her cheeks turned from ivory to a cherry red. "Not that you and Travis weren't good landlords before the bank seized the property. I know that you did everything you could do for us, given the state of your finances."

Bethany deposited the money in the cash register, counted out the change, added spoons and napkins to the bag, and tried not to let her embarrassment at her own deficiencies as a landlord and surprise at Patty's praise of Hank show on her face. "No offense taken."

Patty leaned against the counter and cupped her hands around her mouth, as if imparting a grave secret. "Of course, one of his onlookers this morning was Daphne Miller. You shouldn't let that woman get a jump on you."

Bethany set the bag on the counter in front of Patty. "Hank's our landlord, Patty. I'm not in competition for his attention." But wasn't she?

"Daphne spent the entire afternoon at our store yesterday. And this morning she showed up at ten with coffee. I told Mitch as soon as I saw her, she wasn't there for the antiques. And boy, was I right. It was Hank this and Hank that all afternoon long. He drank her coffee."

She laughed like she told a good joke, but Bethany couldn't find any humor in the image of Daphne pursuing Hank. "She still over there?"

Patty grabbed the bag. "Nah. He put her to work holding boards and handing him nails. She finally got fed up with all the sawdust in her hair and left. Can't say I blame her. You don't suppose a big shot like him would seriously consider a woman like Daphne, do ya?"

Bethany hoped not but shrugged like she didn't care. "What did Daphne do with Gulliver while she was playing the part of assistant?"

"She got wise and left him home, I guess. Hey, these your flyers?" She pointed to the yellow paper, where Bethany had printed the details of the contest and how to vote. She'd included a picture of the cake and one of her and Travis in front of Grandma Lou's, figuring it would add a personal element.

"I'll take some of these and hand them out in our store."

"Great. Don't forget you can cast your vote any time after midnight on Friday."

Patty turned to open the door at the same time it swung inward. She bumped into Travis, who'd come to help Bethany with the dinner hour. "Hey, Travis honey. Sorry about that. I just came for a bite and bit of gossip. Ciao."

"Hey, Patty." The door closed and Travis removed the backpack slung over his shoulder. He blessed Bethany with his usual carefree smile. "Busy day?"

"The usual. How was class?"

"Great, but I have my exam on Wednesday."

Travis would finish his computer degree at a local college in another semester. It comforted Bethany to know that with a degree behind him, he would have employment opportunities if they were forced to close the shop. *God forbid.*

"Are things slow here? Mind if I get a head start on studying?"

Bethany smiled. "Sure. Go sit in the corner where it's quiet. Apple muffin?"

"Sounds great. Thanks, Bethany."

She headed to the kitchen to fetch the muffin and finish emptying the dishwasher.

A tall man with golden hair leaned against the worktable, drinking a glass of her ice-tea, and eating a muffin. Next to him were dark sunglasses and a cowboy hat. He looked up when she entered and flashed her a heart-stopping smile. "We have to stop meeting like this."

CHAPTER TWENTY-FOUR

Bethany advanced toward him with a flushed look on her face. Hank smiled because she couldn't hide her excitement from him, despite how much he knew she fought the attraction. She was happy to see him.

"How'd you get in here?" She had on her grandma's apron again. As she got closer, he saw dark smudges under her eyes. She hadn't slept any better than him.

He winked, making sure to drawl his words, anything to get a reaction. "Oh, it wasn't hard. Scaled an eight-foot fence. Snuck in through the back door. Easy-peasy." He polished off the muffin and set down the ice-tea. "You should try it sometime." He patted his belly. "Great way to stay in shape."

Her lips turned up into a half-smile. She might not want to like him, but she did. He knew it, just as he knew when he would get a choice part.

"Did you get my flowers?" He watched her face and was rewarded with a faint blush.

"I did. They're beautiful. You shouldn't have."

He entwined his fingers with hers and tugged her close. "You're beautiful."

The blush deepened. "Don't flatter me."

Now it was his turn to frown. "I'm not. You are beautiful. And well-deserving of flowers. I'd like to take you out tonight. I have something I want to show you."

She cocked her head to the side, her eyes shining. "What is it?"

"That would spoil the surprise, wouldn't it?"

The doorbell jangled, but they both ignored it.

"I won't get done until nine."

He rubbed his thumb in circles on her hand. She didn't shrink away. He liked the softness of her skin and the calluses under her fingers. "I figured."

"What about Elizabeth? I did agree to stay away from you. She's supposed to help me garner votes in the contest."

Hank's eyebrows drew together. "Don't worry about that. I'll set Elizabeth straight."

"What should I wear?"

He took his time, allowing his warm gaze to peruse her body before moving back to her face. "Tennis shoes. We'll do some walking."

They both glanced at her feet—her white Keds were smudged with dirt, while his Nikes looked brand new. He could almost hear the wheels clicking in her mind, gathering steam.

He tipped her chin until their eyes met. "Don't worry about the shoes. You can wear what you have on. This is casual. So you'll go?"

Say yes. Say yes. Say yes. He held his breath and waited for her to decide.

THERE WERE SO many reasons to say no to another date with Hank. If they were written on folded slips of paper, Bethany could build a bonfire. My God, the difference in their shoes alone was reason enough to keep her distance. His were so fancy they could be on display in a museum.

Her dad used to warn her that her curiosity would spell her doom. Maybe he was right because Bethany found she badly needed to know what Hank wanted to show her. Looking into his eyes, she promised herself she would make this their last outing. "Yes."

He bent his head and pressed his lips against hers, and any remaining thoughts disappeared in a rush of passion. Hank tasted of sweet tea and apples and desire. She spread her hands along the solid planes of his chest and did her best to memorize the hard feel of him so she could pull it out to analyze when she was in bed later tonight. One day, soon enough, all she would have of him would be these few precious memories. She didn't kid herself that Hank would stay in Cleveland. And she couldn't leave Travis and the family business.

He wrapped his arms around her and deepened the kiss. Her body responded like he'd found an on switch. She made a small noise, which he interpreted as consent because he tugged on the strings of her apron until it slipped to the floor. His large hands circled her waist, and he pulled her against the hard length of his body. A sharp noise caught her attention. Her heart jumped, and his hands stilled. They both looked toward the swinging doors. Travis stood in the opening.

Hank pulled her to his side like it was the most natural thing in the universe. He draped a long arm around her shoulders, trapping her. "Hi, Travis."

Concern gathered on Travis's face like a string of thunderclouds before a storm. He pointed at Hank. "Sam's in the dining room waiting for you." Then he cast a concerned look her way. "You okay, Bethany?"

She cleared her throat and tried to step away from Hank, but his arm tightened, so she didn't get far. "Yeah, I'm fine. Hank and I were just . . . er . . ."

Hank smiled. "Getting better acquainted. I'm taking your sister out after the restaurant closes. Don't worry. I'll have her home by a reasonable hour."

He bent, picked up the apron, and set it on the worktable. Then he leaned down, kissed the top of her head, and beamed her a smile as bright as a flare. "If you need me, honey, I'll be in the corner whipping Sam's butt in checkers."

He grabbed the dark sunglasses and hat, which Bethany realized were his latest disguise, and put them on. "Thanks for the muffin and tea."

He strolled by Travis, who stepped aside, then came toward her as soon as Hank had cleared the exit.

"I thought you didn't trust him? Now you're a couple?" Her brother squinted his eyes like he was trying to solve an unsolvable equation.

Bethany turned to the dishwasher to avoid his accusatory stare. "We've only had one date. That hardly makes us a couple."

"The last time you went out with Hank, he upset you. Now you're going on another date? I thought you didn't like him?"

She paused over the dishes. She owed Travis an explanation. "I may have misjudged him."

"So he's not a Hollywood player?"

She filled the canisters with clean silverware. "Did I say that?"

Travis pulled clean glasses from the dishwasher and added them to the open shelf where they were stored when not in use. "Worse. You called him a stud rooster. Said he was after every feathery hen in the hen house, including you."

Bethany floured the worktable and grabbed the pizza dough she'd thawed earlier in the day. Calzones were on the menu, and she wanted to have them in the oven well before the usual customers showed up for dinner. "I may have been hasty."

Travis settled on a stool and watched her work with the dough. "You were kissing him just now—I assume you like him? Or do you always go around kissing men who happen to be our landlord?"

Bethany picked the dough up, twirled it, flipped it, and spread it with her fingers. "I never *didn't* like him. I just wasn't sure if we could trust him. I'm still not. But I am curious about what he wants to show me, and he is entertaining."

Travis gave her a my-big-sister-is-nuts laugh.

She stopped working. "What's the joke?"

"Bethany, you like him. It's okay to say it out loud."

"Don't be silly."

"What's more, most people around here *do* like him."

"What are you saying?"

"He's made friends with all the other tenants. They love all the improvements he's making to this old building. Sam's playing checkers with him, and you know that he only ever plays with you or me. Rosie loves him—he saved Tia's life. The girls adore him. His fans are continually stopping by, hoping he'll make an appearance. Daphne's crazy about him. The guy has no enemies except me. And if I'm honest, I only didn't like him because you didn't."

Bethany raised a shoulder to nudge a curl that slipped out of her headband. "You like Hank?"

"Yeah, I do." He laid a hand on her shoulder and squeezed. "But I won't if he's not treating you right."

Her eyes watered, and she looked away but was too slow.

Travis patted her shoulder. "Ah, Bethany. I want you to be happy. You've been holding things together ever since Mom and Dad died, but you shouldn't have to. Losing the building—it's not your fault. Even if Desmond hadn't made off with the insurance money, we would still have had a tough time keeping the old place afloat. If Hank makes you happy, go for it."

Something hard loosened inside her, and she turned to Travis with a hug. "I'm not sure what I want where Hank's concerned, but have I said you're the best brother ever lately?"

He patted her back and gave her a twisted grin. "I'm your only brother."

"True, so let's just say you're the best only brother a girl ever had."

CHAPTER TWENTY-FIVE

Hank slipped the cowboy hat low on his head and squinted through his sunglasses at the checkerboard.

"King me." Sam let out a bark of laughter, hopping over Hank's remaining man and taking the board. "You haven't played checkers much, have you?"

Hank leaned back in the chair. "Oh, I've played but never against a pro like you."

"I've had lots of practice. Travis and I pick up a game or two every Saturday."

Hank glanced at his phone, pushed his chair away from the table, and stood. "That's enough whooping for tonight. Same time tomorrow?"

Sam chuckled and shook Hank's outstretched hand. "Sure. I'll look forward to dishing out the whooping."

"Them's fighting words, old timer."

Sam collected the checkers and returned them to the box. "You takin' our girl out tonight?"

"Plan to."

"You'll take care of her now, won't ya?"

Hank tipped his hat. "You can count on it, Sam."

"She and her brother don't have their folks any longer to look out for them, so I try and do that. You seem gentleman-like to me, and I do believe you care for her, but don't let me hear of any nonsense now. She don't need any more heartache."

Hank almost smiled at the old man's earnestness. He picked up the empty plates from the calzones and salad Bethany had brought them earlier. "I'll treat her like a princess, Sam. Promise." He turned and headed toward the kitchen, while Sam collected Gypsy.

As always, his heartbeat kicked into double-time at his first glimpse of Bethany crouched over one of the cupboards. Her jeans stretched across her tight behind, and she'd replaced her normal T-shirt with a flowery top. She glanced up when he came in, knocking her head against the open door.

"Ow."

"You all right?"

She stood and rubbed her forehead. Was it his imagination or did she seem nervous?

"Yes, I'm fine. Was just taking an inventory of supplies. Is it time to go already?"

"Not quite. Turn around."

She frowned but did as requested. "Hank, what are you—"

He rubbed her shoulders. "Shh. Relax. We have plenty of time."

"If this keeps up, I'm liable to fall asleep."

"Quiet and breathe." Her skin was soft and warm and damp with sweat, and she smelled of basil, lemons, and oregano. How would she react if he leaned down and kissed the back of her neck? Probably not well judging by the tense set of her shoulders. He continued to work the muscles in her upper back until he felt them loosen. He turned her around. "Much better. Ready?"

She nodded.

"Car's out front." He grabbed her hand and tugged her toward the dining room.

"Wait. Are you sure I'm dressed right?"

"You're perfect." He pulled her along, past the counter where Travis counted money in the cash register.

"You okay to close, Travis?"

Travis's usual scowl was absent. He gave them a thumbs up. "I got it taken care of. Have fun, kids."

Hank raised his eyebrows, but Bethany laughed. "Thanks, best brother ever."

Then they were out the front and slipping into the limousine, while Louis held the door.

"Now can you tell me where we're going?" She rested her head against the back of the seat.

"No, now you can relax and be patient." He smirked and raised a brow. "Any guesses?"

"Dinner somewhere?"

"We already ate dinner. Loved the calzones. My compliments to the chef."

She laughed, low and musical. "Dessert, then? Ice cream?"

Now it was his turn to laugh. "My surprise doesn't include food."

She lifted her head. "More episodes of *Apollo*?"

He threaded his fingers through his hair. "No. You know how much I enjoy watching myself on screen."

"I'm stumped."

"You'll know soon enough. What's on the menu for tomorrow?"

She yawned. "Way to change the subject. Tuesdays, I

usually make meatball subs. They've proved a hit with the younger crowd. And macaroni and cheese for a side."

"Sounds like my next meal. Have you heard from Rosie?"

"Yes, she called me a little while ago. They came home from the hospital today. She sounded worn out but that's to be expected. Tia's doing great." She sat up and looked out the window. The evening sun slipped toward the horizon, casting the sky with a pale pink glow. She could see Terminal Tower in the distance. "We're going downtown?"

"Not quite."

Louis turned onto West 10th Street. She pressed her face against the window. "This is residential."

"True."

"Why are we stopping here? Whose house is this?"

He smiled. "Mine."

~

BETHANY LOOKED from Hank to the white-brick colonial house. Someone had turned the porch light on in anticipation of their arrival.

"You bought it?"

He nodded. "It once belonged to my grandparents. They built it. I'd like to show it to you."

Louis held the door open, and she slid from the car.

"This is amazing." She studied the large house. Four wrought-iron pillars lined the front porch, which was built on a brick foundation. All the windows contained shutters, and stone steps led to the porch with an iron railing on either side. A roof with a large chimney covered the porch, and it looked like a small dormer topped the roof. She couldn't see much beyond that in the dark.

"I stayed here for a month during the summers I visited my grandparents as a kid. Let me show you the inside."

He grabbed her hand and pulled her along, his excitement as contagious as a child on Christmas morning.

The inside was even more impressive. The front room contained shiny wooden floors and a wide staircase that led to the upper level.

"Follow me." He flicked on a light switch and led her through a small kitchen. Built-in cabinetry that someone had painted olive green lined the walls. A black and white checkerboard tile decorated the floor.

Hank pointed to the side wall. "A back staircase used to be in here, but the next owner must have removed it. I would sneak down the steps on warm summer nights when I couldn't sleep and hang out on the screened-in porch, where I could catch a breeze."

"It's wonderful and so quaint. You must have really loved it here."

Hank opened the door onto a long porch, which wrapped around the side of the house. The smell of roses kissed the air. "I did. Come with me. There's more."

And then he was pulling her into the family room, which had a large front window and was lined by built-in bookshelves. To the side, an oversized stone fireplace dominated the space.

"Grandpa told me these stones were pulled from the lake. He and his brother built the fireplace by hand. They also poured the sidewalk out front." Pride rang in Hank's voice.

Bethany rubbed a hand across the massive stones. "They must have been some craftsmen."

"Grandpa knew his way around a toolbox. I feel close to him fixing up your building."

She liked how he said *your* building and not *my* build-ing. "What did he think of his grandson becoming a televi-sion star?"

Hank turned and laid a hand on the mantel, so she couldn't read the expression on his face. "I'll never know. He had a heart attack shortly before I got the role that made me famous. I never got to tell him. I didn't even know he hadn't been feeling well."

She touched his arm. "I'm sorry, Hank. I'm sure he would have been proud of you. But he didn't leave you or your parents the house?"

Hank sighed and the sound carried a world of disap-pointment. "He left it to my mom, but when she died suddenly, and it ended up in my hands, turns out there was a loophole in her will that allowed my dad to claim it. He sold it for cash and didn't tell me."

"That's awful. Did you try to buy it back?"

"Yes, but by the time I found out, the new owners had already lived in the house for six months. They loved the house and the neighborhood and refused to sell to me. I've had a realtor watching the house ever since, in case it came on the market. The day I was late to meet you for dinner—that was the day I found out it was for sale. I had my assistant make a cash offer. Yesterday, the owners accepted and agreed I could come here tonight to show you around."

"That's why you were late?"

"I was late because I was exhausted and overslept. But when I woke, I got the call, which distracted me. I had to talk to my financial advisor about making repairs to the building."

"I wish you'd told me that's one of the reasons you were late that night."

He swiveled toward her and grasped her hand. "This

place is special to me. I wasn't quite up to telling you about it—wasn't even sure it would be mine. Besides, would it have made a difference? You were already worked up about the interview, remember?"

Looking into his eyes, she couldn't lie. "Probably not. But what will you do with it now that it's yours?"

Hank shrugged. "I don't know. Clean it, I suppose. Host a party for my friends."

"Oh." Bethany could picture Hank in all his glory, his Hollywood friends coming to Cleveland for the night to party and then jet-setting out again in the morning.

"You really shouldn't look at me like that."

"Like what?"

His eyes glittered in the dim light. "Like you wouldn't be invited to the party."

"Oh, I wasn't—"

His lips settled on hers—hot, hard, thorough—and all reasonable thought deserted her. The more she kissed him, the more she wanted to go on kissing him. The feel of his lips on hers. The tender way he cupped her face with his hands. His long, lean body and the hardness of his chest pressed against hers. She felt safe, cherished, protected. She felt like she belonged in his arms. Like she came alive when he was kissing her. Like life was more exciting, more pleasurable, more real.

But this was an illusion, wasn't it? Hank was a television star. Somehow, he was tearing down the walls she'd built to protect herself from men like him. Men who took and never gave. Men who wanted her heart but wouldn't give her theirs in return. Men who would throw expensive parties with their fancy friends and then return to their high-class world and leave her behind.

She pushed at his chest until he broke the kiss,

breathing hard. Spending time with Hank was dangerous. She should end things now, before she did something she would later regret. She rubbed her hand across her lips, which stung from the scrape of his whiskers. "We should stop."

His eyes still glittered, but he complied, glancing at his Rolex watch. "C'mon, I still have to show you the backyard. I'll try and keep my hands to myself." He grabbed a flashlight from a table in the corner.

She hesitated, biting her lip.

"Please, Beth. I'd really like you to see it."

What was the big deal about seeing the backyard, if this was their official last date and he kept his distance? She nodded. "Okay, Apollo. Lead the way."

Hank made a face at her use of his television name but placed his hand on the small of her back and guided her forward. The warm heat of his palm sent a tingle to the top of her head and the tips of her toes. A dream formed in her mind. A dream that the pressure of his hand on her back represented far more than a casual relationship. A dream that she was his and he was hers. A dream that there would be a reward at the end of the rainbow for them—a fairytale ending straight out of one of his television episodes.

The screen door clicked behind them, putting an end to her ridiculous thoughts. They stepped into a large, square backyard. A tree towered over one part of the yard, and Hank flicked on the flashlight and led her toward it.

"This tree must be at least a hundred years old. I climbed it once or twice when I was a kid."

She placed her free hand on the scratchy bark and looked up into its tall branches, which glowed white where Hank aimed the flashlight beam. "That's an awfully high tree for one small boy. How did you get into it?"

He stood behind her. She could feel his breath on her shoulder, and she fought the urge to lean against him.

"I was a monkey. I shimmied up the trunk until I could grab a branch."

"What did you do once you were up there? What could you see?"

"The stars. I used to watch until I saw a falling one and wish on it."

"And what did you wish for?" She held her breath, half wanting to know what the little boy Hank longed for and half wanting no answer, so she wouldn't find herself more charmed by him than she was already.

"Truth?" His voice was low and deep, the hushed tone seeming to convey the deepest confidence in the dim light.

She turned to look at him. "Yes, please."

"I wished for a home. I wished that my mom and dad got along and would stay in one place. I wished that I could stay in Cleveland forever and not be dragged across the country, moving from city to city as my dad looked for work."

"Oh, Hank."

"None of those wishes ever came true."

"I'm sorry." And she found that she was. Sorry for the little boy who'd longed for a stable home.

"It's okay. I've given up making wishes on falling stars. Childish really—putting the burden of my deepest desires on something entirely outside my control."

She grabbed his hand and squeezed. "It's not childish. It's wonderful. We have to keep wishing and dreaming. That's the whole point of living. Not everything is within our power to control."

He brought their joined hands into the air. A shiver danced down her spine at the contact. "This is one of the many reasons I like you. You find something good in everything."

She tilted her face up to him. The heat of his body surrounded her. He leaned against the tree trunk and pulled her in front of him, his muscular arms wrapping around her middle. She should move. She shouldn't let her curves relax into his warm heat. But the temptation to enjoy the feel of his arms around her proved too much to resist. She snuggled into his chest and stayed put.

His breath stirred her hair. "Did you ever wish on a falling star?"

"Once or twice."

His fingers stroked the skin on her neck, sending a shiver into her nether regions.

"Yeah? What did you wish for?"

She cleared her throat. "I don't remember." But she lied because she did remember.

Hank's hand stilled. "Why do I feel like you're withholding your wishes?"

"We're not supposed to reveal what we wish for. Then they'll never come true."

He laughed, the sound rich and deep and dreamy. "So your wishes were denied as well. More proof that wishing is childish. I prefer to make my own destiny."

"Like buying this house?"

He turned her to face him and tipped her chin until their eyes met. He looked like one of those famous Greek gods chiseled in stone. For a moment, she forgot to breathe.

"I like to go after what I want. I want you to come to LA with me. I want to show you my world."

CHAPTER TWENTY-SIX

Bethany gazed into Hank's eyes and struggled to convince herself it wasn't wise to go to LA with him. For starters, she couldn't leave Grandma Lou's.

"Before you say no, I'm only talking three days the weekend after next—Friday through Sunday."

"Hank, I can't leave town. I won't be able to keep the pantry open, and people depend on it for food."

"I'll hire all the help you need so you won't have to worry about being away, and since you won't close the business, you won't lose any sales."

"But the expense—"

"I'll pay for your plane tickets and all your travel expenses."

"But—"

He placed the tip of his finger on her lips, silencing her protest. "It's only a long weekend. This isn't a big deal. When's the last time you had a break? You deserve a weekend away from all your responsibilities, don't you?"

She removed his finger and stepped away. "It sure sounds like you've thought of everything."

"I got a call from my agent with some good news for a change. I'm being considered for the role of Robin Hood. I really want this part. I have to fly home to talk to the producers, and I want you to come with me."

"I don't know . . ."

"And I'm up for a major award for my role as Apollo. There's a real chance I could win. I've been invited to the awards ceremony, and I can bring a date."

"Well . . ."

"And I want to introduce you to my brother, Connor. And you haven't met my roommate."

"Roommate?" She took another step backward.

He moved forward. "Yes. He's five, furry, likes treats, and goes by the name of Woodrow."

She refused to smile. "I'm happy you're being considered for the role, and you're up for an award, but my coming with you isn't a good idea. As much as I want to. As much as I'd like to see what your life is like in Los Angeles—meet Connor and Woodrow. Hanging out with you for an entire weekend is just going to make me want what I can never have."

"You *can* have it."

"I won't have a fling with you, Hank. I'm not the kind of girl who sleeps around."

He frowned and moved toward her, and she found herself taking a step backward and then another. She didn't see the tree root behind her and stumbled. Her hands flailed, but strong arms kept her from falling. The rich pine scent of his aftershave filled her lungs.

"For the love of God, I'm not inviting you to my home to have a fling, as nice as that sounds. I'm not asking you to move to Los Angeles. I'm not even asking you to commit to a relationship. There are no expectations. This is just a weekend. A weekend to get to know each other better. If you want, Travis can come too."

"He . . . he can?" Did she even want Travis with her?

"Sure. He deserves a break. You'll both be my guests."

"Well, I don't know. I . . . I need to think about it. Talk to Travis."

"I'll need to know soon. The trip is in less than two weeks. I have to arrange plane tickets."

She swallowed. "I'll give you an answer by the weekend."

"Fair enough. Now that we have that straight, I have one more thing to show you, and then I'll take you home."

It struck her then: Hank pointing out the stars under the tree where he used to make wishes was not an impulsive decision. He'd led her to such a romantic setting to make his case—told her about his dreams as a boy to show her a vulnerable side he didn't share with others, to build a path with her to further intimacies. His goal all along was to get her to agree to a weekend trip to Los Angeles—to his home. And God help her, his plan had worked. She was actually considering the idea.

He wrapped an arm around her shoulders, like they were the owners of the home going for a nighttime stroll, and pulled her along. She was caught up in the whirlwind known as Hank Haverill, and she didn't have the strength of will to withstand the tempest. They headed through the house, where he shut off the lights, and then out to the waiting limo.

"After you, madame." Hank held the door and ushered her inside, before getting in himself and motioning to the driver. "Step on it, Louis."

"Right, sir."

The car accelerated, and they were off to some mysterious destination. Hank tucked her into his side like she belonged there. She could have objected, but when was the last time she'd been held by another human being and felt this content, this safe? Still, it wouldn't do to get too comfortable and oblivious to her surroundings. "We're heading east?"

Hank chuckled and the sound reverberated in her ear. "Good deduction, Watson."

She pushed herself away from his shoulder and pressed her face against the window. "Okay, Sherlock. It's clear you're not going to tell me. So give me a clue. We're going toward the university. Did you go to school there?"

"No, I only spent a year in college—in New York, not Ohio."

"The art museum, then?"

"Nope."

"Wait. This is a cemetery. Why are we in a cemetery at night? Isn't it closed? This is seriously creepy."

"I come here whenever I visit Cleveland. I pay them extra to stay open."

"Why?"

"My mother's buried here."

His explanation was said without emotion. He turned his face from hers, so she had trouble deciphering his expression.

"You visit her grave?"

"I do. I can't introduce you to my mom, so I thought this was the next best thing. I don't visit during the day to avoid questions—I never know if a nosey reporter or curious fan will follow me." He shifted to look at her, his warm gaze traveling across her face and settling on her eyes. "My mother would have loved you. Did I mention she liked to cook?"

Bethany shook her head.

"Her chili was so good I sometimes dream about it." He laughed, the sound almost a caress against her sensitive skin. "She was a strong lady—she had to be to deal with my dad."

"Was your father really that difficult to be around?"

There was a long pause while he gathered his thoughts. "My father wasn't physically abusive. His crime was abandonment and neglect. I was ten when he left. Just a boy."

His voice wavered, then grew bitter. "I begged him to stay. I still remember watching the taillights of his green Ford disappear down the old dusty road in the trailer park where we used to live in Virginia. He never looked back."

An image of Bethany's father, sitting in her high school auditorium, flashed through her mind. Although she'd never had a solo, her dad had attended every one of her high school choir concerts, closing the restaurant early just for her. He'd beam at Bethany from the front center row—her mom and grandparents next to him with their own wide smiles.

The limo stopped but neither moved to open the door.

"Did he ever visit, your dad?"

Hank studied his fingernails. "Once or twice. Each time he'd talk about his new girlfriend and show me a picture of a new sibling. Meanwhile, my mother struggled to keep food on the table and me in shoes."

He flicked a glance her way before looking out the window, and Bethany almost cringed at the harshness reflected there. Gone was the television star who always broadcasted a glowing smile. In his place was a man at war with himself—a man who knew a world of hurt.

The change was so drastic, Bethany blinked, wondering

if she'd really witnessed it. She touched his arm. "I'm sorry, Hank. Not every man is meant to be a father."

Now he did look at her. His face lost all expression. "You're right." He seemed surprised and dumbfounded.

"Hank?" Why did she have the feeling they weren't talking about his father? "Hank, I didn't mean—"

"We're here. Let's forget about my father."

Louis opened the door, interrupting their conversation.

"C'mon," Hank said, unfolding his long legs to climb out of the car.

She scrambled to follow, trailing him to the graveyard. He stopped and swung the flashlight beam on a simple white gravestone. A dozen yellow roses, which could have been plucked that morning, rested in a vase at the foot of the grave. Bethany gazed at the words etched in the stone: *Katherine Anne Haverill, Beloved Daughter, Sister, Mother. If love could have saved you, you would have lived forever.*

"I was in college when she died—completely floored—it happened so fast. I'd talked to her the night before. She said she had a headache, but other than that, sounded like her normal self. I didn't think anything of it. The next day, she was gone. I never got to say goodbye. I dropped out of school —I couldn't concentrate."

Bethany touched his arm. "I'm so sorry, Hank."

He turned to look at her. "Don't be. It's been years since her death. I've had a lot of time to adjust. And dropping out of college landed me my big break in television."

She shivered, and he wrapped one long arm around her shoulders. "Cold?"

"No."

"I didn't bring you here to make you feel sorry for me."

She turned toward him. "Why did you bring me here?"

It was dark, which made it hard to get a good read on his expression. But she knew coming to his mother's grave was not an impulsive decision. He'd planned it, just like he'd planned to show her his grandfather's house and the stars from the tree in the backyard.

She shivered again despite the hot, humid air, which kissed her shoulders. Crickets chirped, filling the silence.

"I brought you here because I've never brought another living soul here."

"No one? Not your dad or your friends?"

"No one. At first, because I couldn't bear to come here when my mom passed away, and later, because I viewed it as private. When you're in the public eye, there's not much considered sacred. I don't want my mother's gravesite to be featured in a magazine or plastered across the Internet."

"Your secret is safe with me, I promise."

"I know. And I know you've read some of those gossipy magazine stories that talk about who I'm dating or will date or ditched. I've had my share of relationships that didn't work out, and I'm not going to apologize or deny my past. But I'm more than the Hollywood heartthrob the media has labeled me . . . that *you* think I am. I want you to see that. I want you to see the real me."

He kissed her then—long, tender, lingering kisses in the moonlight that could have gone on forever as far as Bethany was concerned. When they finally pulled apart, they were both gasping for air.

"Beth," he breathed, framing her face with his large hands.

"Yes," she managed.

"I'm not going to deny I want you. You'd have to be blind not to know how much. But I'll never pressure you to do something you don't want to do. Especially when you're under my roof. You'll be safe with me. Do you understand?"

"Yes." His words sent a sharp tingle through her body, setting it on fire.

"So come to LA with me. No expectations. No strings. I promise, you'll enjoy yourself."

CHAPTER TWENTY-SEVEN

Hank watched as Bethany made her way into her house. His stomach ached, like he'd eaten one too many cookies.

Why had he told her about his father? When he'd planned the evening, he'd imagined describing his mom and glossing over any mention of his dad. But somehow, she had drawn all the anguish of their strained relationship out of him. He'd known he had bitter feelings, but until tonight, he hadn't registered the pain behind them.

Some men aren't meant to be fathers. Her words, uttered as they were during Hank's description of the horrible father who'd abandoned him as a child, sliced into his core with all the heaviness of an ax. Wasn't he like his father—a string of women a mile long but emotionally unavailable to those who mattered? If he ever settled down, wouldn't he also make a careless, absentee father? Being an actor was not conducive to family life.

"Let's get moving," he said to Louis after Bethany closed the front door.

The car pulled away from the curb, and his cell phone

buzzed. He checked the number and frowned. *Connor.* Although it had been over a year since Connor first arrived on his doorstep, he still hadn't adjusted to the idea of having a brother. He had been alone far too long.

"Hello, Connor. Is Woodrow all right?"

"Hey, big guy. Woodrow's fine. He's had a long walk, a bath, and lots of treats."

Hank frowned. "You shouldn't feed him too many treats. The vet said it could affect his mood."

"Yeah, well, they make him happy. If you ask me, he bit your ex because she had it coming to her."

"Why are you calling?"

"Does there have to be a reason? I just thought I'd check in."

"How much do you need?"

Connor coughed. "Ten thousand. I'll pay it all back. I promise."

"That's what your dad says."

"He's your dad too."

Hank groaned. "Don't remind me." It wasn't fair to treat Connor like their father. "I told you I'd pay for tuition. Just let Pamela know the payment's due, and I'll have her take care of it."

"I really will pay you back when I graduate."

"It's not a big deal, Connor. I can afford it." He ignored the twinge inside at yet another drain on his bank account. "Was that it?"

"Well . . ."

"What happened? Did you wreck your car?"

"No, I didn't wreck my car. I just . . ."

"Girl troubles? Don't think I'm the best one to advise you there, but I'll try."

"No, Hank. I just . . . I want to wish you a happy birthday. I know it's tomorrow, but you're in a different time zone, and I have exams and will be cramming tomorrow and stuff."

A strange feeling filled him—almost a warmth. "You . . . er . . . thank you."

He hadn't thought about his birthday. Pamela usually sent him a card signed by the rest of his staff. Blackie would sometimes buy him a drink. His father hadn't called on his birthday in years, and there was no one else to remember or make a fuss except his fans, who tended to post their best wishes on social media or send him fan mail, which Elizabeth hired a firm to answer.

"I thought maybe we could hang out together or something when you're back in town. When are you coming home?"

"You sound like a nagging wife."

"Elizabeth says you're infatuated over a girl."

"Elizabeth needs to mind her own business." He was going to have to talk to his publicist and set a few boundaries.

"I've never heard you sound this defensive over a girlfriend."

Hank sighed, wishing he did a better job of reining in his temper. "I'll be home the weekend after next, and her name is Bethany. She has a brother about your age. I'm hoping to bring them with me."

"You really like her, don't you?"

"She's not hard to like."

"You never said that about Melanie."

Louis pulled the car into the drive. He would drop Hank off and then return the car to wherever he stored it.

"Yes, well, you'll see what I mean when you meet her."

"This sounds serious. You think she's the one?"

"One what?"

Connor sighed loud and long. "The one you're going to marry someday."

"What are you talking about? I'm not getting married." Why would his brother think he was planning a long-term commitment? Hank cleared his throat, which had become clogged. "Listen, Connor, I gotta run. Thanks for watching Woodrow. I'll see you in about ten days."

"Thanks for paying my tuition, big guy."

"It's nothing." He ended the call but stared at his phone without really seeing it. Was that where this friendship with Bethany was leading—to marriage and kids one day? Connor hadn't met Bethany, and even he sensed that a woman like her wanted commitment—a commitment Hank doubted he could offer.

He closed his eyes and pressed his head against the back of the seat, but he couldn't stop the cold trickle of fear from entering his gut and spreading through his limbs. To distract himself, he picked up the phone and called Elizabeth. He may not be the marrying kind, but he would do what he could to ensure Bethany's dreams for Grandma Lou's came true.

BETHANY ADDED peanut butter brownies to the display case and wiped her palms on her jeans. Only crumbs remained from her latest batch of Grandma Lou's chocolate cake with buttercream frosting. She eyed the knife and fork on the clock above the counter, which pointed to eleven. The lunch crowd hadn't yet arrived, and Rosie and the girls were eating lunch at their usual booth in the corner.

She took an uneven breath and headed toward the kitchen. There were no more tweaks to Grandma Lou's recipe. The time had come to submit their contest entry. Even though she had until midnight on Friday, she couldn't wait a second longer.

She hurried to the kitchen and set up her laptop. She keyed in the contest entry website and began completing the short form. Business name—check, recipe—check, photographs of the cake—check, electronic signature verifying the recipe was an original first served in their café— check. She entered all the information and then hovered her hands over the keyboard. "Grandma Lou, here goes nothing," she whispered.

She clicked the mouse and hit enter. The button went gray before the page morphed into a time-clock, counting down the minutes until the voting would begin. Excitement curled in the pit of her stomach like a wriggling worm.

She exited the screen and moved to the next task. In a busy kitchen, there was no time to dwell on any one job. She pulled freezer containers from under the worktable and began filling them with the pumpkin cookies she'd iced earlier.

"Did you know today's Hank's birthday?" Rosie asked, breezing into the room with a stack of dirty dishes and proceeding to load the dishwasher.

Bethany glanced up, surprise creasing her forehead. "No, I didn't. Are you sure?"

"Well, unless he's lying. It was his excuse for ordering a chocolate donut with sprinkles this morning. He stopped in on his way to do repairs over at Jim's Jewelry. He said there's a hole in the wall that needs patched."

Bethany sealed the first container and started on a second, swallowing the guilt clogging her throat. How come she hadn't known it was Hank's birthday? "You've sure been spending a lot of time talking with Hank lately." Ever since he'd saved Tia's life, now that Bethany thought about it. "He didn't mention it was his birthday. I feel bad I didn't get him anything."

"He's a good man. He's been kind to us. The girls were thinking we could bake him a cake. He loves your supernatural whoopie pies. Why don't you make a giant one?"

Relief at the suggestion made her hands tremble. She would give Hank a celebration like he'd never had before—a personal one that spoke to their friendship and the stories he'd told her about his family. "Rosie, you're a genius. I'll get started right away."

She called to Tia and Tana, who were playing with a set of blocks in the corner. "Girls, put on your aprons and come and help me. We're going to make Hank a special birthday cake."

"Yay!" the girls chorused, running to find the little aprons Bethany had sewn for them last Christmas, which were stored in a cupboard low to the ground where they could reach.

Bethany pulled ingredients—flour, sugar, salt, baking soda, cocoa, butter, vanilla, buttermilk, and one large egg—and set them on the worktable, then pulled out the large mixing bowl.

"Tia, you can add the flour, baking soda, and salt. Tana, you'll add the sugar, cocoa, and vanilla. And I," she placed the mixing bowl in front of them, "will add the butter, buttermilk, and egg."

Bethany scooped the dry ingredients, and the girls took turns adding their measuring cups to the bowl and stirring.

Soon they were pouring batter into the cake pans and placing them in the hot oven.

"While we wait for the cakes to bake, let's make the filling. We want it to be nice and airy, so we'll whip it a lot."

They had finished mixing the filling and were just beginning to frost the layers when Travis entered the room. "Whatcha baking?"

"We're making whoopie pie cake," Tia said.

"It's Mr. Hank's birthday," Tana said.

"Is that right?" Travis asked, grinning at Bethany. "This sounds like you're getting serious."

Bethany rolled her eyes and placed a layer of cake on top of the filling. "It sounds like nothing of the sort. Girls, get the sprinkles ready."

Travis got a spoon. "I think you need a taste tester." He scooped some of the glistening frosting on to his spoon and popped it into his mouth. "Mmm-mm. Your supernatural filling is the best there is. How's the contest entry coming along?"

"Well, I submitted it this morning. Be sure to cast your vote starting after midnight and spread the word. Right now, though, I'm more concerned with how we'll get Hank into the shop to celebrate his birthday."

"Not to worry on that front," Rosie said, breezing into the kitchen with a stack of dirty dishes. "Sam's here for an early dinner, and he mentioned Hank's challenged him to a game of checkers tonight."

Joy made her hands light as she opened the top on the tub of sprinkles. "Perfect. Let Sam know what we're planning and spread the word to all the tenants. I want this to be a birthday celebration he'll remember."

～

HANK MASSAGED the back of his neck and headed toward Grandma Lou's. After a full day of physical labor, he looked forward to sitting down and enjoying whatever homemade dish Bethany had cooked up today. He opened the door to its familiar jingle and squinted at the balloons taped to the counter.

"Surprise! Happy Birthday!" A slew of familiar faces came from behind the counter and the kitchen.

Hank stopped moving and paused in the doorway, stunned into silence. A happy birthday banner stretched across the back wall, and balloons in a variety of colors were taped to the walls. Sparkling streamers hung from the ceiling.

Hank nodded at Mitch, Patty, and Angel, and there was Sam, who grinned at him, his gold tooth flashing. Tia and Tana grabbed his hands and tugged him toward the table in the center of the room. Rosie, Travis, and Bethany stood to the side of the table, which held a giant chocolate cake on a white stand. Other guests Hank recognized as frequent customers or those who owned businesses in the building clustered around the table with drinks in their hands. Behind them, steam rose from a pasta bar set in the corner.

Hank looked at Bethany. "You did all this for me?"

Her eyes sparkled. "I had helpers. The girls and I wanted it to be a surprise. Happy birthday, Hank."

Tia handed him a card. He studied the drawing. On the outside, someone had sketched a picture of a large bumblebee, which had been colored in with a yellow marker. The card read, "Hap-Bee Birthday." Inside were the signatures of what must have been everyone who'd ever stepped foot in Grandma Lou's.

"Do you like it?" Tana asked.

Hank couldn't stop his smile. "I've never had a better

card," he said, and he meant it. "How'd you know I like bees?"

"Our mom drew it. We colored it," said Tia.

"Come and make yourself a plate of pasta," Bethany said, eyes shining. "But first, we have to sing happy birthday." She lit a single large white candle in the middle of the cake. "C'mon, everyone. One, two, three . . ."

A chorus of voices rang out—some couldn't carry a tune, but Hank thought it was the sweetest melody he'd ever heard.

"You must make a wish," Rosie said.

Hank closed his eyes and wished. He wished Bethany would always look at him this way, her face soft and eyes glowing with affection. He wished all his friendships were honest and true, like the ones he'd made in Tremont. He wished the moment could last forever.

"Aren't you going to blow out your candle?" Tana asked.

Hank opened his eyes and blew; the candle winked out. Bethany cut a large slice of the cake down the center and handed him the first piece. He forked a cream-filled bite into his mouth. "Wait—is this a giant whoopie pie?"

Bethany giggled and nodded, and the girls squealed, and the entire room erupted into laughter.

Then there were slaps on his back and pasta and cake to eat and presents to open. Angel presented him with a black rose, Paula and Mitch gave him a homemade jar of spaghetti sauce with a bag of pasta, and Rosie had knitted him a pair of socks she said she'd started after he'd saved Tia's life. Travis and Bethany presented him with a small, narrow wrapped box on behalf of everyone in the restaurant.

He raised an eyebrow at Bethany. "What's this?"

She shook her head like a magician who refuses to

reveal her secrets. "I'm not spoiling the surprise. Open it and find out."

So he did.

Inside the box were two tickets to tomorrow's Cleveland Guardians' baseball game—club seats. Travis snatched the construction worker hat from Hank's head and replaced it with a Guardians' ball cap.

"I don't know what to say." And Hank did not. But he tried to express his feelings anyway. "I've never had a celebration as nice as this one. Thank you, everyone."

"Can I have your autograph?" a shy girl with brown pigtails asked, holding up a napkin.

He smiled. "Sure thing." He set the napkin on the table and signed it with a flourish.

Later, after he'd collected himself enough to give a small speech, and jokes were made and the last piece of cake was eaten and the guests were leaving, Hank cornered Bethany in the kitchen. She was stooped over the dishwasher. He cleared his throat. "I don't think I've ever had a better birthday celebration. Thanks for all you did to make it special."

She stood. "I'm so glad, Hank. But it was nothing. You deserve it for all the work you've been doing around this old place."

He pulled her into his arms. "It was more than nothing. You made me a special cake. You remembered how much I like baseball. You bought me two tickets—I assume you won't make me go on my own?"

She eyed him like a detective bent on solving a case. "As friends?"

"Of course." Hank held his breath.

She must have decided in his favor because she tipped her head to the side like a little bird, smiled, and batted her eyelashes. "Oh my. Are you inviting me to a baseball game, Hank Haverill?"

"I am," he drawled. "Is that a yes?"

"I'd never pass up a game of baseball."

And that, Hank thought, was the icing on an already fabulous supernatural whoopie pie cake.

CHAPTER TWENTY-EIGHT

Bethany marveled at how fast she'd gotten accustomed to being driven around town in a limo. Hank was waiting for her in the back of the big black car when she arrived home from Grandma Lou's at 6 p.m. the next day. He rolled down the window as she approached, his golden blond hair peeking out from under his baseball cap and a lazy smile on his face. "Get in, slow poke, we don't want to be late for the game."

Louis came from the front to open the door for her. "Hello, Bethany."

She handed Louis a brown paper bag with a smile.

He arched his eyebrows. "What's this?"

"I brought you a pumpkin muffin. Made it fresh this morning."

"Why, that's awfully kind of you. Thank you."

She smiled and nodded, then slid across the cool leather seat toward Hank.

"Travis covering for you at the restaurant?" Hank asked, after Louis had closed the door. His cell phone buzzed, but he ignored it.

"No, he had an exam today and some errands to run, but Rosie's handling the dinner hour."

"Hey. What are you doing all the way over there?"

She scooted a few inches toward him, breathing in his cool mint smell. "Hey yourself."

He sniffed the air in front of her. "You smell like apples."

"I baked a pie." She made a face. "You know baseball, apple pie and all that. I thought, maybe you and I . . ." A sudden shyness had her stuttering.

Firm fingers lifted her chin until their eyes met. "Whatever you're selling, I'm buying."

She licked her suddenly dry lips. "I thought we could go back to Grandma Lou's for apple pie. After the game."

His eyes settled on her lips, and he quirked his mouth into a slow smile. "And you worried I'd say no? You had me at 'you and I.' Throw an apple pie into the equation, and I'm a goner."

She couldn't stop an answering smile from lifting the corners of her mouth. "You'd think I'd know you have a major sweet tooth by now."

"Sweetheart, you and pie are about the best things to come my way in a long time. Maybe ever."

"I didn't mean . . ."

He wrapped a long arm around her shoulders and tucked her into his side like a football. "I know what you meant. And I meant what I said. Pie without you is just pie."

Before she could respond, Hank's cell phone buzzed again. He glanced at the number and stiffened, his face hardening into a furious mask. *Sorry*, he mouthed, letting her go and turning toward the window.

"How much?"

There was a pause. Bethany was close enough to hear the loud male voice on the other end.

"What kind of greeting is that?"

"The only kind you'll ever get from me."

"I'm not calling about money. Well, not exactly. Listen, your brother mentioned that you're getting serious about a girl."

His jaw tightened. "Why do you care?"

"I'm concerned about you. Your last girlfriend is suing you for millions. The one before that spread lies about you on social media. This one sounds like she doesn't have two cents to rub together."

Bethany cringed. They were talking about her.

"None of which is your business." Hank sounded bored. "Is there anything else?"

"Yeah, happy belated birthday. Linda and I are planning a trip to Los Angeles in September."

He straightened. "You're kidding." The bored tone vanished.

"I'm perfectly serious. We can celebrate then."

"No."

"Now hear me out. I know I wasn't around much when you were younger, but I didn't have my head on straight back then. I'm in a good place since I last talked to you. I got a promising lead on a new job, and if this comes through, we'll buy a house once we save a little dough. If we can afford the plane tickets, we thought it would be fun to come for a visit."

"Still no." Now he sounded mean. Bethany shivered.

The voice on the other end pleaded. "I thought you'd be happy. You're always on me about staying put and holding down a job. Son, it's only a brief visit. Surely, you can spare a little time for us. It's the perfect opportunity for you to meet your sisters and stepmom. They're anxious to get to know you."

"I'm not interested in getting to know them. I gotta go."

"Hank, just think about it, will you. We'd all like to see you and Connor. I'll call you later when you've had more time to consider the idea."

"Now wait—"

The call ended, and Hank stared at his cell phone for a full minute before glancing at Bethany. Fury banked like hot coals in his eyes.

"Your father?"

"Yes, sorry you had to listen to that." His voice oozed acid. "Dear old Dad wants to visit me in Los Angeles."

She pressed a hand on his arm. "Hank, I know you probably don't want to hear this, but your dad's request sounded reasonable. Maybe you should visit with him while he's in town. Don't you want to meet your sisters?"

Hank narrowed his eyes. "If your ex called you up and wanted to come for a visit with his new girlfriend, would you let him?"

A cold chill crawled up her back. "That's not the same. Besides, this isn't about me."

A muscle clenched in his cheek. "You're right. It isn't about you. It's about me. My relationship with my dad isn't up for discussion."

"I . . ." She sucked in a breath at the sting. He was right. They hadn't known each other long enough. It was none of her business. "I was just trying to help. I didn't mean to get too personal."

For a long moment, Hank didn't speak, and the silence between them grew awkward.

She searched her brain for a safe topic. "It's been years since I've been invited to a baseball game. My dad used to take Travis and me as kids a few times a year—back when they were called the Indians. One time, we caught a fly ball. I think Travis still has it in his bedroom." She rambled but couldn't seem to stop herself. "Did you know the team was originally called the Naps? That was a tribute to one of the popular players in the early 1900s. His name was Napoleon, or Naps for short."

Hank brought her hand to his lips and kissed her fingertips, which erased every stray thought in her head. "I'm sorry. I didn't mean to snap at you. My father is a sore subject."

Bethany shivered and pulled her hand from his. "I know. I didn't mean to upset you. Especially when we're enjoying your birthday gift. Can you forget I said anything? I'd really like us to have a good time."

Hank sighed, the sound a lot like the steam from her pressure cooker at the end of its cycle. "Listen, I know you meant well. But that man doesn't deserve to call himself my father. He was never there for me growing up. Not once. He has no right to call me out of the blue and tell me he wants to come visit me in LA with his wife and my half-sisters, whom I've never met, and expect me to accept them. It's too much to ask."

"I understand, but . . ." Bethany said and swallowed. She did understand. But she also knew that if his father was looking for forgiveness, Hank owed it to himself to hear him out.

Hank stretched his hands behind his head. "But what? I can see you're dying to give me your opinion." He closed his eyes. "Go ahead. I'll try not to lose my temper."

How could she make him understand? Bethany clenched her hands in her lap and studied her nails. She'd chewed them to nubs worrying about the family business.

Looking at them helped her get out the next part with barely a tremor in her voice.

"Desmond took every bit of money I had in my savings account, including the money Travis and I got from our insurance policy after our parents were killed. This was the money I was planning to use to keep Grandma Lou's afloat. He knew what I was trying to do, and yet he betrayed me anyway. I thought we were going to spend the rest of our lives together, but . . ."

Hank opened his eyes and squinted. He looked every inch a god—a curious, questioning one. "But what?"

"He never intended to marry me." An aching embarrassment washed over her like a wave rushing to shore, leaving a cold chill behind. She shivered. "He didn't love me—all he wanted was my money."

Hank turned her face to meet his sharp gaze. "He's a fool. I'm sorry."

Bethany's face heated, and she twisted until he released her chin. She looked out the window rather than meet his knowing eyes. "The only other thing he found attractive was my cooking skills. To say I'm bitter is an understatement. It's been two years, and I'm still furious. I loved him—trusted him. He betrayed me in the worst way possible."

"He deserves to be behind bars. Why didn't you hire a lawyer?"

"Don't you think I tried? I gave him joint access to the account. In the eyes of the law, he didn't do anything wrong. He had a right to the money. It was my fault for trusting someone who didn't deserve my trust. Poor Travis has had to suffer the consequences of my poor judgment."

"I don't think your brother blames you for what happened."

Bethany gripped the seat and tried to ignore the heat in

his gaze, which drew her toward him like a powerful magnet. "He doesn't. But I do. I can't forgive myself. Desmond never once asked for forgiveness. He never once admitted he was wrong. But your father has."

She finally had the courage to look his way.

He studied her from under hooded eyes. "So, because my father said he's sorry for years of neglect, you think I should forgive him?"

She put her hand on his. "No, Hank. What I'm saying is you should hear him out. Let him visit. Give him a chance to explain. Maybe something he says will ease your anger . . . help you understand his neglect. It's a gift you give yourself."

He studied her hand. After a few moments, he placed his other hand on top of hers and rubbed his thumb across it, sending a warm tingle through her skin. "I'll think about it."

"All right." She would have to be satisfied with his answer. She could hear her mother's voice in her mind: *Baby steps, sweetheart, baby steps.*

They were quiet for the rest of the ride until Louis parked the car in front of the stadium.

"Let's go." Hank threaded his fingers through hers and pulled her along until they reached the club seat section. "This place looks amazing. Much different than the last time I was here." He tugged at her hand. "C'mon, the game's about to start."

They found their seats, but not before helping themselves to hotdogs smothered in stadium mustard, golden french fries, and giant sodas.

Hank gazed with rapt attention at the players on the field, but Bethany found herself distracted by a little boy in front of her with straight black hair and a gap-tooth grin. He kept smiling at her over his mother's shoulder. Then there was a middle-aged man a seat over with long white hair and his belly hanging over his belt buckle, drinking a beer. And —the girl seated three rows in front of them on the right— was she staring at them? The girl tapped the arm of her friend next to her, who turned her head to take a peek. Bethany looked away.

Then the seventh inning stretch came and craziness ensued. The girl and her friend asked Hank for his autograph, then the man next to her did the same, and soon, a small crowd circled them, all demanding Hank sign whatever they had to offer. In some cases, it was their shirt, in others, a napkin. A lady asked Hank to sign her forehead, which he laughed and did. Bethany shifted her weight from one leg to the other and wondered how Hank continued smiling. Thank goodness the game resumed, and everyone returned to their seats.

"Sorry," Hank said, offering her a lopsided grin.

"It's okay," she said, but seconds later she wished she'd held her breath.

The cameras on the field panned to them, and the next thing Bethany knew, her giant mug appeared on the big screen next to Hank's. She stared in horror, but Hank tapped her shoulder. When she turned to look at him, he offered her a slow smile, as if he saw the big screen as an opportunity rather than cause for alarm.

"It's the kiss-cam. We can't disappoint them."

Before she could fully grasp what he planned, he kissed her in front of the entire stadium. The kiss was short but thorough, and when he separated from her, there were cheers and clapping all around them.

Hank's grin seemed satisfied, but Bethany felt her cheeks grow hot and her heart and lungs freeze. She sipped her drink and kept her eyes down to avoid looking into all the faces turned her way. A few minutes later, the game resumed, and she let out her breath bit by bit. Her heart resumed its normal thumping in her chest.

She poked Hank in the side and put her hand over her mouth so no one else could hear. "Tell me we didn't just kiss in front of thousands of people."

Hank laughed but kept his voice low, thank goodness. "Okay, we didn't kiss in front of thousands of people. More like a million, if they broadcast to the viewers at home."

She narrowed her eyes. "This doesn't concern you?"

"Not at all. It concerns you, I take it?"

"Hank, people are going to think we're an item."

He laughed again, and she had the urge to slap the silly, satisfied grin off his face. She might have, too, if it weren't his birthday outing, and if it didn't remind her of all the female leads in every dramatic film she had ever seen. She gripped her drink and gritted her teeth.

"Why do you care what they think? We are an item." He nudged her arm with his. "Aren't we?"

She rolled her eyes. "No, we're not."

"Then why do you kiss me?"

"We shouldn't be kissing at all."

His lips drooped into a pout, but it didn't detract from his good looks. If anything, it added to his charm. "Look me in the eyes and tell me you don't like kissing me."

Her eyes met his blue ones. "I don't like kissing you."

He chuckled. "Liar, liar."

Bethany's lips twitched. The truth was she did like kissing him, and they both knew any denial was a lie.

CHAPTER TWENTY-NINE

Maybe it was the homemade apple pie and vanilla ice cream she and Hank ate after the game or the tender way he looked at her when he kissed her good night—like she was his girl. Or maybe it was the slew of messages left on the restaurant's voicemail from reporters who'd seen the kiss-cam and wanted an interview. Whatever it was, she went to bed with a jumble of confused thoughts in her brain.

Bethany tossed and turned most of the night, wrestling with vague dreams of being lost in an amusement park. No matter how much she searched, she couldn't find the way out.

In the morning, she woke with a headache and blurry eyes, but a firm decision in her mind. She would not go with Hank to Los Angeles—despite how tempting the invitation was, despite how much she liked him, despite the attraction sizzling between them and how much he made her laugh. She was not cut out for Hollywood—look how she'd freaked out about the kiss-cam. Hank needed someone who could deal with his high-profile lifestyle. And she had responsibilities here. This was not the time for a vacation. Voting would begin soon, and she needed to promote Grandma Lou's as much as possible.

She ran a hand through her curly mop and gazed in the bathroom mirror at the dark smudges under her eyes.

Mistake, mistake, mistake.

The single word echoed in her mind like the lyrics of a song she couldn't shake. She rehearsed what she would say to him as she took a shower and got dressed, her stomach quivering. *Hank, I can't go with you. I'm sorry. I don't want to leave the restaurant. It would be wise if we don't see each other outside of business.*

By the time she arrived at Grandma Lou's, she'd worked herself into a jittery mess as she went over all the reasons that visiting Los Angeles with Hank was a bad idea. She grabbed a knife from a drawer and began dicing vegetables for minestrone soup

He's out of my league, he'll grow bored with me, he'll break my heart. Her hand shook, and she sliced through her glove and into her thumb instead of the carrot she held. She hissed and dropped the knife. A bead of blood oozed from the wound.

Mistake, mistake, mistake.

She stripped the gloves, washed her hands in the sink, and scrounged for a bandage in the back cupboard where she kept a few first-aid items.

Travis came in as she applied the bandage. "You cut yourself?"

"Yeah, I wasn't paying close enough attention, I guess. Um, Travis, before you head out, could you give me a minute? I want to talk to you about something."

"Sure. What's up?" Travis pulled out a stool and sat.

Bethany set the knife to the side. She didn't want any more accidents. "Hank's invited us to California. To his home."

Travis leaned forward in his chair. "Seriously? To hang with him?"

"I'm planning on turning down his offer."

"Why? If you're worried about Grandma Lou's, don't be. I bet we could get Rosie to cover for us."

"That's not necessary. Hank said he'd hire someone to oversee things while we're away, and he'd pay for our travel expenses. He thinks we both need a break."

"Why shouldn't we take him up on it? It's been a long time since we've had a vacation from this old place." He cast his gaze around the kitchen like he was seeing it with fresh eyes. "Besides, we could never afford a trip on our own. I thought you liked Hank. You said you trust him. Why wouldn't we go?"

She put on some fresh gloves, picked up the knife again, and resumed cutting the carrots, careful to keep her movements slow and steady. "I do like Hank. I just don't think we should leave Grandma Lou's right now."

"But why? You need a break. I need a break. Sounds like a perfect opportunity."

"You want to go to California?" Bethany eyed her brother. He rarely asked for anything.

"Not if you don't want to."

"That's no answer."

The doorbell jingled, indicating the arrival of their first customer of the day.

Travis slid off the stool. "Keep cutting. I'll take care of whoever it is."

Bethany finished chopping the vegetables, then added

them to the pot of broth on the big stovetop. She ditched her gloves, but something dragged on the floor—her shoelace had come untied. She started to bend over when Travis came through the swinging door, carrying a giant bouquet of sunflowers in a cobalt blue vase.

"I think Hank really wants you to visit him in California." He set the vase on the worktable, handing her a small card.

Bethany forgot about her shoelace and read the scribbled note in Hank's bold hand.

Sunflowers to remind you how bright the sun is in Los Angeles. Thanks for the birthday gift. Wishing on a star. Hank.

She swallowed and nestled the card among the blooms. *Mistake, mistake, mistake.* "He's going to be disappointed."

"We also got a paying customer. Elizabeth's looking to buy a carafe of coffee to go. Will we sell it that way? She brought her own carafe."

"Sure." The doorbell jangled. "I'll get the pot and see who else is here. You can take out the trash. It's overflowing."

Travis nodded, and Bethany wiped her hands on her apron, grabbed the pot of coffee, and went to fill Elizabeth's carafe. Hank's publicist stood by the kitchen door in a pale peach number, tapping her French-manicured nails against the counter.

"You're up bright and early," Bethany said, trying for a friendly smile. She suspected she was not Elizabeth's favorite person right now. "I'm, um, sorry about breaking our agreement to keep away from Hank."

"Pshaw." Elizabeth waved her hand like it was no big deal. "Hank's hard to ignore."

Bethany lifted the pot of coffee in the air. "Travis said

you're looking for an entire pot of coffee? It'll be twenty for the pot."

"That's a little steep, isn't it? But all right. I only get the best for Hank. I know how much he adores his coffee." She tipped the lid open on a black carafe. "Fill her up."

"I'll be right with you," Bethany called to the fair-haired gentleman who'd leaned over to peer into the donut case. "All donuts are two dollars apiece."

She finished filling the carafe and eyed the credit card displayed on Elizabeth's cell phone, which she held out for payment. "Sorry, I'll need your actual card."

Elizabeth sighed and dug in her purse for her card, handing it to Bethany. "Oh my, he's easy on the eyes."

Bethany had turned to swipe the card, but Elizabeth's words made her pause. She followed her gaze and almost dropped the pot of coffee. The gentleman raised his head, and she got a good look at his sandy hair, square jaw, and dark glasses.

Desmond. Did she speak? She must have because he moved toward her.

Elizabeth raised her penciled eyebrows. "You two know each other?"

Bethany barely registered her words. "Why are you here?" The words came out as black and bitter as the coffee grounds she'd dumped in the trash.

"I came to apologize, and hopefully to make amends."

"You need to leave."

"Won't you please hear me out?" Desmond walked forward, one hand stretched in front of him as if he thought she would slam the empty coffee pot over his traitorous head. Which wasn't a bad idea. "I have an idea on how we can save Grandma Lou's."

She stilled. Why would he think Grandma Lou's was

closing? And what was he doing here after all this time? Had he seen the kiss-cam? That would explain his sudden appearance. "Let me guess . . . by stealing more money from me?"

"I'll just leave you two to reminisce," Elizabeth said, grabbing the carafe and heading out the door. "Enjoy your day."

Bethany advanced from behind the counter, still clutching the empty pot, and Desmond took a step backward.

"Now hold on a second," he said.

"Out. If you don't leave, I'm going to call the police."

Desmond took another step backward, eyeing the pot. "I just want to help you."

What he wanted was money. And he thought he could find it because he believed she and Hank were an item. "I'm counting to five. One—"

"Please. I've got a spot reserved for you on my cooking show. I want to do a live feature on Grandma Lou's. To ask for votes for the contest."

She stopped moving. "How do you know about the contest?"

"Elizabeth mentioned it. She said you were desperate to save the building."

"When were you talking to Elizabeth?"

"I ran into her in town and followed her here just now."

Convenient. She snorted and rolled her eyes.

"Listen to me. You're going to need my help. With the media attention the show will bring, you can gain the votes you need to final in the contest."

She tightened her grip on the pot and kept moving. "Two. I'm not that desperate."

Desmond straightened his shirt and frowned. "Now,

don't let your ego get in the way. I'm sorry for the way I left."

Bethany curled her lip. "And taking my money? Are you sorry about that?"

"Why would I be? We were engaged, and it was a joint account. It was as much my money as it was yours. But if you're still stewing over that, let me make it up to you by featuring your restaurant on my show."

Bethany took another step forward. "Three. What? Are ratings down? Four. You have to be insane," she hissed, "to think I'd go anywhere near your show after what you did to me."

It all happened so fast. One minute she was advancing on Desmond, pushing him toward the exit, the next she tripped on her shoelace she'd forgotten to tie and slammed into his chest, dropping the pot, which rolled toward the counter without shattering. Before she could stop him, his arms caught her, pressing her close. She struggled to catch her breath, stunned at the familiar feeling of his body and the cinnamon and ginger scent from the tea she remembered he always drank.

"I have thought of you every single day since I left Cleveland. I made a terrible mistake. I know it now. I'd like to make it up to you. Remember how good it used to be between us?"

She opened her mouth for air, and he thrust his lips onto hers.

The door opened and a tall man with broad shoulders and golden hair stood in the entrance. He drew his brows together until they met in the middle, then he crossed his arms like the Greek god Apollo himself. All he needed was an arrow to complete the picture.

~

ANGER BURNED BRIGHT, erupting like a solar flare in Hank's gut. He crossed his arms so he wouldn't punch the man in front of him.

He'd come to Grandma Lou's this morning, hoping Bethany had decided a relationship with him was worth the risk. That, after he'd poured out his deepest secrets to her under the stars, she would agree to the trip to LA. Instead, he found her kissing another man—and not just any man but her former fiancé—the Chef King—who had betrayed her trust and run off with her money.

"Hank, it's not what it looks like." Her face flushed red, and she punched at the guy's chest. "Let me go, Desmond."

Hank took a step farther into the room. "What does it look like? Like you're reacquainting yourself with an old flame?"

The Chef King trapped Bethany's fists by crushing her against his side with one arm. He pushed his glasses up the bridge of his nose and extended his other hand like he was greeting an old friend. "You're Hank Haverill, aren't you? I believe our shows are affiliated with the same television network. I'm Desmond Mitchell. Perhaps you've seen my cooking show."

Hank didn't shake the proffered hand. Instead, he watched Bethany's expressive face shift from frustration to fury.

She stamped on Desmond's foot until he released her. "Time's up. Get out of my restaurant."

"Bethany, be reasonable. I was just trying to help you. I saved you from a nasty bruise."

She pointed at the door. "No, you assaulted me. And I'd

rather have the bruise. Go and don't come back. I never want to see you again. Not even on television."

Desmond frowned. "Fine. Never say I didn't try to help. I'll go." Then he turned to Hank. "Just so you know, she's a liar."

Bethany gasped, outrage in every aspect of her curvy form. Desmond had already turned his back and was walking out the door.

Hank reached out a long arm, snagged Desmond's shoulder and turned him around in one smooth motion. "Apologize."

"I already tried that with her, and she wouldn't have it."

"With good reason, from what I've been told." He tightened the vise he had on Desmond's neck and pushed him toward Bethany. "Say you're sorry and then take yourself outside and don't look back. Or do you want to be one of the unlucky ones who can say they've been clocked by me?"

Desmond hesitated, his fists clenched and face a deep red. "Fine. I'm sorry. Are you happy?"

"Tell her, not me. And sound like you mean it." Hank squeezed a little harder until Desmond gasped, turning three different shades of purple. He cranked his head toward Bethany.

"I'm sorry. I'm sorry. Please, make him stop."

"Let him go, Hank," Bethany said, glaring at Desmond. "I don't need his apology. It wouldn't be sincere, anyway."

Hank shrugged and released Desmond, who turned and scurried to the door like a small, nervous rat. At the last moment, he must have realized he was far enough away from Hank's reach to dredge up enough courage to turn and sneer at Bethany.

"I'll look forward to the day this place closes. Won't be

much longer, from what I hear. Heard talk you plagiarized your contest entry."

The door clanged shut behind him, and Hank glanced toward Bethany. She stared after Desmond, a stunned expression on her face.

CHAPTER THIRTY

Hank led Bethany to the nearest chair, fighting a desire to chase after Desmond and use him as a punching bag. Some guys were just plain assholes. "Are you okay? Sit."

Bethany didn't answer but did as he asked. Her eyes shifted from Hank to the front door.

Travis came from the kitchen, a stack of plates in his hands. "Is she all right? What happened?" He set down the plates with a thunk.

"Your sister had an unexpected visit from her ex-fiancé." Hank crouched next to Bethany. "Place your head between your knees. Travis, get her a glass of water."

Travis rolled his hands into fists. "That jerk was in our restaurant? He's got a lot of nerve after what he did. I'll kill him."

Bethany raised her head. "I'm okay, Travis. Don't fuss. Please."

Travis looked like he yearned to charge from the restaurant and tackle Desmond in the street, but his sister's pale face stopped him. He glanced at her, nodded, and hurried to fetch the water.

She looked at Hank, her gaze wide and concerned and frightened. "He said he met Elizabeth in town and followed her here. She told him about my contest entry, and he offered to help me garner votes by featuring me on his show. But what did he mean about me plagiarizing my entry? Why would he say that?"

Hank rubbed her back. "He's just making trouble. Don't listen to him. I should have clocked him when I had the chance. And I'm not happy with Elizabeth for talking to him."

A wry smile surfaced on Bethany's face. "Much as I appreciate your willingness to fight for me, I'm glad you didn't. You don't need to be getting mixed up in this craziness. Can you imagine the headlines?"

He placed his hands over hers. "I *am* mixed up in this craziness. I would do much more than pound Desmond for you. Are you going to be all right?"

Her smile widened until he caught a glimpse of her teeth. "Yes, how can I not be? I have two knights in shining armor come to my rescue." She took the glass of water from Travis, who had returned from his mad dash into the kitchen.

The door jangled, and they all looked up. A young mom pushing an infant in a stroller entered with two toddlers. The sight did more to restore Bethany's equilibrium than Hank's efforts had accomplished.

"My soup," Bethany said, pushing herself to her feet. "I need to check on it. Travis, can you help Francesca? She has her hands full. I'll be right back." She scurried toward the kitchen before Hank could stop her.

He followed behind. Funny. He was always a step behind, trying to catch up. When he entered the kitchen,

Bethany was at the stove, stirring a large silver pot. He sniffed the air. "Beef noodle soup?"

She looked at him as if she'd totally forgotten he was still in her café. "Minestrone for the lunch crowd." She wiped her forehead with a paper towel. "Are you hungry? That's the least I can do—"

He pulled the ladle from her fingers and set it in the pot. Then he tugged her into his arms and held her close, looking into her wide, gray-green eyes. "Yes, I'm hungry. But not just for food. You need a break from this place. Will you come to LA with me?"

IT WAS the shock of seeing Desmond again that turned her no into a yes. At least that's what Bethany told herself later, after she and Travis closed the restaurant and returned home. She happened to agree with Hank—the surest way to recover from the turmoil of confronting Desmond was a change of scenery.

Bethany yanked the brown suitcase, which had been her father's, from the storage area in the basement where it lay hidden under a mountain of clutter and dragged it up two flights of stairs into her bedroom. The metal handle was worn, and there was a dent in one side, but otherwise, the suitcase was in decent shape.

She sat on the bed and studied her hands and admitted what she preferred to deny. It was more than a change of scenery that had her saying yes to the weekend in Los Angeles. No, it had been Hank himself. He hadn't given a scrap of attention to Desmond's claim about her, although she'd been so mortified and furious about the whole scene that she'd scurried into the kitchen. No, he'd defended her honor and then worried about her, anxious to know if she would make the trip. How could she refuse?

She crossed to her dresser, plunged her hands into the top drawer, and pulled out two pairs of panties and bras in a decent enough shape for travel. Then she crouched to peer into the bottom drawers. Hank had told her not to fuss over what to bring, so she considered the stack of jeans and T-shirts, which made up her day-to-day wardrobe. They would have to do, but she would pack one nice outfit, in case they went somewhere special.

Her cell phone buzzed, and she stood and grabbed it from her dresser top. Her pulse quickened when she saw the identity of the caller. "Hello." Did she sound as breathless as she felt?

"I love the sound of your voice."

Hank's familiar drawl had her heart fluttering, so she stepped backward and sank onto her bed. "Hi, Hank."

"Listen, remember when I mentioned I'm up for an award?"

"Yeah."

"Well, the award ceremony is a black-tie affair. I don't want you worrying about an outfit. I'll have my assistant pick you out something nice."

Bethany tried not to let the trickle of excitement coursing through her veins sound in her voice. "Well, I can't afford a fancy dress, so thank you, Hank."

"I've made all the arrangements for our trip. We'll fly in a private plane next weekend—you, me, Travis, and Elizabeth."

Elizabeth was coming, too? Elizabeth had been responsible for Desmond coming to her restaurant, and Hank knew it. Her stomach rolled like she'd swallowed a bucket of pebbles. "Okay."

"Why do you sound like I made you eat something you detest? You're not changing your mind about coming with me, are you?"

"No, I'm not. I told you I would. I think this trip will be good for Travis and me. It's just—Elizabeth's not my favorite person."

Hank sighed, the weary sound traveling through the phone line and into her ear as if he were sitting next to her. "I know, and I'll talk to Elizabeth about overstepping. But she's been with me since the beginning. I'm her only client, and she's extremely dedicated. In the early days, when we had nothing, I told her if she stuck by me and I made it big, I wouldn't leave her behind. She's sacrificed a lot to see me successful. She's used to flying with me when we travel to the same location, so it would seem unusual to fly separately."

Bethany sank onto the mattress and gripped the soft blanket she kept at the end of her bed. "I don't mean to make a fuss."

"You're not. You have nothing to worry about. I'll make sure she plays nice."

"I'll be fine."

"I don't like that word, 'fine.' When we're talking about you and me, you can wipe that word from your vocabulary. You'll be more than fine, I promise. I'll sit next to you and rub your back and ply you with champagne. You won't even know Elizabeth's there."

She laughed. "You make it hard to refuse."

"Seriously, Beth, I'll be with you every step of the way. I want you to relax and have a fun time. I want you to come home dreaming about the next time you'll visit. I want you to trust I'll take care of you."

She took a breath and held it. "You may not want a next time after spending a full weekend with me."

"Woman." The single word in his deep voice carried through the phone line, tickling her insides. "We'll enjoy our time together. Trust me."

Her heart fluttered like a butterfly taking flight. The thought of a next time with Hank was too incredible to believe. So she stopped herself from going there—from focusing on what couldn't be. She thought of the wish she'd made under a falling star the night Hank hadn't shown up for their dinner. How she had wished against her better judgment that he was the real thing, even though she'd known in her heart that her wish was foolish. But maybe she had been wrong.

"Still there?"

"Yes."

"Good. You have a whole week to pack. Get to bed. You need your sleep. I'll see you tomorrow."

"Hank?"

"Yes?"

"Thanks for defending me today . . . with Desmond."

There was a pause, and then finally, Hank's voice. "Sweetheart?"

"Yes?"

"It was my pleasure."

CHAPTER THIRTY-ONE

"You can't be serious." Elizabeth took a breath.

Hank could hear her startled gasp through the line. It was Saturday morning, and he was in the gym at his rental. He put the phone on speaker and turned off the treadmill.

"This is an important audition. Blackie says Robin Hood is up for grabs, and you have a great shot at the role. Don't you care? You have to be all in, Hank. You're letting your infatuation with this restaurant owner distract you. You wouldn't believe the flood of social media posts and reporter calls that kiss-cam generated. We have to be careful how we play this, or the press will have a field day."

"Her name's Bethany, and I'm not distracted, Elizabeth. I'm returning to LA, aren't I?"

"The only reason you're returning is because *she* agreed to come with you. It's like you've totally forgotten how important your career is to you. To all of us."

"I've not forgotten my career. I just took a temporary hiatus. It's not like there was anything exciting happening until this audition and the awards ceremony." He grabbed a towel and wiped the sweat from his forehead.

"Hank, we've all worked far too long and far too hard to watch you throw your career away. You can't take a hiatus when you don't have a steady income. Now's the time we have to maintain your heartthrob image and work really hard to land your next gig."

Hank plopped onto the sofa and dragged a hand through his hair. He set the phone on the table in front of him and eyed it like it was a scorpion about to strike. "You're not telling me anything I don't know, so you can skip the lecture. I have something more important to discuss. Have you been meddling in Bethany's personal life?"

"I have no idea what you're talking about." Elizabeth sounded exasperated.

Hank watched the waves crest the shoreline outside the window of the rental property he called his temporary home. "So you didn't talk to her ex-fiancé?"

"I didn't say that. I ran into him once in town. He's got his own television show. It's always wise to make connections with other celebrities. You never know when they'll come in handy."

Hank rubbed his chin and shook his head, although he knew Elizabeth couldn't see him. "Did you tell him Bethany's business was in financial trouble, and she'd entered a contest?"

"The subject may have come up. We talked more about what you both had in common and how you could help one another. I told him you'd purchased the building his ex-fiancé used to own. He expressed interest in featuring Bethany on his new television show. That's all. Seemed like a win-win for all of you, which you know I always strive to achieve. Why are you getting so worked up?"

Anger, hot and hard, pulsed through his veins, surprising Hank. When was the last time he'd felt this passionate about anything? "I don't want her hurt, that's why. He confronted her today, and it wasn't pretty. She was badly shaken up."

"You mean to tell me he lied about wanting her on his show?"

"No, I mean, she doesn't want anything to do with him—which is totally understandable. The guy took her and her brother for a ride—stole their life savings and used it to move to New York and break into television. He's a real jerk, and I don't want him around her. So do me a favor and don't meddle in her affairs any further, okay."

"Okay, okay. Calm down. I won't *meddle* as you call it, although I prefer to think of it as helping her achieve her goals and achieving ours at the same time."

Hank gripped the couch cushion and worked to keep his voice even. Elizabeth was only doing her job. "I shouldn't have to tell you this, but I will anyway. Please keep your interactions with her and her brother to a minimum. I want them to have an enjoyable time in LA. Regardless of what you think of her, or how she might impact my career, Bethany's a good person. I don't want to see her hurt any more than she already has been."

"Right. Like hanging out with you in LA won't hurt her? I've seen the way she looks at you. The woman's half in love. What's going to happen when she's all the way there after you show her a good time? You're not the settling down type, Hank. You think that won't hurt her?"

Hank rubbed his aching head and took deep breaths to try and slow his thumping heart. "It won't happen." But even as he said the words, he recognized the lie. Didn't he want Bethany to fall for him? Didn't he hope to take things further? He was male after all, and she was an attractive female. Their relationship wouldn't remain platonic forever.

A memory of her as she'd looked the other morning in the kitchen at Grandma Lou's came into his mind as if he'd conjured the vision from a crystal ball—her face white, her lips puffy as if she'd been gnawing on them with worry, her gray-green eyes half afraid, half longing, wide with unshed tears. She had gazed at him like a recovering alcoholic with a bottle of booze—knowing she must not have it, while at the same time, realizing it was within her grasp, and difficult to resist. Elizabeth was right. If Bethany didn't have feelings for him yet, she would soon. It was only a matter of time.

Elizabeth let out a grunt. "You pay me to be straightforward, so that's how I'm going to be. Bethany Parker isn't Melanie Wilson or any of your other starlets. She won't understand your lifestyle, let alone accept it. She won't know how to handle the press. She won't move to LA and leave her family behind when you crook your little finger. You can tell yourself she won't fall in love with you, but she will. And then she'll cry her little heart out when you're forced to leave her behind. Is that what you want, Hank?"

"No, of course not. I don't want to hurt her." But wouldn't he, if he continued his pursuit?

"That's what will happen, unless you're prepared to give this girl a ring, relocate to Cleveland, and throw a big fat white wedding. And we both know marriage and weddings aren't high on your list of priorities after your crappy childhood."

"Okay, point received. Listen, I gotta run."

Hank ended the call and paced back and forth between his weight-lifting bench and the windows. Outside, a seagull perched on the cast-iron patio table, basking in the sunshine and looking for a handout.

He picked up a pair of forty-pound weights, turned to the mirror, and curled his wrists, flexing his biceps.

He wanted to ignore Elizabeth's words. What did she know about relationships? As far as he knew, she'd never had one. She was a classic workaholic who never made time for dating. She couldn't possibly know if Hank was capable of a committed relationship or not. Could she?

His stomach twisted and his arms ached. A vein stood out in his bulging muscles. Sweat dripped down his face. He placed the weights back on the rack, breathing hard.

Bethany was an adult. She knew what she was getting into coming to LA with him, didn't she?

He gazed at his reflection in the mirror. It was hard to lie to himself. She was halfway in love with him, and what he felt for her went way beyond friendship. He might almost believe he loved her if he thought he was capable of that emotion. He had promised her she would be safe with him, and he'd meant it. But the longest any of his relationships had ever lasted was six months. Bethany wouldn't be safe if she fell in love with him. And she would. It was in her eyes, in the way she looked at him, in her smile, in her kiss.

He grabbed another white towel from the stack and wiped the sweat from his forehead. He cared about Bethany. More than he'd thought he could ever care about someone else. But Elizabeth was right about him. He never stayed in love for long. He always went through a period of infatuation, but eventually, he grew bored, and they would fight, and that ended the relationship. Melanie had said the problem was him—he wanted his own way and wasn't willing to compromise.

He grimaced at his reflection. He only ever hurt the women who fell for him. He wasn't capable of loving another. He didn't have the gene that other men seemed to have that allowed them to settle down with one woman. He would be an absentee husband like his father, invested in his career and not paying attention to the people who loved him the most.

He balled the towel up and made a basket into the hamper as a hard ache settled in his chest. In the end, he would destroy her. And despite all his other failings, that knowledge wasn't something he could live with.

BETHANY SLAPPED the eraser against the chalkboard easel and wiped yesterday's menu from the board. Now that she had made the decision to leave Grandma Lou's for the weekend, she was eager to make the trip.

She wrote the lunch special in her curvy handwriting—which she thought looked like a little girl's, but Travis said looked friendly—and suppressed a shiver of excitement. She was going to see Hank's home—all the places he loved. She and Hank would get to know each other better, grow closer. He would reveal sides of his life the public didn't get to see. Maybe her wish under the stars had a chance of coming true after all? Maybe they could have their own happily ever after?

She crossed the *T*s and dotted her *I*s. Last night, she and Travis had logged on to the computer to learn about Los Angeles and write down all the sights they might want to see or visit. Travis got excited over Dodger Stadium and Venice Beach, while Bethany yearned to see Malibu. Earlier, before the lunch crowd showed, Travis had covered for her while she went to a nearby discount boutique. She had splurged and bought herself a new hot pink sundress, hat, and pair of sunglasses for the occasion.

She finished the last line and then carried the easel outside and positioned it near the door. Hopefully, the promise of her homemade vegetable lasagna and garlic toast would draw in the lunch crowd.

She stepped inside and headed toward the kitchen when the door let out its familiar jingle. Her mind conjured Hank, but when she turned to see who had entered, it was only Sam and Gypsy. She swallowed a mixture of disappointment and annoyance with herself for being so infatuated that she expected to see Hank around every corner.

"What's this I hear about you leaving town?" Sam took off his hat and held it in front of him as if he was paying his respects.

Gypsy curled around her leg and meowed, knowing it was the surest route to attention. Bethany did not disappoint, bending to rub behind her ears before answering Sam's question. "News sure travels fast in this town. I only agreed to the trip a few days ago. How'd you hear about it?"

Sam tipped his head to the side in what Bethany knew was his way of gauging her well-being. "Travis mentioned it when I got my coffee this morning. Seemed pretty darn excited about it. You're not?"

Bethany couldn't stop the grin from taking over her face. "I am too, Sam. It's been years since either of us could afford a vacation. Hank's promised to make the trip fun and is paying for all our expenses. How could we say no?"

Sam flashed her a broad smile. "I'm real happy for you. I can't think of two kids more hardworking and deserving. It's nice to see you excited about something for a change and not so worried. Although, I don't know what I'll do without my favorite girl around."

"It's only a couple of days. Hank's bringing in help on Friday, so you'll still get your home-cooked meals." Bethany had already talked to the general manager, as well as the chef and servers Hank had hired to run the kitchen while she was gone. They'd all seemed highly confident. She'd written out lengthy instructions, which they promised to follow to a T, including instructions on how to treat loyal customers like Sam.

"I'm more worried about your sunny smile. It always brightens my day."

"Well, you just grab a seat over in the corner, and I'll bring you a piece of lasagna fresh from the oven."

Sam did as she instructed, and Bethany hurried into the kitchen to dish out the lasagna. That was the last opportunity she had to dwell on the coming trip. Rosie and the girls arrived, and Bethany fussed over them, relieved to see Tia back to normal and Rosie with her calm smile in place. And then a group of tourists entered, looking for Hank, who of course hadn't yet put in an appearance. The fans all wanted coffee and whoopie pies because they'd heard they were Hank's favorites.

At noon, Travis returned from a few errands to help serve and clean up, and before she knew it, it was the dinner hour.

"Has Hank been in?" Bethany asked Travis when he headed into the kitchen during a short lull, to help her with the dishes.

Travis slung a dishtowel over his shoulder. "Haven't seen him. Did he tell you he would be?"

"Not directly." Bethany grabbed a pair of oven mitts, opened the oven door, and reached for the peanut butter oatmeal cookies, flinching when her hand got too near the hot tray. "Ow." She ran cold water in the sink and thrust her burned fingers through, which offered immediate relief. "I just assumed he'd stop by for something to eat."

"Don't get worked up. He'll probably show after the supper crowd. You know how he comes and goes."

But Travis was wrong. When Bethany wiped down the last dirty table and totaled the day's earnings, Hank had still not appeared in the shop.

She was halfway home when her cell rang. "Hank? Is everything okay?"

"Sorry, this is Pamela Harris, Hank's assistant. He's tied up and asked me to call you on his cell."

"Oh. What's wrong? Where's Hank?"

"Hank's fine."

The woman sounded normal, which did much to quell the sick feeling in her tummy.

"He needs to cancel your visit to LA. He had an unexpected opportunity come up this afternoon and had to fly home early. He's involved in meetings until late tonight. But he wanted you to know he's really sorry for the change in plans and maybe he can make it work another time."

Bethany narrowed her gaze at the road. "He's . . . he's coming back to Cleveland, isn't he?"

"I wouldn't know," the woman said. "We didn't discuss his future plans. I'm sure he'll give you a call when he can."

"Oh, okay." Bethany ended the call and threw her phone on the seat, right next to the bag with the sundress she would now need to return. She couldn't afford to spend money on an outfit for a trip she wouldn't get to take.

She hunched over the steering wheel and gasped at the sharp ache in her side and struggled to see through the stream of tears clogging her vision.

CHAPTER THIRTY-TWO

Hank watched his assistant hang up with Bethany out of the corner of one eye—with the other, he studied the script in front of him. He should be more excited. According to Blackie, the producers wanted him for the role. They would sign the contract tomorrow night. So why did his weary heart beat out of sync, and his temples ache, and his eyes burn like he hadn't slept in months?

Bethany must hate him now.

"You're all set." Pamela stood in front of him, her tablet in her hands and a question on her serious face. She looked efficient and calm and ready to balance his checkbook or order takeout or unpack his luggage if he asked her to.

He had never really studied her face before. If she let her dark hair down and allowed it to curl naturally and used a bit less makeup, she would look a little like—

"I stayed as close to the truth as I could, like you asked me to. Do you need something further?"

He closed his eyes, as if the motion could shut down his restless thoughts, and leaned his head against the cushions of the brown leather couch. He could hear Bethany scolding him for being rude, but he refused to acknowledge the phantom voice. "How did she sound?" His throat scratched like sandpaper.

"Fine."

There was that word again—fine. Hank had hired Pamela because, unlike Elizabeth, she didn't ask questions or let her personal feelings show. Most of the time, it was what he wanted, but not now—now he needed color. "Fine, how?"

"She was worried something had happened to you. I reassured her you were well. She asked if you'd be in touch."

She paused, waiting for his acknowledgement. He didn't give her one.

"Well, if there's nothing more, I'm going home now." Pamela's voice moved away from him, heading toward the door. He wanted to yell at her to stay and commiserate with him but what would be the point? It wouldn't change anything. Bethany would still be two thousand miles away in Tremont, and he would still be at his home in Los Angeles, saving her from his lustful self.

"I've updated your electronic calendar with the rest of your schedule for the week. Blackie asked me to remind you —you have dinner at Antonio's with your lawyers and the producers tomorrow at seven. He doesn't want you to be late. I believe they want to hammer out the finer details of your contract. And Elizabeth has you committed to the awards show for Sunday. It's at the Palace Theatre."

Hank grunted, and Pamela must have taken the sound for an acceptable response because he heard her open the door. "Good night, Hank."

Then the door clicked shut and silence reigned. But even that seemed too much. His thoughts circled like screeching gulls to the phone call. He couldn't handle talking to Bethany himself, so he'd taken the coward's way out and made Pamela do it. He knew from the one-sided conversation that Bethany had asked Pamela whether he would return to Cleveland.

Hank opened his eyes and threw the script on the shiny glass coffee table. The motion interrupted Woodrow, who napped by Hank's feet, his head over his paws. He looked up, but when Hank didn't stir to give the black Lab his normal pat on the head, he closed his eyes for another snooze.

Could he ever return? He didn't know, but he suspected the answer must be no. The place held too many memories now. Too many aching, precious, soul-stirring memories. He couldn't even get excited about staying at his grandparents' house, which he now owned. If he did, he would be sorely tempted to see Bethany. He would need to fight his attraction to her all over again. Far better to sell the Parker building and break things off now while her heart was still intact, and he had enough self-control and honor to do the right thing.

He stood and headed to his well-stocked bar, which housed sparkling crystal glasses, copper shakers, and large amounts of liquor. Woodrow followed him, his paws clicking on the hardwood floor.

Hank would memorize his lines later. What he needed now was a stiff drink—maybe more than one. Maybe he would get so drunk he would pass out.

He filled a glass with ice crystals so clear he could see through them and poured himself a measure of whiskey. It seemed as if he'd left his happiness behind when he'd made the decision to leave town after talking to Elizabeth. But he'd needed to cut Bethany free before he destroyed her life. Before he broke her heart.

He held the glass up to the light and studied the golden liquid. Elizabeth was right. He was not marriage material. And Bethany deserved the whole shebang—diamond ring, fiancé, big wedding, honeymoon in an exotic locale. She deserved someone who could love her like she deserved to be loved—someone who didn't have the press hounding them twenty-four hours a day. She deserved someone who would stay by her side and support her dreams and let her shine without stealing the spotlight for his own selfish needs. She deserved someone who could give her children one day—a family.

He downed the drink in one healthy swallow, enjoying the familiar burn in his throat. Maybe he would go out tonight—anything to forget a pair of gray-green eyes. Maybe he would enjoy all that the city of dreams had to offer.

He hurled the glass across the room, where it hit the wall and shattered into a zillion pieces, startling Woodrow, who barked and ran in circles.

If only his well of dreams hadn't run dry.

HOW SHE MANAGED to make it home in one piece, Bethany wasn't sure. Perhaps her guardian angels decided to do their job for once and guide her. Maybe she relied on muscle memory and drove on autopilot. She didn't recall how she pulled into her driveway and made it inside the house and to her bedroom. She only knew that she found herself lying on her bed, hugging her pillow, and crying buckets of tears.

Bethany plucked a tissue from the box on her nightstand and blew her nose. Why would Hank cancel the trip to Los Angeles after he'd spent so much time convincing her to come with him? She must have done something to offend him. Had he thought about Desmond's barb about her being a liar and believed him?

Or was she jumping to conclusions? Would Hank return to Cleveland and renew his invitation? Maybe he really did have to leave town early and cancel their plans abruptly. But if that were the case, wouldn't he have told her himself? Having his assistant call had been so unlike him—so cold and impersonal.

Pride came to her rescue, and she drew herself up and tossed the tissue in the trash can. As her dad used to say, no sense crying over something she couldn't change. But what an idiot she had been, believing Hank cared for her.

She swung her feet over the side of the bed. She would not fall apart because she had been gullible and believed his line about wanting to show her a side of himself the public didn't get to see. She had believed there was more to the man than the superstar mantle he wore like a badge of honor—believed his lies about giving her time, not wanting to rush her, and wanting her friendship.

She padded over to the dresser and pulled out her softest pajamas, contemplating her reflection in the mirror. Her eyes were red-rimmed and glassy, and the tip of her nose was pink.

Once again, the girl in the mirror had trusted a man who didn't deserve her trust.

This time, though, she had lost more than her foolish pride. This time she feared she had lost a piece of her foolish heart.

CHAPTER THIRTY-THREE

Hank put on his tuxedo and straightened his bow tie. Elizabeth had insisted he wear a lavender shirt to match his date, who happened to be his *Apollo* costar, Heather. She was sweet and pretty and wore a lavender dress, but she wasn't Bethany.

He rubbed his temples, but it didn't lessen the pounding headache—probably brought on by a guilty conscience. He scrounged in the medicine cabinet for two aspirin, which he tossed down with a glass of water.

He picked Heather up in the limo, traveled with her to the Palace Theatre, and exchanged boring pleasantries. Hank was grateful that Heather liked to talk, and that she only required him to say yes or no or the occasional maybe. The moment they got out of the limo, she threw her arms around his shoulders and kissed him at the same moment a photographer snapped their picture. Hank knew the embrace was purposeful on her part, since it was good for their careers if fans thought they were an item. And then they were admitted to the auditorium and seated at the front of the stage.

She leaned toward him and whispered, "Do you think you'll win best actor?"

"Maybe." His answer seemed to satisfy her.

A few minutes later, his name was called, and he moved to the podium to accept the award, his chest swelling with pride and relief. He had worked hard on *Apollo*, and the win would help to solidify his place in Hollywood. Elizabeth and Blackie would be delighted at this turn of events and the boost to his career.

An hour later, they came out of the theatre to the flash of cameras and well-wishes from the crowd. "Hank, how does it feel to be voted best actor in a television series?"

"It feels good," he said, placing his hand on Heather's back to guide her through the onslaught of press.

"There's a widely circulated picture of you kissing a woman on a kiss-cam at a Guardians' baseball game not long ago. Are you dating anyone special?" A tall woman with fake eyelashes thrust a microphone in his face.

He'd been asked this question many times over the years, so he knew how to play the game. He widened his smile and winked at the camera. "Not at the moment. But you never know."

"What about you?" The lady pushed the microphone in Heather's face. "You're on the god Apollo's arm tonight, and you're both recently single. Wouldn't you like to make this a permanent arrangement?"

Heather was a veteran in front of the camera too. She cocked her head his way and batted her long, dark eyelashes. "I've been told we have chemistry on set."

"So there you have it, folks," the lady with the microphone said into the camera. "The god and goddess are out tonight, and they make quite a pair, don't they?"

Hank figured the camera panned in for a close-up, so he

kept his grin firmly in place and guided Heather by the elbow to the waiting limo. Once they were inside, he went for the liquor between the seats.

Heather put her hand on top of his. "You know, we could see if our chemistry on set extends into the bedroom."

Hank stilled. "Aren't you planning to get back with your ex?"

"No, that ship has sailed. And I know you and Melanie are no longer an item, so, what do you say? My place or yours?"

Hank pulled his hand out from under hers. "Sorry. I'm not looking for a good time right now." He made himself a gin and tonic.

"It's Melanie, isn't it? You still have feelings for her."

"Yes." He did have feelings for Melanie—ones of relief. But he wanted to spare Heather's pride, so he didn't bother elaborating.

She slid her hand onto his thigh and stroked. "If you change your mind, Apollo, you have my number. Call me."

He ignored her hand. "Can I get you a drink?"

Heather moved her lips into a little pout. "Vodka and cranberry—heavy on the vodka."

And that ended that.

Later, when he was home, lying in bed at ten o'clock, he asked himself why he'd refused Heather's advances. They were both single and consenting adults. Except he was not single—not really. It had only been a few days since he'd left Cleveland, but he tortured himself thinking about Bethany, where she was, who she was with, whether she hated him. He wondered if she thought of him whenever she looked up at the stars, like he thought of her.

He brought her white sweater to his nose, the one she'd

dropped in his rental home the night he'd made her dinner, and breathed in her lemon and vanilla scent until he slept.

BETHANY WOKE to the sound of her cell phone alarm piercing the quiet morning. She groaned and found the time. Was it six o'clock in the morning already on a Thursday? She tried to drum up her normal optimism for the day ahead, but all her enthusiasm had vanished when Hank had left town.

She rubbed her tired eyelids and forced them open. She couldn't fall apart because Hank had disappointed her. She had chores, responsibilities, a living to earn. She had enjoyed her life before Hank slid across her countertop. She would enjoy it again one day—just maybe not at this particular moment.

Travis knocked at her bedroom door. At first, he'd taken Hank's desertion much better than she had, preferring to think it was only temporary. Until yesterday, when they had seen on the news that Hank would play Robin Hood on the big screen and filming would start in a few weeks. Travis had sworn then and given her a hug, offering to work late so she could have the evening off.

"You awake?"

"Yeah. C'mon in." She pushed her feet over the side of the bed and sat, staring at the floor.

He opened the door. "I'll go in for you this morning. You can join me when you're feeling up to it."

She studied the concerned expression on his face. "I'm okay. You don't need to take on my work."

"Yeah, I do." He handed her his phone. "You were right about Hank. He didn't waste any time."

The photograph caught her eye—Hank kissing a beautiful dark-haired woman and the headline: *Apollo Actors Rumored to Be Dating*. Blood rushed to her temples. He'd kissed his costar—the woman she'd watched him kiss on screen that evening not so long ago, when he'd made her dinner and asked to be her friend, and they'd watched an episode together. She fought to breathe. "It doesn't matter," she managed.

But it did. She knew it, and Travis knew it, although he didn't say anything more, probably not wanting to upset her further.

They said little on their way to Grandma Lou's, but once they got there, he took on the task of greeting customers, allowing her to disappear into the kitchen.

She eyed the clock—the knife seemed to take forever to move a millimeter. Was it still only eight o'clock? Five customers visited the restaurant, but only three could afford to pay for meals—the others were looking for handouts from the pantry. Maybe it was time she stopped treating her customers like family. If they kept this up, they would be out on the street by the end of the month. But at least they still had the contest—finalists would be announced tomorrow, and if they won, it would be the lifeline they needed.

She tugged at her cotton T-shirt. She always dressed for comfort, but today her clothes felt too snug, too sticky. Today, she pined for her parents' calm advice. Today, she wanted to scream and cry and flail her arms about and have a good old-fashioned temper tantrum. But she couldn't afford to have an emotional breakdown. So she donned her apron and headed to the kitchen for her own brand of therapy. She pulled out the flour, baking powder, sugar, salt, milk, cream of tartar, and cold butter to make her dad's homemade biscuits.

By the time Travis left to pick up supplies, and Rosie and the girls arrived at eleven, she had just pulled the first golden, flakey tray from the oven.

"Oh, my. Are those homemade biscuits I spy?"

Bethany removed her oven mitts and wiped her hands on a towel. Already, she felt a million times better. "Today is a biscuit kind of day."

Rosie raised an eyebrow. "That bad, huh? Girls, give Miss Bethany a hug."

The girls ran toward Bethany, and she crouched to take them into her arms. Above their heads, her gaze caught Rosie's.

Her broad smile seemed forced in place. "*Ay caramba.* I'll get the jam. Nobody is ever sad eating a warm biscuit with homemade strawberry jam."

And that was the truth, Bethany thought when she bit into the buttery crust and a little jam dribbled down her chin. But when the biscuits were consumed and the jam wiped from her face, all the misery she felt at Hank's abandonment returned tenfold.

"Girls, run and look in my purse in my locker. See if you can find my tissues."

Tia and Tana ran to do their mother's bidding, their feet pattering as they hit the wood floor.

"You're in love with him, aren't you," Rosie said, handing her a napkin and patting her back.

Bethany realized she was crying, a slow trickle of wet tears. She wiped her eyes and blew her nose, but the trickle kept coming.

"I didn't want to be," she said. "I did everything I could not to."

"*Querida,* don't blame yourself. You couldn't have stopped from falling for Hank even if you were gagged and tied to the stove with your apron strings. Love knows no boundaries. Some things are meant to be."

Bethany swiped at the annoying tears with the napkin and hiccupped. "Yes, I could have. I should have kept my distance. I should have listened to Elizabeth. She said Hank would break my heart. She warned me to stay away, but I ignored her."

"Bah. The woman is a cold-hearted snake. You listen to me. We have a saying where I come from. *Cuando alguien te da comida preparada con tanto amor, te está dando un pedacito de su corazón.* When someone gives you the food they cook with so much love, they give you a piece of their heart. You couldn't have stopped yourself from falling for Hank the minute he took that first bite of tomato soup. You couldn't have stopped him any more than you could have stopped taking care of me and the girls. That's just the kind of woman you are. It's what makes you special, *cariño.*"

The tears were coming faster now, rolling down her cheeks in warm rivulets, like a summer rainstorm.

"Honey, you didn't do anything wrong, you hear me? Hank had his reasons for leaving, and I'm pretty certain they had little to do with you. Don't blame yourself."

Bethany couldn't keep up with the napkin, so she stopped trying. "It's just—I really care about him, Rosie. I thought he cared about me. How could I have been so wrong?"

Rosie embraced her, patting her head like a baby and placing it on her shoulder, where it made a wet patch. "I don't know, honey, I don't know. I think Hank does care about you as much as he is able to. I know he couldn't take his eyes off you most of the time. This turn of events is real strange."

Now the sobs began. Great big body-heaving sobs she

couldn't contain. All the pain she held inside welled up and spilled over like a plugged sink with the water running. She couldn't stop crying even if she wanted to, which she didn't. She hugged Rosie and shuddered in her arms and allowed the deluge to wash over her.

"Let the tears flow, honey. Let them all flow. Tears are *bueno*. Tears are *muy bueno*. They'll help ease your pain better than any medicine I can give."

"Miss Bethany, are you sad 'cause Mr. Hank left?" Tia returned with a wad full of tissues. She handed them to Bethany, who managed a nod.

"I'm sad, too," Tana said. "Mr. Hank was nice."

"C'mon girls. Let's give Miss Bethany some space." Rosie released her from her comforting embrace to usher her daughters to the dining area. She turned at the swinging doors. "You just sit and rest. I'll take care of things out here until you've got yourself together. It may not seem like anything could ever be right again, but trust me, the passage of time will help. You've got the contest to look forward to. Won't they announce the finalists tomorrow?"

Bethany managed a nod.

"It's one day at a time, *amiga*. That's all."

Bethany tried to smile, but it was too much. So she nodded and blew her nose into the tissues and tried to think about what to do next.

CHAPTER THIRTY-FOUR

"You need to eat," Blackie said, sipping a Guinness. He wasn't much older than Hank, but a premature white spot on his dark hair gave him the appearance of maturity. "Elizabeth said you've lost weight."

They sat in a booth in Hank's favorite restaurant, known for its exclusivity and extraordinary seafood. Hank studied the menu, but nothing seemed appetizing. "You sound like a father."

Blackie cackled. "I am a father. For God's sake, eat, my man. Even my three-year-old eats better than you."

Hank sighed. Nothing tasted as good as Bethany's cooking. His cell phone buzzed next to his hand. His father. He ignored it. "Quit your nagging. I'll order a hamburger."

Blackie raised his glass. "A toast."

Hank clinked his glass against Blackie's, but more from habit than celebration.

"To your recent success. And—I have a buyer eager to cut a deal."

"Cut a deal?"

"For the Cleveland building, of course. If you're not

going to convert the structure into a fitness center, then you'll need to sell it. I have a buyer."

"I'm not interested in selling."

"They're willing to pay top dollar."

Hank sat forward and fingered his glass. "Who is it?"

"It's not a single person, it's a conglomerate, a real estate company who'll turn it into a high-class apartment complex. They like the location, so near to downtown."

Hank pressed his lips together. "No."

"Now, Hank—"

"I said no. End of discussion. I'm not selling to a real estate conglomerate."

"You'd be foolish not to. They're willing to offer one and a half mil—more than the building's worth to you and triple what you paid for it. You'll make a killing."

"I'm not interested in making a killing. I want to make sure whoever owns it will allow the tenants to continue renting."

"You'll never find a buyer willing to make that deal. Whoever owns it will make more by turning it into something new than continuing to rent the space."

His cell phone buzzed again. His dad was persistent. This was the fifth time he'd called today. The old man must be desperate for money. He bit his lip to stop from hurling the device across the room. "I won't have it turned into something new."

"Be reasonable, Hank. The building needs attention. You can't continue to own it without investing in it. It's an expensive proposition. I urge you to reconsider."

"No. End of story." He raised his hand. "I mean it."

"All right," Blackie grumbled, downing the contents of his glass.

Hank's cell phone buzzed again. Across from him, Blackie glowered. "You need to answer that?"

"Nah, it's no one important." Hank silenced the call, picked up his glass, and followed Blackie's example, but it couldn't dull the pressure behind his eyelids.

BETHANY TOTALED the money in the drawer for the third time and tried to stop the butterflies from coursing through her system. It had been nearly two weeks since Hank had left, and there was no way they would have enough to pay next month's rent and buy the supplies needed to keep the place open. She groaned before she realized Travis could hear her.

"What's wrong?" he asked, pausing from his job sweeping the floor.

She busied herself by checking the bakery items. There were two chocolate donuts and one banana muffin left in the case. "We need to be on the list when they announce the finalists tomorrow."

"Why do you sound like the voice of death?"

"Travis, if our names aren't on the website, we're going to have to close Grandma Lou's at the end of the month."

Travis leaned on the broom. "I know he's a slime for leaving you and all, but maybe we can use Hank's guilty conscience to buy us some time on our rent? He'd probably give us an extension to make the payment."

She swallowed and pretended her heart didn't lurch and shift inside her chest at Travis's suggestion and stuck her chin in the air. "No way. I can't face him right now. Not after the way he left."

"I wasn't suggesting *you* call him."

"I said no, Travis." Her voice shook, and she hunched against the counter to stop the trembles.

Travis shot her a concerned look.

"I won't call Hank, and you can't either. He's made it clear he's moved on. We need to as well. Call it pride or whatever, but I won't burden him with our problems. Let's just keep our fingers crossed we win, okay?"

"LOOK TO YOUR LEFT," Blackie said out of the corner of his mouth. "Looks like we're about to have company."

Hank turned his head to the side and suppressed a groan.

"Why hello, Hank. Heard you were back in town," Melanie said, leaning over the table and granting him a full frontal view of her chest.

"Hello, Melanie. I see the grapevine is alive and well. I've only been back a week or so."

She gave him a sly look, causing goosebumps to form on Hank's skin. "Heather said you missed me. Did you miss me, Hanky?"

Hank's insides cringed at the use of the pet name. He tightened his jaw so he wouldn't be tempted to say something he would later regret. Why had he ever thought Melanie attractive? The pounding in his head intensified. He nodded toward Blackie. "You remember my agent?"

"Yes, of course I remember you." She presented Blackie with what Hank called her don't-waste-my-time smile and shook his hand. Then she leaned toward Hank and kissed his cheek like they were dear friends and she hadn't screamed expletives at him the last time they'd talked. Hank tried to keep the surprise at her greeting off his face.

"I heard you'll be playing Robin Hood on the big screen. Congratulations. That's quite a role."

"Yes, it is."

"Now you're back in town, let's do lunch and catch up."

He raised an eyebrow and gave her his famous Apollo frown—the one he used before he vanquished the enemy. "You want to catch up?"

"Well, of course I do. You and I had something special together, didn't we?"

"Melanie, you're suing me for millions of dollars. Anything special we had is long gone."

"Now, Hank, let's not be overly dramatic. I'm dropping the lawsuit. You know I only filed it because you broke my little ol' heart." She pressed her hand against her chest, drawing his eye there. "When Heather told me how you felt, well, you know I want to let any past mistakes go, to see if the flame between us can be rekindled." She leaned toward him, smelling of jasmine and roses. The name of her perfume, "Bolt of Lightning," popped into his head— probably because the ounce he'd bought for her birthday had cost him more than his electricity bill for an entire year.

Hank wrapped his fingers around his glass and watched the ice melt. "I thought you were dating Brent Chambers?"

"My, you *have* been out of touch, haven't you? Brent's old news. I'm a free agent." She squeezed his bicep. "I see you're still keeping your gorgeous bod in shape." She straightened, granting him a sweet but false smile. "We were good together once, Hank, weren't we? We could be again. But don't wait too long. Give me a call, okay." She left in a perfumed flurry.

Blackie guffawed. "That's some woman. Looks like Robin Hood has put you back on Melanie's A-list. Better strike while your iron's 'in the fire' so to speak . . . eh, Apollo?"

Hank released his pent-up breath. "Don't be an ass." His phone buzzed, and he groaned. His dad wasn't giving up. "Sorry, I'll be right back." He stood and headed toward the bar, where Blackie couldn't eavesdrop on his conversation.

"Hank, I'm here," his father's voice came through the phone.

"Where's here? In LA?" An icy hand pressed against his lungs. He pulled out the nearest bar stool and sank onto it.

"Where else? I told you we were coming to visit, remember?"

"You said you'd call me about visiting."

A hoarse laugh rang through the phone. "That's what I'm doing right now. Calling you. I'd like to come see ya, son."

"You need money."

"No, that's not why I'm calling. We're on the way to your house from the airport. We should be there in . . . Linda, what's the GPS say?" His dad sounded excited.

Hank heard a faint voice, which must be his stepmom, in the background.

"Thirty-eight minutes."

Oh my God. His father, stepmom, and half-sisters were on their way to his house. The icy hand clutching his lungs moved to his heart and squeezed.

"You there, Hank?"

He heard Bethany's voice in his head, as if she stood next to him and wasn't halfway across the country. Compassionate and kind Bethany who had been betrayed by her fiancé. *Let him visit. Give him a chance to explain. Maybe something he says will ease your anger—help you understand his neglect.*

The hand gripping his heart eased.

"Hank, I know you blame me for leaving the way I did when you were a kid. I'm real sorry about that time. I've got a lot of regrets. Hank?"

It's a gift you give yourself, Bethany urged in his mind. Warmth pulsed through his veins. He drew in a breath. "Yeah?"

"I'm in a better place now. Got a new job, and it's going well. Your stepmom and sisters want to get to know you. I'm just asking you to give us a chance to be part of your life. What do you say, son? Can you spare a few hours for a visit?"

Hank gripped the phone and listened to the sound of his heart thudding in his ears. "All right, Dad."

CHAPTER THIRTY-FIVE

Bethany's finger paused over the computer mouse, and she eyed the cursor, which blinked at her in the address line like an annoying gnat. Sweat made her hands slick on the keys as she typed the name of the contest.

Please, Big Guy Upstairs, let Grandma Lou's final.

Travis leaned over her shoulder in their tiny kitchen at home and eyed the laptop screen. "No more stalling, Bethany. Refresh the page. It's ten o'clock at night. They have to post the finalists before midnight. The site must be updated by now."

Bethany swallowed and wiped her hands on her jeans. "Here goes nothing." She pressed the enter key. The page went white before refilling the screen. Her heart thudded in her ears and her eyes blurred for an instant as her gaze traveled past the opening paragraph and narrowed on the list of ten finalists, which came into focus with sudden clarity.

1. *Spun Sugar*
2. *Heartland Bakery*
3. *Slice of Heaven*

4. *Baker's Dozen*
5. *Valentino's*
6. *Cosmic Cooking*
7. *King of Tarts*
8. *Great Lakes' Cakes*
9. *Flakey Layers*
10. *Grandma Lou's*

"There's our name! We're finalists," Travis said, his fingers tapping the screen.

Relief spilled into her quivering stomach like a spring rain, and her heart skipped, sang, and performed a wild happy dance in her chest cavity. She shot from her chair, which fell to the floor with a loud thump, grabbed Travis's hands, and jumped into the air, squealing like a kid on Christmas morning. "We did it. We did it. We did it."

"What's this we? You did all the work."

"No." Bethany turned to Travis, shaking her head. "*I* don't own Grandma Lou's. *We* do. I couldn't have worked on our entry without your help in the restaurant. It was a team effort. We did it together."

"Whatever you say, Sis. I didn't have a doubt we'd final, though."

"At least we have a shot at the prize money."

Her cell phone rang, and she checked the number, but she didn't recognize it, so she silenced the ringer and let it go to voicemail.

"I don't know how I'll ever get to sleep tonight," she said. "What if we celebrate our contest final with a glass of wine? That usually makes me sleepy."

"Good idea. I'll pour us each a glass. I think there's still a bottle in the fridge."

Bethany's phone buzzed, indicating the caller had left a

voicemail. She found the message and tapped the playback button.

"Hello. This is Francine Richmond from the Fresh & Easy baking company. Please call me at your earliest convenience. My number is . . ."

The phone slipped through her shaking hands and crashed to the floor.

Travis paused in the act of pouring the wine. "Is that . . . ?"

"Yes. Fresh & Easy. Yes." Bethany scrambled to find the phone. She sat and pressed the phone icon to return the call.

Travis set the glasses on the table and sat across from her, his gray-green eyes reflecting her excitement and nervousness.

"Hello, this is Bethany Parker. I'm returning your call." Her words ran faster than Daphne's dog after cupcakes, her stomach tightening like it was slowly being squeezed in a vise.

"Yes, hello, Bethany. This is Francine Richmond, chief marketing officer at Fresh & Easy baking company. Sorry for the late-night call—I'm overseas, and there's a bit of a time change. But I have what I think will be exciting news for you, and I didn't want to wait another moment to share it. Your recipe for Grandma Lou's Chocolate Cake with Buttercream Frosting has been selected as the winner in our baking contest. Congratulations."

Bethany released her breath all at once. Adrenaline poured through her veins. "Wow. That is amazing news. I'm . . . I'm so excited. I can't begin to tell you how much. Thank you."

"Not only did your recipe receive more than ten thousand likes on our website, but we've made your chocolate cake in our test kitchen, and our chefs and tasters agree it turned out fabulous."

"I'm so glad you liked it."

"We loved it. We wanted to alert you early that you're our winner so you can prepare for potential media calls. However tempting it will be, it's extremely important you don't share this exciting news for another forty-eight hours, okay?"

"Certainly, I won't."

"Not until we have a chance to distribute our press release. Then you'll be free to share. We'll email you full details and give you permission to share the news once we've posted an announcement on our website. Congratulations again, Bethany. We're so pleased you entered our contest with such a wonderful recipe."

"I'm honored to win. Thank you again."

Bethany ended the call and dropped the phone like a hot coal.

Travis's eyes met hers. "We won the contest?"

She shrieked and shot up from the chair. "Oh . . . My . . . God! We won. We actually won, Travis. I can't believe it. This is like . . . like some sort of amazing dream." She held out her arm. "Pinch me, please, and tell me this is real."

Travis jumped up and hugged her. Then he pinched her arm and laughed, his face glowing with excitement. "I'll do better than pinch you. This calls for a toast."

He picked up one of the glasses he'd set on the table and raised it high in the air. "To our dear Grandma Lou and her famous chocolate cake with buttercream frosting."

Bethany smiled and clinked her glass with his. "Hear, hear." She gulped the wine like it was fruit punch. She was going to need quite a bit if she had any hope of sleeping a wink tonight.

~

THE SOUND of tires on pavement had Hank reaching for his whiskey glass. He reminded himself to cut back on his alcohol consumption, but not today. Today, he was meeting his dad and stepfamily after years of avoidance. "Connor, they're here. Get the door, will ya?"

"Sure," Connor agreed, closing the textbook he'd been studying and leaving the room, an eager bounce in his step. Connor didn't share the depth of his bitterness toward their father, although Hank knew there must be scars buried deep.

Voices echoed in the foyer. He drained his glass and set it on the bar, his heart tripping into high gear. What had he been thinking to put himself through this? *Give him a chance to explain. Maybe something he says will ease your anger . . . help you understand his neglect.* Bethany's gentle voice in his head centered him, reminding him why he had agreed to the difficult reunion.

And then his dad entered the family room with Connor close on his heels. His stepmother and sisters—strangers—followed behind, looking around his home with *oohs* and *ahs*.

His father crossed to stand in front of him, much frailer and grayer than the last time Hank had seen him. "Son, it's good to see you."

Hank nodded, not up to giving the old man a hug. "How was the drive?"

"Long, but we made it. You remember my wife, Linda."

"A pleasure, Hank," Linda said, with an agreeable smile.

She had silvery blonde hair, rosy cheeks, and a laugh that seemed sincere. "We are so happy we could come for a visit. Your father talks about you night and day. You must know how proud we are of you and your success. Thank you for making time for us. We know you're busy."

"I'm glad we could make it work." Hank nodded and smiled, wondering if he meant it.

"And these are your sisters, Willow and Glenna," she said, turning to the two teens. "Girls, this is your brother Hank."

"Hi," Glenna said, with a small, awkward smile. His youngest sister couldn't have been more than thirteen, with a narrow, little face and stick-straight blonde hair falling past skinny shoulders. She tried hard to hide a mouth full of metal.

"Hi, Glenna," he said, smiling. "Nice to meet you."

"I can't believe I finally get to meet my big brother, the superstar," Willow interjected, diverting his attention. The older girl offered him a quirky smile, so much like Connor's. If he remembered right, Willow was a senior in high school and a center on the volleyball team. She was tall and thin with a clear complexion and the confidence that comes with athleticism. "Can I get your picture? My friends are never going to believe it when I tell them where I am."

She held up the camera on her cell phone, laughing, and he obliged, draping a casual arm around her shoulder, while she snapped the picture. Then he offered the same to Glenna, who wasn't as bold as Willow, but clearly wanted a photo too.

Awkward greetings over, they sat around the family room, while he plied them with sodas from the bar, and Connor offered them a tray full of snacks. Then they discussed every topic he could think of—the best attractions to visit while they were in Los Angeles, life on a college campus, the Hollywood lifestyle—until it was time for them to leave.

"Son, thanks for having us," his dad said, pulling him into an awkward hug. "I'm really glad we got to see you."

"Me too, Dad. Me too." And this time, Hank discovered, he meant it.

"HEY, BIG GUY, WHATCHA DOING?" Connor said when Hank picked up his call.

"Connor, what's up?" Hank asked. "I'm about ready to go on *The Talk*."

"No kidding. Well, I won't keep you."

"I've got a few minutes. Everything all right?"

"Yeah, everything's good." Connor cleared his throat. "Was just going to say it was a good visit with Dad the other day."

"Yeah." Hank swallowed the dryness in his throat. It had felt good to meet their stepmom and sisters and to have a conversation with their dad that didn't involve money.

"I know you still don't trust him. But it was nice, wasn't it, to be all together like that?"

"Yeah, I guess. Where are you?"

"I'm on my way to your house. Thought I'd take Woodrow for a walk . . . I know that was hard for you and all. To talk to Dad and Linda and meet Willow and Glenna. But you did good. Dad seemed really proud of you. You okay?"

Hank straightened the collar of his shirt and frowned at the phone. "I'm good. Why?"

"I don't know. You still seem . . . unhappy or something."

Or something. He swallowed the sudden lump in his throat. "Just working. I'm all right."

"You don't seem like it. Seems like every time I talk to you, you're sad and angry. Is it the girl you dated in Cleveland? You know, the restaurant owner. Whatever happened to her?"

Hank shifted his rear end on the extra comfy couch in his dressing room. "Nothing happened to her. She's still in Cleveland, as far as I know."

"Did she break up with you or something? Is that why you're depressed?"

"No." The single word came out sharper than Hank intended. He drew in a breath and lowered his voice. "I'm not unhappy, Connor. I'm getting my career back on track, that's all. You want me to be able to pay your college bills, don't you?"

"Not if it makes you miserable."

Hank gritted his teeth. "I'm not miserable. Not at all. I was just named best actor in a TV show. Rehearsals have begun for *Robin Hood*. What the heck would I have to be miserable about?"

"See, that's what I mean. You sound like you've been sentenced to prison."

And he felt like it too. Hank rubbed his jaw. "Your imagination."

The door opened, and Elizabeth stood in the entrance.

"If you say so." Connor didn't sound convinced. "Mind if I hit the gym while I'm at your place?"

"Go for it. Listen, gotta run." Hank ended the call and stood.

"Los Angeles is good for you, Hank. Your hair and

makeup look great." Elizabeth crossed his dressing room, her long legs encased in expensive-looking trousers. Not a wrinkle marred her ivory silk top. She looked cool and controlled and confident as she removed an invisible piece of lint from his shirt. "You're on in five. Are you ready?"

Hank tilted his thumb in the air, and a few minutes later, he settled his bottom on the cushy black leather chair behind the microphone at *The Talk*, the hottest podcast in television and film. He took a drink of water and prepared for the first set of questions from the host, Jessica Flowers.

He passed his gaze across the studio audience and settled on an olive-skinned face near the front. *Not Bethany.* Reason dictated it couldn't be her, but he leaned toward her, his heartbeat stumbling and skipping before resuming its steady cadence. *It wasn't her.* But he could not stop his entire being from hoping.

Hank's gaze moved past Bethany's look-alike before circling back to study her face in more detail. *Definitely not Bethany.* Her skin was too dark, jaw too long, cheeks too narrow, lips too thin. He dropped his gaze to his hands and swallowed the disappointment shooting its way into his churning stomach.

Every seat was filled in the studio, which held at least one hundred people, not to mention the millions of listeners and subscribers, all eager to know what he thought.

Would another station pick up *Apollo*? *Highly unlikely.* (That ship had sailed.)

What kind of car did he drive? *A Porsche 911.* (A splurge when he'd landed the role that made him famous.)

What did he eat for breakfast? *A protein shake.* (He longed for one of Bethany's chocolate donuts with sprinkles.)

Did he and Heather date? *No, they were good friends.* (He wasn't certain he would ever date again.)

Jessica cleared her throat. "Hank, what's the last show you watched on TV, and why did you choose to watch it?"

A picture of Bethany, cheeks pink and hair tucked behind her ear as she slept on his shoulder, tugged at his memory. He forced a shrug and a grin and downplayed his answer. "Mine, actually."

"Do you always watch your own shows?"

"No, I usually avoid them."

The crowd laughed, but Jessica persisted. "Oh, really? Intriguing. So tell us, why did you watch your own television show?"

"A friend who hadn't seen it asked to watch it with me."

"A friend, eh? A female?"

Hank shifted and unscrewed the cap on his bottle of water. He took a swig to wet his dry throat and forced a grin. "What other kind is there?"

"Now you have us all intrigued. Who is this mysterious friend? Anyone we'd know?"

"No," Hank said, his smile fading.

"I read you purchased a building in Cleveland, Ohio, where you were born. You've been seen around town with the previous owner, Bethany Parker. Was she your audience of one?"

A picture flashed on the confidence monitor in front of him—the picture from the kiss-cam at the baseball game. Heat flooded his body. Beads of sweat broke out on his forehead. The photo exploded on the giant screen behind him, and the studio crowd whistled and cheered.

Hank cleared his throat and spoke into the microphone, keeping his tone strong and even. "She's a tenant in the building. She and her brother own a restaurant called Grandma Lou's. I highly recommend their whoopie pies."

The audience laughed, but Jessica persisted. Hank wanted to wring her nosey neck, but he plastered a smile on his face and pretended he found the conversation humorous.

"From the photo, you clearly like each other. Is Bethany Parker anything special to you?"

Hank wiped his hands on his pants and spoke into the microphone. "Just a friend."

"Oh, then you probably aren't aware her business won a national baking competition today? Sadly, the company sponsoring the contest announced shortly before we went on air that her entry was disqualified due to plagiarism. Apparently, she broke the contest rules when she entered a recipe shared by the Chef King last month on his television show."

Hank's throat closed up and his mouth went dry. "No, I hadn't heard," he managed.

CHAPTER THIRTY-SIX

The jingle of the door had Bethany looking up from the counter for incoming customers. Early this morning, Fresh & Easy had announced the contest win and customers had been stopping in all day to congratulate them. Grandma Lou's phone had been ringing nonstop, so she finally took it off the hook so they could get stuff done and sent her cell phone to voicemail.

A burly man hidden behind a large video camera entered the restaurant, accompanied by a woman holding a microphone. Bethany recognized the woman from the local news—the one who'd shown up on the day she met Hank, to interview him outside the building.

She wiped her hands on her apron and swallowed hard. The local station must be here to interview her. "Can I help you?" Bethany smiled at the visitors, who moved forward in tandem. One of them held a camera, which, from the flashing green light, appeared to be rolling.

The reporter thrust the microphone toward Bethany's chin. "Why did you plagiarize your recent contest entry?

Are you upset you're no longer the winner of the baking contest?"

Fear gripped Bethany's body with icy tentacles. "What are you talking about?" Her stomach quivered and the room tilted, forcing her to cling to the counter to stay upright. She closed her eyes until the spinning room settled, and she could open them again without getting sick.

"Your restaurant's entry, Grandma Lou's Chocolate Cake with Buttercream Frosting, was originally shared by Chef King Desmond Mitchell as part of his television show last month."

She didn't know whether her face reflected surprise or looked as blank as her thoughts. The reporter's words might have been in a foreign tongue for all she could understand. Seconds ticked by while she registered the hard look in the woman's cool blue eyes and the flashing of the television camera pointed in her direction and the slickness of her hands where they gripped the wood countertop. Then the wheels in her mind shifted into high gear, and she realized the seriousness of the accusation.

"I *didn't* plagiarize our entry. The recipe was my grandmother's." How had she not known that Desmond had shared it? Of course, she'd been a little busy trying to keep the restaurant afloat, and in general, she avoided watching Desmond's show because it only made her angry.

The reporter tilted her lips in a suspicious smirk. "Fresh & Easy announced your recipe from all the entries as the winner of the contest this morning and then rescinded the announcement a few hours later, after they learned your entry violated their contest rules. It has proven to be a duplicate of Desmond Mitchell's."

They rescinded the announcement. Bethany's throat closed, and she had a sudden, urgent need for air. A sharp ache took up residence in her chest, right above her pounding heart. They must have tried to leave a message, but with the shop phone off the hook, and her cell calls going to voicemail, she hadn't gotten it. "He stole it. Desmond stole my grandmother's recipe." Her voice trembled, making her sound guilty.

"Those are serious charges. Desmond Mitchell is a well-known public figure and host of a popular television cooking show. Do you have proof what you say is true—that he stole your recipe?"

"Yes, I . . ." Her throat constricted further, cutting off her air supply. She swallowed the dryness and tried to explain. "I have the recipe, written in my grandmother's handwriting. I added a few notes to it on the side, in pencil, but most of it is in her handwriting. Is it sufficient?"

The reporter's eyes widened, so she looked almost interested, and she nodded. "I'm sure our viewers would like to see your grandmother's recipe. Can you show it to us?"

"Yes, I keep it in the kitchen with my grandma's cookbook. Follow me."

She led the reporter and cameraman into the kitchen and rummaged on the shelf above the pantry until she found Grandma Lou's fat red cookbook stuffed with snippets of recipes in her spidery handwriting. Then she carried it with her into the dining area and opened the book on the counter. The recipe for her chocolate cake, which should have been on top, was nowhere inside. Warm heat flooded her cheeks. "It's not here." She flipped through the pages in the book, searching desperately for the familiar scrap of paper with stains from cooking.

The reporter shot her a pitying glance, like Bethany needed a remedial course in lying. Then she turned to look into the camera.

"You heard it here first, folks. She may be known as a talented baker in this neighborhood, but Bethany Parker, owner of Grandma Lou's Kitchen and Pantry in Tremont, is in hot water over the recipe she submitted to a national baking competition. Today, Ms. Parker's recipe was selected as the winner of the half-a-million-dollar prize money. In a strange twist of events, the Fresh & Easy baking company announced that Parker had entered a recipe widely attributed to Chef King Desmond Mitchell, Parker's former fiancé. Unfortunately for Parker, her entry has been removed, and she'll no longer have a shot at the prize money. The new winner has not yet been announced. I'm Susan Winchester, reporting live from Tremont."

The moment the green record light stopped blinking, Susan set down the microphone on the counter and peered into the display case. "I'll take a vanilla swirl brownie and a cup of coffee to go. And Joe, here"—she gestured to the cameraman—"will take a whoopie pie."

"I'm sorry, I need a second," Bethany said, grabbing her cell phone where she'd set it behind the counter and pulling out a chair to sit. Her limbs trembled and her head was full of the air which seemed to have escaped her lungs.

She searched her voicemails until she found the message from Fresh & Easy and listened to Francine explaining that her entry had been disqualified after they'd received an anonymous tip saying her recipe had been previously published. Fear grabbed her heart and squeezed with a cold fist. The whole world thought she was a liar, that she had stolen the recipe from Desmond. How would she ever convince anyone to believe her?

The reporter watched her, one hand on her hip, while Joe headed out the door. Bethany figured he was returning his camera to the white van parked out front.

"That was live on the news just now?" Bethany asked.

Susan slapped a ten-dollar bill on the counter. "As live as a newborn baby, honey." She pulled out the chair next to Bethany and sat. "You didn't steal the recipe, did you?"

The oxygen seemed to return to the room all at once, and Bethany took a cleansing breath. "No, I didn't."

"Listen, for what it's worth, I believe you. I have a good instinct about these things. But my job as a news reporter is to leave my personal feelings out of it and tell the facts."

Bethany looked around Grandma Lou's. The worn tables, rickety chairs, wood countertop, and antique register gave the place an ancient, rustic charm. Donuts drizzled in melted chocolate, homemade fruit pastries, and today's special pumpkin muffins tempted from the display case. Shelves with the rhubarb jam she'd canned last summer, the teas she ordered from a British catalogue, and her grandmother's tea set lent an old-fashioned charm to the atmosphere.

A single tear slid down her cheek. It was time to admit what she'd been denying ever since Desmond left town. She couldn't keep running a business that was part charity without pulling in a profit, no matter how much she loved it —no matter how homey she had made it or how much of her own personality she had stamped into the fabric of the place. She and Travis must close the door on their grandparents' legacy and say goodbye to their neighborhood friends. They must put this chapter of their lives behind them and build a new one. *Somehow*.

She sucked in a quivering breath. They must be strong, but dear Lord, she felt so weak.

She swiped at the tear, trying not to draw attention to it, and stood to fetch the treats and pour the coffee. The busyness settled her nerves, and she returned with the disposable cup of hot coffee and the brownie and whoopie pie in a paper bag, and set them in front of Susan, giving her the change.

Bethany stuck out her chin. "I know you're only doing your job, but I didn't plagiarize my entry. I've been making that recipe since I was a small child. It was my grandmother's favorite cake. No one ever made it quite like she did."

"Honey, if you show me proof, I'm more than willing to present both sides of the story." Susan opened the bag, pulled out a piece of the brownie, and popped it in her mouth. "Oooh, this is good. Did you make this?"

"Yes, this morning. I don't know what other proof I can show if I can't find the original recipe."

"Do you have any credible witnesses who'd be willing to speak up in your favor?"

"My brother, Travis—"

"Someone other than family."

"Well, I've served the recipe to some of my customers in the past."

"That's what I'm talking about. Will any of them have seen the original recipe in your grandmother's hand?"

"I don't know. I can't remember ever showing it to any of them, although I've served the cake in the restaurant from time to time, and they all seemed to enjoy it."

Susan ate another piece of brownie and stood. "I have to get back to the station. But see if you can find the recipe or if any of your customers remember seeing it. If you can get a few credible witnesses, I'm willing to give you airtime to tell your side of the story. If you're telling the truth, it could clear your good name and your restaurant's reputation with it."

Bethany sighed and tried on a smile, but she couldn't make it stick. In all her imaginings of the worst that could happen, she had not imagined this. Not only had she failed to win the contest, but her personal integrity had been destroyed along with that of her business. There was no way she could ever recover. She and Travis must close the doors to Grandma Lou's.

Her lip quivered. "Thank you, Susan. I appreciate your willingness to share both sides of the story."

"Here's my card. Call me when you're ready."

CHAPTER THIRTY-SEVEN

Hank shifted in the driver's seat of his Porsche and did his best to keep the anger from his voice. "Bethany Parker would *never* steal a recipe and enter it into a contest. She's the most honest, respectable, kind, and considerate woman I've ever met. You're making a mistake."

The Fresh & Easy representative Pamela had managed to track down for him after he'd left the studio was apologetic, yet unwavering. "Sir, we appreciate your support of Bethany Parker, but I'm afraid the rules of the contest are quite firm. The winning recipe must be an original. The fact of the matter is Desmond Mitchell shared the same recipe for chocolate cake with buttercream frosting on a nationally aired television production months *before* the entry was submitted by Bethany Parker in our contest."

"Yes, because he *stole* the recipe from her."

"Can you prove it?"

"If I can, will you reinstate her entry as the winner? This accusation of plagiarism will destroy a good, honest woman's reputation and the reputation of her business."

"If you have concrete evidence, of course we will reconsider. We'll delay announcing her replacement for a few days, so you have time to submit your evidence. Can you do it?"

"I'm sure going to try," Hank said, clutching the wheel. "I'll be in touch." He hung up the phone as the light turned green and stepped on the gas, only to apply the brakes a few minutes later. Los Angeles traffic was its usual tangled mess.

He tapped his fingers on the steering wheel and studied the brake lights on the car in front of him. There was no way Bethany had cheated on her contest entry. Desmond had to have stolen it.

He squeezed the wheel like he wished he could squeeze the life out of the Chef King right now. If he had known the extent of his treachery, Hank would have tossed the jerk out on the street the minute he'd spotted him annoying Bethany. He should track the thief down now and teach him a lesson or two. It wouldn't help Bethany restore her reputation, but it sure would help Hank release his pent-up anger.

Traffic began to move again but crawled along at a snail's pace. It took almost an hour before he pulled into the exclusive gated neighborhood where he lived in the Hollywood Hills. Hank used the time to call Blackie, the producers, and a private investigation firm that had a reputation for getting answers fast. He'd worked himself into quite a stew by the time he arrived home.

The first thing he noticed was Connor's Honda Civic in the driveway with Elizabeth's shiny red Mini Cooper parked next to it.

Hank entered his house from the garage to hear raised voices coming from the great room. He paused in the entrance to listen.

"You should be happy," Elizabeth was saying. "Hank's

got his dream role now, and you'll continue to be able to mooch off him for the rest of your college expenses."

Connor's voice rose a notch. "Sure, he's helping me with school, but I'm not mooching. I intend to pay every penny back when I graduate. My point is, he's not happy."

"How would you know if he's happy or not? You've only known him for a year. I've been with him for almost fifteen. I think I'm a better judge of his happiness. Trust me, landing the role of his dreams makes him happy."

He was about to enter the room, but Connor's next words stopped him cold.

"Can't you see he's in love with her? That's why he's been moping around and giving one syllable answers to everything he's asked. The big guy's in love, and he doesn't even know it."

For some reason, Connor's assertion, which he would have scoffed at a few months ago, had him shaking in his custom-made Oxford shoes.

"Hank in love," Elizabeth said with a laugh. "Never. Your brother's left a trail of broken hearts a mile in every direction. But he's never *once* been in love. You of all people should know why."

"What do you mean?" Connor asked, sounding puzzled.

Hank found himself moving forward to make sure he heard whatever rationale Elizabeth would give.

"Oh, for Pete's sake. Because you both have abandonment issues, that's why. You're afraid of intimacy. That's why Hank's relationships never last. He doesn't feel like he's deserving of a woman's love or support, so he finds a way to sabotage his relationships. You're both running scared and probably will be for the rest of your lives. This isn't complicated."

Connor mumbled something, but Hank couldn't hear it. His brother must have been farther from the entrance than Elizabeth, who responded.

"You're lucky you've had Hank to lean on, but outside of his dog, Hank's had no one since his mom died. He's afraid of love and commitment and all those things that come with a real relationship. The only way he knows how to show love is by footing the bill. That's why he's paying for your education. Trust me, he's not in love with Bethany Parker. He wouldn't know how to be."

And every word she spoke rang true, Hank realized, except for one.

"I FAILED, TRAVIS," Bethany said.

She'd sat him down at one of the tables at the close of the business day and confessed the ugly truth and shared the official-looking email she'd received earlier in the day from Fresh & Easy. "We've been disqualified from the contest. Desmond used Grandma Lou's recipe on his TV show, so they rejected our entry. I'm sorry, Travis. I've called Fresh & Easy to try and explain, but they're asking for definitive proof that Desmond stole the recipe, and I don't have it."

"What sort of proof would they need?"

"Someone who would have eaten the cake in our grandparents' day, more than one customer who remembers seeing the recipe, a written confession from Desmond himself. I tried to talk to Desmond, but he won't take my phone calls. I've interviewed everyone who's come in today, but no one remembers seeing the recipe or eating it back in the day. I even called a lawyer to see if they'd take this on pro bono, but they told me we don't have a case. I don't know what else to do. I'm sorry."

"It's not your fault," Travis said, patting her arm. "It's Desmond's. He's a horrible scum of a human being." He pushed his chair from the table and stood, his hands clenched into fists at his side.

Alarm shot through Bethany, stealing her breath. "Where do you think you're going?"

"To kill him. I'm going to find the weasel and squeeze his neck with my bare hands. Then maybe he'll think twice about stealing from anyone ever again." Travis turned and headed toward the door.

She stood up so fast her chair almost toppled over. "Travis Parker, stop this instant. It's too late. They've already disqualified our entry. We have to come up with proof in the next day or so, or we're done. Getting in a fight with Desmond will only make it worse."

He turned. "I don't see how it will make it worse. It will sure make me feel better."

"What we need from Desmond is a sworn confession. Beating him up will make it look like we're in the wrong. I don't want you hauled off to jail. That won't help us with the contest."

Travis considered her logic for a moment and, with a gusty sigh, returned to the table. "There's really nothing we can do?"

"Short of a miracle, no. My only consolation is knowing Grandma Lou's recipe *was* good enough to win."

"You're darn right there. That's why Desmond stole it." Travis patted her shoulder. "So this is it, then? We'll need to close Grandma Lou's before the end of the month?"

Bethany sighed and rubbed her eyes. "If we don't figure out some way of redeeming our reputation and winning the contest in the next couple of days, yeah, it's over. They'll select a new winner. We'll have to be out by the end of the month."

"Have you reconsidered talking to Hank? Maybe he'd give us an extension on the rent?"

Bethany shook her head. "No, and I don't intend to. Even if Hank agreed to waive next month's rent, we'd still have to close. The sad truth is that even with the boost in sales since Hank's been in Grandma Lou's, we just aren't making enough money to stay open."

"It's okay, Bethany. I'm getting my diploma after next semester. I'll be able to find a job that pays well. Perfect timing. We'll get by. I know we will. We'll do it like we've done everything else . . . together."

"That's right." Bethany smiled and gave her brother a hug. "I can't do it without you. You truly are the best brother ever."

"Don't you forget it."

"Never."

Despite the loss of their livelihood, she still had Travis. Together, they would find a way to survive. Maybe they would carve a new life out for themselves.

HANK MOVED toward the entrance of the great room, his limbs shaking. Everything Elizabeth said about him was true—he was afraid of intimacy, he loved his career, he was thrilled to land the role of his dreams, he didn't know how to love. Except she was wrong about one thing.

He did love Bethany Parker.

My God, Connor was right. He couldn't stop thinking about her, was miserable without her. He had loved her the moment he'd spied her, eyes closed, savoring a bite of choco-late cake. How had he ever thought himself immune?

Hank leaned against the wall to steady himself. He hadn't thought he could fall in love because he had believed what Elizabeth said about him. He had believed he was undeserving. That he was like his dad—selfish, egotistical, incapable of loving another. Unable to remain faithful. Unable to be a good father. Although his dad seemed to be making an effort, there was no guarantee the changes were permanent.

He forced a breath and stepped into the room, his gaze taking in Elizabeth, who relaxed on the couch, her long legs encased in skinny jeans, and Connor, who stood with his arms crossed in front of the bay window, his face creased in frustration. A wave of adrenaline shot through Hank like he'd stepped in front of a camera and was about to give the performance of his career. Except this was no studio. This was his home. And his next lines were unrehearsed.

"Hank, I was wondering when you'd get here," Elizabeth said, her expression serene.

Not a line of concern marred her smooth face. If he didn't know better, he would believe she and his brother had been discussing the weather and not his capacity to love another human being.

"Connor and I were just catching up before he returns to school."

Hank ignored Elizabeth and focused on his brother, who had on a UCLA T-shirt and a pair of gray sweatpants. He looked like he'd been hitting the gym. A tuft of curly blond hair escaped from under his red Angels ball cap. "Thanks for taking such good care of Woodrow while I was gone."

Connor raised his blond eyebrows at the faint praise,

but Hank moved forward until he stood in front of his brother, man to man. "I haven't been the best big brother to you, have I?"

Connor took off his ball cap and scratched his head, a question in his blue eyes, so much like Hank's own. "You didn't know I even existed until last year. You've been fine."

There was that word again, *fine*. How come everyone in his life wanted to say everything was fine? He shook his head. "No, Connor, I've not been fine. Not in a good long while. You were right about me. I've been unhappy and unaccepting of you. I've been grumpy and mean and distant. But with your help and a little luck, I hope to get beyond fine."

Connor straightened, a slow smile filling his face. "Whatever you need, big guy."

Hank laughed. "Right now, I need a drink."

Elizabeth spoke from behind him. "Whatever are you two yammering on about? Hank, did something go wrong during the podcast?"

He turned to face Elizabeth. "You can say that."

Instead of elaborating, Hank walked to the liquor cabinet and found the rum. Time to rehearse his next lines. He wanted to get this right. He poured the drink and added coke and ice.

Elizabeth stood and moved toward him. "The interview was going fantastic when I left early to change clothes and come here. Was it something to do with Melanie?"

Hank downed half of the drink. "Bethany was accused on national television of entering someone else's recipe in the baking contest. You know, the contest she hoped to win to repurchase her building?"

Elizabeth fixed him with a serious look. "That's unfortu-nate. I did what you asked of me and helped her get the votes she needed to final. It's not my fault she didn't submit a qualified entry. Why are you so upset?"

"I'm upset because she's been wrongly accused. But it doesn't matter that she didn't win. I plan to give the building back to her."

Elizabeth's penciled eyebrows jerked toward her brow line. "That's ridiculous. Why would you do a thing like that?"

"Because he loves her, that's why," Connor said, a broad smile lighting up his face. "I told you he loved her. That's why he's been all mopey and mean."

"Impossible. Tell me you don't think you're in love with Bethany Parker, Hank. That's not going to do a thing to help your career."

Hank took a final swig of his rum and coke and contemplated Elizabeth's worried face. "Ah, that's where you're wrong, Elizabeth. Loving Bethany is going to change my career completely."

"What do you mean Bethany Parker's going to change your career completely?" Elizabeth asked, gazing at him with a mixture of horror and concern. "Hank, you're not thinking of giving up acting for her, are you?" She stood facing him, hands on her hips and eyes wide with disbelief and panic.

His gaze flicked to Connor who remained by the window, a broad smile still on his face.

"No, I'm not giving up my career."

She lifted her hands toward the ceiling. "Oh, thank God. For a moment there, you had me worried. I thought you were going to tell me you're moving to Cleveland. I don't think I could stomach living in that horrible city."

Hank folded his arms across his chest. "Oh, I *am* going to move to that horrible city."

Elizabeth gasped, the sound a sharp contrast to Connor's bark of laughter. "You can't be serious."

Hank returned his glass to the bar and poured himself a bolstering drink. "More serious than I've been about anything in a long time. I own a house there, which I've been fixing up, and I plan to relocate. But don't worry. I'm not ending my career. I plan to invest in a business. But not a fitness center. I'll open my own production studio."

"Have you lost your mind?"

"No, I believe I've found it. I plan to talk to Blackie and the producers tonight, so don't think of calling them. I'll convince them to complete the filming in Cleveland."

Elizabeth advanced toward him like a soldier preparing for battle. "Why would they agree? Filming has already begun in California."

Hank stood his ground. "Because I'm prepared to walk, and I suspect they'll prefer I didn't. As you said, filming has already begun. But early surveys of public perception show Apollo is favored for the role. They won't want to lose me. Don't worry, I'm not expecting you to come with me to that horrible city."

Elizabeth stopped moving. Now her eyes shifted like a deer cornered by a mountain lion. Hank almost felt sorry for her, but he smothered the feeling. Elizabeth had tried to harm the woman he loved.

"What are you saying?"

"I'm letting you go, Elizabeth."

"You're joking."

"I wish I was. I thought I could trust you. But you interfered with Bethany winning the contest."

Elizabeth drew herself up like she smelled a rotten fish. "I did nothing of the sort. I had absolutely nothing to do with Bethany Parker entering a recipe shared on her ex-fiancé's cooking show. That was accomplished before I ever met the woman."

"Maybe so, but you *were* responsible for the little reunion with Desmond I witnessed before I left town. You must have thought she would take him back. I suspect you discovered Desmond had aired the recipe on his show and didn't bother warning Bethany that her entry would be disqualified. What else did you do to ensure she lost the contest?"

"These are ridiculous accusations. Hank, please. I work my tail off for you. Are you really going to punish me over something I had no control over?"

Hank locked his eyes with hers, so she would know he meant business. Connor remained a silent observer. "Yes, I am . . . unless you're willing to come clean about your involvement."

She uncrossed her arms. "What do you want to know?"

CHAPTER THIRTY-EIGHT

Bethany wiped tables for the last time and tried to keep herself from breaking into tears. It had been two days since the news had reported that they plagiarized their contest entry, and she and Travis had done everything they could to save the business, but it still wasn't enough.

She slapped the dishcloth on the wood and scrubbed the surface until her wrist ached. Life was so unfair.

The back door slammed shut, and Travis shuffled in from the kitchen. "I've finished moving the boxes into Mitch and Paula's van. There are only a few things I haven't packed. Are you gonna be okay?"

"Yes." She took off her rubber gloves and tossed them next to the bucket of soapy water along with the dishrag.

"You're slinging things around. Are you sure?"

"No, Travis, I'm not sure of anything anymore. I've been trying to be strong but this . . ." she looked around the empty restaurant, "this is awful."

Bethany collapsed onto the nearest chair and rubbed her hand across her eyes. She couldn't bear to look at the empty shelves and walls devoid of pictures. "We've had so much sadness over the last few years. Losing Mom and Dad, having all our money stolen, and now, Grandma's recipe, by Desmond—who knows what else the rat took from us?—then watching Hank leave town and losing this old place. My heart can't take any more."

Travis pulled out the chair opposite her and sat. "I have an idea. We shouldn't go out like this, all sad and depressed. Let's do something fun."

Bethany put her chin in her hands and wrinkled her nose, giving him an are-you-crazy look. "I can't dredge up excitement when I'm depressed. I need to wallow."

"Let's whip up one last batch of Grandma Lou's Chocolate Cake with Buttercream Frosting in her kitchen. We'll make a hundred cupcakes and hand them out to all our loyal customers. Desmond may have robbed us of the contest win, but the recipe still belongs to us, right? Let's not let the creep steal our joy. This will be a wonderful way to honor Grandma's memory and all the great times we've had in this building. We'll gorge ourselves on cake and drown our sorrows in milk. What do you say?"

Bethany smiled and sniffed and blew her nose with a tissue she dug from her pocket. "You had me at cupcakes."

Travis stood. "Let's go then. I didn't pack the mixer. We'll have to dig out the ingredients and the measuring spoons and cups and baking pans."

He headed into the kitchen, and Bethany followed. This would be the last time she would ever cook in their kitchen. Who knew what the new owner would turn it into?

They pulled the ingredients from the boxes and the milk and eggs from the cooler. Bethany combined flour, cocoa powder, baking soda, baking powder, salt, sugar, and brown sugar in the mixing bowl. Travis added oil, milk, and eggs. Then she picked up the vanilla and handed it to

Travis. "Do you remember when you first smelled vanilla and begged Grandma to let you taste a spoonful?"

Travis groaned and measured the vanilla into the teaspoon. "How could I forget? I never understood how something that smelled so good could taste so bad. What about the time your hands were wet, and you filled ice-cube trays and got your knuckles stuck to the ceiling of the freezer?"

Bethany giggled. "Mom said I was the only kid she knew who could get frostbitten in the middle of the summer. They were something, weren't they?"

Travis added vanilla to the mixer. "Mom and Grandma? Yeah, they were."

"Mom, Dad, Grandma, Grandpa. I can't believe they're all gone now." She poured boiling water, her hands trembling. "They would hate what's happening. Grandpa said he started the restaurant on a wish and a prayer and a two-thousand-dollar loan he got from his uncle. All that hard work down the drain."

Travis emptied the batter into the cupcake pans and put the pans in the oven. "Don't blame yourself, Bethany. I don't. Even if we have to close the business, no one can ever take our memories from us. We keep those memories alive whenever we make the old recipes."

"What do you mean, *if?* Are you still holding out hope? There is none, Brother. Better let it go now."

"There's always hope. You never know what can happen."

Bethany shrugged. If Travis wanted to keep hope alive for a little while longer, who was she to burst his bubble.

While Travis washed the dishes, Bethany turned on the mixer and sifted in powdered sugar a little at a time until familiar peaks began to form in the buttercream frosting. "I do blame myself for the restaurant closing," she said. "None of this was your fault. It pains me you'll suffer the consequences too."

"I'm okay. Closing Grandma Lou's is hitting you harder than me. You're the one who inherited Mom and Grandma's cooking skills. I'm just your sidekick. If it weren't for Desmond, you would have been set to keep this place running forever. Besides, think of all the cake I've gotten to eat over the past few years."

As if Travis had ordered it to happen, the timer went off on the oven, indicating the cupcakes were done. Bethany grabbed the hot pads to remove the pans, and then she and Travis played cards and waited for the cupcakes to cool. By the time the dishes were back in the large plastic container, and they had resumed their seats on the stools, the cupcakes were ready to frost and eat.

"You first," Travis said, pointing to the nearest cupcake.

"Nope. We'll do it at the same time." She handed her brother his own. "On the count of three. One, two—"

A pounding sounded at the front door, and Bethany set down the cupcake and looked at Travis. "Who could that be?"

Travis quirked his eyebrow and stood. "I don't know. Let's go find out."

Bethany reached the door first and opened it. "Elizabeth? I'm sorry, but we're closed."

Elizabeth's hair was so windblown, it looked like she'd won a race. "Can I come in? Please, I'd like to talk to you."

Bethany gestured for Elizabeth to step inside. She was followed by Susan Winchester, the reporter from *Channel Ten News*, the cameraman from last time, and dozens of spectators, some of whom Bethany recognized as customers. "What's going on?" Bethany asked, the hair on the back of her arms rising as if in revolt. The last thing she wanted was to be on camera. She didn't care if she never saw another one in her lifetime.

"I owe you a heartfelt apology. I've made a terrible mistake," Elizabeth said.

"What's with all the cameras?" Travis asked, beating Bethany to the question.

"I've asked them here." Elizabeth stood by the counter, turning to face the camera. "I have a confession to make, and I want to be sure it's recorded and shared on television."

"Why?"

"You'll understand in a moment. Trust me, there's a good reason."

Bethany couldn't imagine what would be good enough to require a news story she would welcome, but Elizabeth had already turned to Susan Winchester.

"Let's roll."

Susan smiled at the camera. "As we reported earlier in the week, Grandma Lou's Kitchen and Pantry, and its owners, Bethany and Travis Parker, were eliminated from being named the winners in a national baking competition sponsored by Fresh & Easy, makers of high-end cooking utensils. Up for grabs? Five hundred thousand dollars in prize money. Today, this story has taken an amazing turn, with Bethany Parker's entry being reinstated, and the Chef King's integrity being called into question."

Bethany's stomach churned like her mixer, starting out slowly and moving into high speed. She stared at Susan Winchester, trying to make sense of the reporter's words. Her heartbeat stuttered, her thoughts frozen in space and time.

Susan turned to Elizabeth and held the microphone in

front of her. "I'm here with Hank Haverill's publicist, Elizabeth Fortenay, who first reported the thievery, resulting in Grandma Lou's entry being disqualified. Elizabeth, can you describe for our viewers how you figured out the Chef King had stolen the Parkers' family recipe?"

Bethany and Travis leaned forward like spectators at a racetrack.

Elizabeth held up a piece of paper, which all eyes, and the camera, zoomed in on. *Grandma Lou's recipe!* How had it landed in Elizabeth's hands?

"I met the Chef King, Desmond Mitchell, when I was in town assisting my client, Hank Haverill, with his newest business interest. Hank had purchased the historic Parker building as an investment. Bethany Parker, one of the former owners, mentioned the contest on more than one occasion to Hank and me, so we were well aware that she intended to enter her grandmother's recipe in the contest."

Bethany strained to hear Elizabeth even though the place was so quiet you could have heard a whisper.

"But in my conversations with Desmond, he described the recipe to a tee and insisted it was his paternal grandmother's, whose name was Louise Mitchell. He told me he'd shared it on his television show not too long ago and sent me a link to the episode, so I knew what he said was true. I took the Parkers' only copy of the recipe in their grandmother's handwriting, intending to return it to the person I believed was the rightful owner, Desmond Mitchell."

Bethany gasped. Travis looked like he was going to kick someone. Bethany laid a restraining hand on his arm.

Elizabeth turned to where they stood by the counter, and the camera followed her movement. "I owe both of you a sincere apology. When I took the recipe, I thought I was preventing you from capitalizing on the theft of a treasured family recipe. I had no idea I was assisting a thief."

Susan Winchester thrust the microphone under Elizabeth's nose. "How did you discover your error—that the Chef King actually stole the recipe from the Parkers and not the other way around?"

Elizabeth nodded at the camera, her look apologetic. "From my client, Hank Haverill."

Bethany's heart skipped several beats before thumping madly in her ears.

Elizabeth continued. "When Hank learned Bethany was accused of plagiarizing the Chef King's recipe, he was convinced of her innocence. Two days ago, he hired a firm of private investigators to get to the bottom of this. They interviewed a number of elderly Tremont residents. Dozens of them came forward in support of the Parkers. Many are here today."

She gestured behind her, and it was then that Bethany registered how many people had entered the shop. There must have been at least thirty, and there were even more outside the building.

Elizabeth continued. "Several of those interviewed recall enjoying the cake when Grandma Lou Parker first shared the recipe in her kitchen in the early 1950s. As it turns out, Desmond's paternal grandparents were in grade school in the 1950s, and his grandmother's name is Rosalind and not Lou. But to dispel any doubt, the private investigator interviewed Desmond's grandparents, who are still living. They had no idea their grandson had claimed the recipe was theirs and have issued a statement denying any knowledge of it, as well as an apology on their behalf."

"So, what does this mean for the Parkers?" Susan asked. "Have you shared your findings with Fresh & Easy?"

Elizabeth smiled at the camera. "We have. I'm happy to tell everyone that the company has reinstated Grandma Lou's as the winner of their contest today."

Elizabeth gestured behind her toward a woman with dark curls, who'd been standing in the shadows. She stepped up to the microphone, a large cardboard check in her hands, and gestured for Bethany to join her.

"My name is Francine Richmond, chief marketing officer at Fresh & Easy. On behalf of the company, we want to congratulate you on your winning entry, Grandma Lou's Chocolate Cake with Buttercream Frosting. We are proud to present you with this check for five hundred thousand dollars. Congratulations."

Francine held the check out to Bethany, but Travis had to guide her forward until she clutched the giant cardboard rectangle in her shaking hands. Was this really happening?

Travis's grin was wider than that of a kid with a cupcake. A ray of hope sparked in Bethany's mind like someone had swung a flashlight beam over the dark cavern of despair she'd been living in for the last month.

The camera operator trained his camera on her and snapped a few photographs. Bethany hoped she was smiling, but she had a strong feeling her face still showed some of her shock at the turn of events.

"What will you do with the money?" Susan Winchester asked Bethany and Travis. "Do you plan to keep the restaurant open?"

Bethany cleared her throat. "Yes, that's the plan."

"What do you think of the Chef King stealing your recipe and then making it seem like it was his? Are you angry?"

"I was angry at first, but honestly, all I feel right now is sadness. He must have been desperate to steal someone else's work."

"Well, I'm certain I speak for all Clevelanders when I say congratulations. We hope you'll remain a fixture in this neighborhood for many more years to come." She turned toward the camera. "For *Channel Ten News*, good night and sweet dreams from Tremont."

The camera guy swept the room a final time before turning off his camera.

Travis cupped his hands around his mouth. "Hey, everyone. How about some of Grandma Lou's chocolate cake in cupcake form . . . on the house."

The crowd cheered.

"Mitch, why don't you run and get a few gallons of milk and plastic cups from the corner store?" Paula asked her husband, who nodded and offered Bethany his normal quiet smile.

Mitch headed out the door, while Travis went to get the cupcakes, and Bethany turned to Elizabeth. "Thank you for setting the record straight."

Elizabeth wrinkled her nose. "Oh, don't thank me. Thank Hank." She flipped a hand over her shoulder, as if . . .

Panic plunged through Bethany's veins like she'd been shot with adrenaline.

CHAPTER THIRTY-NINE

Bethany looked toward the front door. A flood of people entered the small space—customers, friends, neighbors—all carrying trays of food and coolers of drinks and calling out their best wishes. Was she dreaming? Grandma Lou's had been empty only an hour ago. Now it was filled with noise and chaos and life.

"Where have all these people come from?"

"Hank invited them." Elizabeth motioned toward the door again.

There was Sam, looking dapper in a new bow tie, and Tia and Tana, along with Rosie, holding a banner that read: *Home of the Award-Winning Grandma Lou's Chocolate Cake with Buttercream Frosting.* And behind them . . .

Her breath left her in a rush. She stumbled and would have fallen if Travis, who'd returned from the kitchen to set a large tray of cupcakes on the counter, hadn't grabbed her arm and held her up. Standing just beyond the girls was a tall, broad-shouldered man with golden hair and eyes bluer than the sky on a summer day. He stared at her with all the apprehension of a man unsure of his welcome.

It seemed as if the background noise fell away, that the friends patting her back and offering congratulations didn't exist, and only she and Hank were in the room. Travis said something, but she couldn't hear him. Her stomach wound tighter than the trussed-up turkey she and Travis made last Thanksgiving. She tried for anger, but all she could feel was a mind-numbing, jaw-dropping relief. She covered her mouth with her hand and swallowed the sob threatening to erupt.

Hank looked good. More than good, he looked achingly real. His hair might have grown a tad, and he might have dropped a few pounds, but he still resembled the man who'd repaired her dishwasher and made her dinner and wished on stars and bought her flowers because he said she was beautiful and deserved them. The same man who'd kissed her and begged her to come to Los Angeles, then disappeared without a word of explanation.

She swallowed, but it didn't ease the dryness in her mouth. She blinked, but her eyes still burned. She had thought she would never see him again—like it had all been a glorious, impossible dream. Now, here he was, in the flesh.

She kept a hand over her mouth as another sob rose in her throat, as if she could keep all the emotion of the last month contained. Every time she'd caught glimpses of Hank on television or in a magazine, he had a beautiful woman by his side. Bethany figured he had moved on and forgotten her. Yet here he was.

"Beth." He came toward her and waited—for what, she didn't know. Did he expect her to run into his arms because he'd helped her win the contest?

He was wrong. She pressed her lips together and kept her arms at her sides, so she wouldn't be tempted to hurl herself into his hard embrace. He'd left what seemed like a lifetime ago, with no communication, no "I'm sorry but I can't see you anymore," no "let's remain friends." If anyone was owed an apology, it was her.

Still, because of his actions, Grandma Lou's was saved. He had somehow convinced Elizabeth to confess her role in the deception, which proved Bethany's innocence and allowed her to win the contest. She should be grateful, shouldn't she? And all eyes were on them. She needed to maintain some semblance of calm.

"Hank." She forced his name past chapped lips.

He took another step forward, and then another, until he towered over her. "Beth," he said again in his dear, familiar voice—the one that caused her to go all shivery inside with excitement. The same shiver she got when she watched an incredible sunset or pulled a recipe she'd never tried from the oven.

She wanted to lean her head against his broad chest and feel his arms wrap around her, but she didn't dare. He held his hand out as if he meant to touch her face, but she turned her head to the side. "Why have you come back?"

His eyes took on a strange cast, almost vulnerable, and he dropped his hand. "You won the contest. I thought . . ."

Bethany kept her face calm, while inside she fought a battle for control. Did he really think he could waltz back into her life after weeks without contact and not expect her to need a solid explanation? "Is that the only reason? Because you helped me win a contest?"

"Woman." His eyes warmed again, and his cool breath vibrated her hair. "Is that what you believe? I only came back because you won a contest?"

She stayed put, but her eyes locked with his and drank him in. "What am I supposed to think? You skipped town and had your assistant call me. You didn't even give me the courtesy of a personal phone call. Now you appear in Grandma Lou's on the day we're closing and I . . ." She infused her voice with steel. "Well, I don't know what to think."

"I made a mess of things with you, didn't I? I wasn't thinking clearly. But I am now, and I promise you, I'm not leaving this time."

"You're staying in Cleveland?"

"Yes. If you'll have me. I've missed you. You can't begin to know how much. These past few weeks have felt like decades."

But she did know because she missed him too. Something glorious unfurled inside her like a ship's sail caught by the wind. Still, she held herself in check. What if he lied? What if she misinterpreted his words? What if he only meant he wanted to go back to being her handyman land-lord? What if this was some ploy to make her lose her heart only to have him crush it? "Why did you leave in the first place?"

He reached for her hands, and the warm sensation of his large palms connecting with hers tore at her heart until it was almost more than she could bear. He threaded his fingers through hers, and she dropped her gaze to their joined hands.

"I was saving you from myself."

She sucked in air. "What made you think I needed saving?"

Now his fingers tipped her chin until she couldn't look anywhere but into his glorious eyes. She saw flecks of light blue in his irises and the gold-tinged brown of his thick eyelashes.

"I didn't want to hurt you. I was under the misconception that I wasn't capable of loving another—of loving you. I thought I was like my father, and I'd break your heart. I couldn't do that to you."

She kept her gaze fastened on his, afraid to move, afraid to breathe, afraid to dream. "Misconception? So you now believe you *can* fall in love with me?"

He circled her pulse point with his thumb. "No, I don't believe it."

Alarm tingled in her stomach and a cold dread danced down her spine, erupting in a wave of anguish. Her body seemed to sag and draw inward. "You don't?" she whispered.

He quirked his lips into a smile—the smile of a conquering hero—and drew her into his arms. "I know it. I've loved you from the moment I first saw you taking a bite of chocolate cake, and I promise, I'll love you until your last."

HANK WATCHED her as she took in his words. He saw the moment her eyes went from wild hurt to the beginning of hopefulness to steady belief. He didn't waste another moment on words then. Instead, he grabbed her hand and led her through the crowd, ignoring the hoots and hollers, and pulled her into the kitchen. Once inside, he drew her into his arms and kissed her.

His cell phone buzzed, but he ignored it. It wasn't hard. He was a starving man stranded on a desert island who'd finally spotted water. The first taste of her didn't quench his thirst . . . not by a long shot. Hank was certain he could spend an entire lifetime kissing her, and he would never grow tired. But he forced himself to separate from her lips because they needed to breathe, and he needed to stare into her sparkling eyes and make sure he hadn't imagined the love he saw glowing in them.

Her lips parted. He strained to hear her words.

"I love you, Hank."

Ahh. The sweet, sweet sound. No other words could make him feel more alive.

"I tried to fight it, but I couldn't. I think I fell in love with you that first day, when you asked me to keep you company while you devoured a whoopie pie. And then you scaled an eight-foot fence to see me."

Her cheeks flushed a delicate pink, but she didn't look away. "I have you to thank for all of this, don't I?"

He kept his eyes fixed on hers, so she would know he spoke the truth. "I never imagined Elizabeth would go as far as to discredit you. I am sorry. I should have realized what was happening much sooner. When I discovered what she'd done, I was furious. I gave her an ultimatum—either come clean and turn this around or lose her job and her reputation. She chose the former. She believed the lies Desmond told her, which is why she did what she did."

"Hey, you two, why are you hiding in here?" Travis came through the door, stopping when he saw them, a grin spreading over his face. Rosie and the girls weren't far behind. "When's the wedding?"

Hank smiled like a crazy man, and he didn't much care that he had a small audience. He filled his lungs, and reached into his pocket where he'd placed his mother's modest ring, which he'd paid extra to have a jeweler embellish with a larger diamond at short notice—was that only this morning? It felt like a lifetime ago. Then he clasped both of Bethany's hands in his, turned her to face him, and got down on bended knee, right smack dab in the middle of the kitchen.

"Beth, will you marry me?"

CHAPTER FORTY

Bethany drew in a shaky breath and gazed at the sparkling diamond ring and the man who presented it to her. For the first time since she'd known him, Hank looked afraid—like all his future joy and happiness hinged on her answer.

She laid her palm against his cheek. The smell of his musky cologne reached her nostrils. "Yes," she said. Her voice wobbled, so she tried again. "Yes, I'll marry you."

His face broke into a broad smile, and he kissed her hand and then slid the ring on her finger. He stood and hauled her into his arms and kissed her again. He only let her go long enough to accept a hug from Travis.

"Welcome to the family," Travis said, slapping him on the back.

Hank shook his hand. "I'm mighty proud to have you as a brother-in-law."

Rosie squealed and hugged Bethany. The girls squeezed her legs and then rushed to hug Hank, who crouched low and pulled them into his arms and up into the air. "What do you think? Will these two do as flower girls?"

"I can't think of anyone better or prettier to do the job," Bethany said.

"What's a flower girl?" Tana asked.

"It's a girl who walks down a carpet at a wedding and hands out flowers," her older sister answered, sounding official.

"Will you excuse us a moment, girls?" Hank asked, setting them down. "There's someone I really want Bethany to meet."

Hank pulled her to his side and through the double doors that led to the dining room. They moved through the crowd, smiling and greeting the friends and customers who had crowded into Grandma Lou's. Finally, they reached the entrance, where a tall young man stood, a grin on his face. He looked like a younger version of Hank.

"Is this . . . ?"

"Bethany, I'd like you to meet my brother, Connor."

Connor held out his hand. "Pleased to meet you, Bethany." His blue eyes, so much like Hank's, twinkled with warmth and laughter.

Bethany found herself leaning toward him. "So you're Connor," she said, flicking a glance at Hank. "It appears, Apollo, you have some competition in the looks department."

Connor flashed a quick smile at Hank. "I think I'm going to like your girlfriend, big guy."

"Fiancée," Hank corrected.

Connor cupped his hands around his mouth and twisted to look at Bethany, pretending to relay a closely guarded secret. "My brother's been grumpier than a starving bear these last few weeks. Thanks for agreeing to marry him and ending our misery."

She glanced at Hank. "You missed my cooking?"

He winked, his blue eyes crinkling at the corners. "What can I say, woman, I'm addicted to your whoopie pies."

"So it *is* my cooking you fell in love with." For a moment, a vulnerable feeling she hadn't realized she possessed opened inside her.

Hank's face grew serious, and his eyes latched on to hers. "Sweetheart, I was only joking. I fell in love with the whole amazing package. I promise, your talent in the kitchen is just the sweet, sweet icing."

Joy filled her like a hot air balloon, tickling her insides until she laughed aloud. She had almost forgotten the feeling. It swept her away on a tide of happiness, swallowing her insecurities in its wake.

"Do you have a sister?" Connor asked, bringing her back to earth with a start.

She smiled. "No, just a brother. Come with me, and I'll introduce you. You're about the same age. I think you'll have a lot in common."

HANK WATCHED with pride as Bethany pulled Connor across the room to where Travis was chatting with a few of the other tenants. Now she was his once more, he wanted her all to himself. He started to follow, but someone grabbed his arm. *Elizabeth.* She must have been listening to their conversation.

"Hank, I want to apologize. I am truly sorry for meddling, as you call it. I never meant to hurt you or Bethany. I thought I was protecting you. And now I see I was wrong. And I hope I've shown it by making amends. She's perfect for you. Can you forgive me?"

The well of happiness in his heart was much too large to hold a grudge. "Yes, Elizabeth, I can, if you promise never to interfere again in my personal life."

"I won't. I swear it. I've learned my lesson." Elizabeth arched a brow. "Well, I may have one teeny-weeny suggestion."

Hank laughed. "All right. I can see you're dying to offer advice. Out with it."

"Maybe you and Bethany ought to produce a healthy line of bakery items. Somehow, I don't think whoopie pies quite fit your public image."

He grinned. "That's actually not a bad idea. I'll talk to Bethany and see what she thinks."

Elizabeth smirked and gestured toward the lady from Fresh & Easy. "Hank, let's snap a photo with Francine, shall we?"

He paused long enough for the photo, knowing Elizabeth would be sure to post it to his Instagram that evening. He scanned the crowd for Bethany, spotted her, and moved forward, but he could hear Elizabeth talking to Francine above the din of the crowd.

"Despite the snafus, I've managed to turn this contest win into positive media coverage for your company," she said. "I could be a real asset if you're in need of a publicist?"

Hank shook his head and grinned. He had no doubt Elizabeth would turn the entire event to her advantage. He spotted Bethany talking to Sam and joined her.

"Well, hi there, Hank. I'm real happy for you," Sam said. "I knew you were smitten with my girl the day you showed up in your overalls and hat to fix her dishwasher. I told Bethany then and there you were in love. She didn't believe me, but you do now, don't you, girl?"

"You were right, Sam."

"When's the wedding. Have you set a date?"

"It's much too soon. We just got engaged," Bethany said.

"As soon as we can make it happen," Hank said, glad to see Bethany didn't argue. If he had his way, they would be married within the month.

They spent the next hour traveling from group to group, with Bethany introducing him to any of the customers he hadn't met. She called each one by name, their faces lighting up as she asked after their families. Then he ate a cupcake and drank a glass of milk when all he really wanted was to have her to himself.

But of course, it wasn't until much later, when the good-byes had been said and the well-wishers had departed and Louis had dropped them off at Hank's grandfather's house, which was now his own, that his wish came true.

She sniffed the air as he opened the front door. "Why do I smell paint?"

"Close your eyes. You'll know soon enough."

He led her into the dining room and had her stand in the middle of the floor, beneath the antique chandelier. "Keep your eyes closed now."

Hank found the remote, dimmed the lights, and pressed play on the home stereo system. Then he took her into his arms as the first strains of "When You Wish Upon a Star" by Louis Armstrong came over the speaker.

"You can open your eyes now."

She blinked and looked around the renovated house.

"Surprise," he whispered.

He'd had the decorators add sunflowers to all the rooms and touches of purple before he'd left Cleveland, since it reminded him of Bethany. The mantel on the stone fire-place had been refinished, the wood floors polished, and the walls painted a subtle gray. A plush green couch occupied one corner and a leather recliner the other. Elizabeth had given him the photo she'd snapped of the two of them—Bethany looking alarmed and him looking determined—framed. He'd placed it on the built-in shelves next to the fireplace along with a framed kiss-cam photo from the baseball game.

She twisted in his arms, looking everywhere at once. "My God, Hank, it's so beautiful, what you've done with the place."

"You like it?"

"How could I not? It's lovely."

"Lovely enough to live in with me . . . after we're married?"

Her misty green eyes looked wide and mysterious and more dazzling than the stars in the night sky outside.

"Yes, yes, it is. I think I'd follow you to the moon right now, if you asked." She laughed, the sound soft and dreamy. "This house is much more convenient."

A thick bubble wedged in his throat. "Thank you for agreeing to be my wife. Thank you for making my dreams come true. I want you to know you were right and I was wrong."

She cocked her head to the side. "About what?"

"So many things. About wishing on stars. About forgiveness."

"You believe in wishes now?"

"How can I not when I have you? All I did last night was wish on stars, terrified you'd reject today's proposal."

"Meanwhile, I was wishing you'd propose and figuring it was an impossible dream. Who did you forgive?"

"Elizabeth . . . my father. If it's okay with you, I'd like to invite them to our wedding. My stepmom and sisters too."

She nodded. "Of course, Hank. They're family. I'd love to meet them." She wrinkled her nose. "I'm not so keen on Elizabeth, but I think not even she could spoil our happiness."

He laughed and tightened his hold. "Now we have that out of the way, kiss me, Beth. Please. Then all my wishes *will* come true."

She tilted her face toward him, and he bent his head, and their lips met somewhere in the middle, while overhead Louis Armstrong crooned, echoing the desires of his heart.

EPILOGUE

One year later

"Hurry up now or we'll be late. We don't want to miss the grand reopening of Grandma Lou's. Do I look okay?" Bethany eyed her pink dress in the hallway mirror. She wanted to look professional but also embody their new line of healthy bakery products. But it was hard to find a maternity dress that covered the ready-to-pop mountain that was her stomach and still looked pretty.

Hank smiled from the recliner, stretching his hands behind his head. "Like a dream come true."

"You always say that." She fastened the pink pearl earrings he'd given her as a gift on their wedding night nine months ago. They'd gotten married in a quiet ceremony in Hawaii with just their families and close friends present, but had a larger reception for everyone else when they'd arrived home.

He stood and came toward her, and as usual, she felt a

little thrill to think he was her husband. His hands came down on her shoulders, and he pulled her against his hard frame so they both looked in the mirror together. "I say it because it's real. You are my dream come true, Mrs. Haverill, and don't you ever forget it."

He splayed his hand across her stomach, and they both felt as the baby kicked.

"Did you feel that?" She placed her hands over his.

"I did," he breathed against her neck. "Our child will be a fighter like her mother."

She turned in his arms. "He'll be a Greek god. After all, this is your child."

He smiled, revealing a dimple. "How do you know it's a boy?"

"I don't. I just picture a little boy who looks like you."

"You know you've made me the happiest man alive?"

"Yes, but I'll never grow tired of hearing you say it."

"Then I won't. Ever." He held out his arm. "Are you ready, princess?"

"Yes," she said, and took his arm. "I am."

"Then let's climb into the royal chariot."

Normally, he drove, but tonight was a special occasion, so he'd called for the limo. After months of renovations, they would celebrate the updates to the building and announce some exciting changes to Grandma Lou's menu with much public fanfare and some national news coverage.

A few minutes later, the limo was at the restaurant's front door, but Hank asked her to wait until he could escort her to the entrance. Camera crews lined the sidewalk. A large gold ribbon with "celebration" written in block letters covered the doorway. He held out a hand and flashed her his confident smile. "Showtime."

Although she would never get used to the cameras and

paparazzi that followed them around snapping photos, Hank was in his element. He looked dapper in a pair of gray slim-fitting slacks, shiny black boots, and a white short-sleeve dress shirt that showed off his biceps. Bethany was content to hold his arm and let him deal with all the questions.

Elizabeth stood near the entrance with Travis and Rosie. And there were her helpers, Sean, Liam, and Declan, looking classy in the khakis and dress shirts she'd bought them for the occasion. "Hello, boys, you're looking good," she said.

They grinned and elbowed each other in the ribs.

"Hank, Bethany," Elizabeth interrupted. "We're all set inside."

Rosie gave Bethany a hug. "Nervous?"

She nodded. "A little."

Travis patted her shoulder. "Don't be. You'll do great. Here, I think you'll be needing these." He handed Bethany a large pair of scissors.

"Don't you want to do the honors?"

"I wouldn't even think about it. You did most of the work." Travis winked. "Tell you what, you cut the ribbon, and Rosie and I will watch to make sure it's done right. Deal?"

Bethany rolled her eyes. "Oh, all right. But you should know better than to irritate a pregnant woman."

"Get ready. Looks like you're on."

Susan Winchester, the reporter from Channel Ten, greeted them, microphone in hand. "Hank, you and Bethany spent months, not to mention lots of cash, to make improvements to this historic building for all the tenants. Now Grandma Lou's is set to provide Clevelanders with even more food options. Tell us, what's so special about the new menu?"

He paused on the steps and turned to face the camera. "My wife is incredibly talented. She knows locals love their baked goods. But I know many fitness buffs can't enjoy them on a daily basis because of the calories and sugar. Besides improvements to the building, we're unveiling a new line of products that everyone can enjoy, without adding inches to their waistline."

"That's fantastic. What are you calling it?"

"Food of Gods. Take it from me, even the gods never tasted bakery items this good, and good for you."

"Hank," another reporter called out from the crowd, "congratulations on the new Robin Hood movie and opening your own production studio. Are you excited to become a father?"

"I'm thrilled."

"You've said in the past that your own father wasn't much involved in your formative years. Are you worried at all if you'll make a good father?"

Hank hesitated, and because Bethany was holding his arm, she felt his muscles tighten. Why did reporters always ask needling questions? "Hank will make a terrific father," she said and turned to Susan Winchester. "Are you ready, Susan? We have a ribbon to cut."

"We're rolling."

"Okay, Cleveland," Bethany said. "Welcome to the newly renovated historic Parker building." She clipped the ribbon amid cheers from the crowd.

"C'mon inside and help yourself to free samples," Travis said.

The baby lurched in her belly and a stabbing pain shot

through her lower back. "Oh, my goodness. Hank! I . . . I think it's time."

"Now, Beth?" His eyes looked a bit wild.

"Yes." She nodded, as another pain gripped her. "Now."

"What are we waiting for? Out of our way." He motioned to the line of reporters. "My wife's having a baby."

Bethany was too busy counting breaths and fighting the stabbing pains to pay any more attention to what was happening around her. The next hour was a painful blur. By the time they arrived at the hospital and were escorted to a room, her contractions were close together, and the nurse said it wouldn't be long. The reporters tailed them but were kept outside, thank goodness.

Then the nurse set up an IV, and the anesthesiologist showed up to give her an epidural, and her doctor arrived and told her to push. And then . . .

And then there was a loud wail.

"It's a girl," the doctor said.

The nurse swaddled the baby in a blanket, and Bethany caught a glimpse of the most beautiful little face she had ever seen.

"A girl?"

"She's got her mother's lungs," Hank said, squeezing her hand. Tears rolled down his face. "She looks like you."

"Congratulations, you have a daughter. Would you like to hold her?"

"Yes," she said. "Yes, please."

And then the baby was wrapped in a pink blanket, and Bethany stared into a precious pair of blue eyes—blue like Hank's.

The nurses and doctors left them to get acquainted.

"Do you want to hold her?"

Hank shook his head. "I don't want to hurt her."

"You won't, Hank."

He held out his arms, and she laid the tiny bundle in his hands. He cradled the baby to his chest. "What shall we call her?"

"I don't know. All I ever thought of are boy names."

"I have a suggestion. What do you think of Stella? It means star."

"That's beautiful, Hank. I love it. And for a middle name, how about Katherine, after your mother . . . Hank?"

He didn't answer, Bethany realized, because he was too choked up.

"What's the matter, Hank? Are you worried about being a father?"

"Nah, it's not that." He gazed at her over the top of little Stella's head, his heart in his eyes. "I just realized another wish I made has come true."

"To have a baby?"

"To have a family."

And that, Bethany thought, was more than enough dream-come-true for both of them.

THE END

ACKNOWLEDGMENTS

Dear Friends,

As I reflect on the journey of writing this book over the past six years, I am filled with gratitude for the incredible people who supported me along the way. Writing a book is much like running a marathon—both can be a solitary pursuit, filled with ups and downs. However, it was the encouragement and insights from each of you that helped me cross the finish line.

I would like to extend my heartfelt thanks to early readers who took the time to provide invaluable feedback. Your suggestions were instrumental in shaping this story.

A special thank you goes to Harpeth Road publisher, Jenny Hale, whose keen eye recognized the "heart" of my manuscript. Your thoughtful suggestions were truly spot-on and helped refine the narrative in ways I could not have envisioned on my own. I am thrilled that my story found such a wonderful and supportive home.

I am also immensely grateful to my agent, Elizabeth Winick Rubinstein, and my editors, Emma Sherk, Megan McKeever, Lara Simpson, Lottie Hayes-Clemens, and Kendra Olson, whose expertise and dedication brought this story to life. Your guidance was vital in crafting a polished and engaging final product.

And last but not least, to my family, especially my husband, Barry, for putting up with me during the long journey to publication and encouraging me along the way.

I couldn't have done this without all of you. Thank you for believing in me and my story.

With all my appreciation,

Amanda

A LETTER FROM AMANDA UHL

Hello,

Thank you so much for picking up my novel, *The Icing on the Cake*. I hope you enjoyed the story, and it offered you a sweet escape.

If you'd like to know when my next book is out, you can sign up for new Harpeth Road release alerts for my novels here:

www.harpethroad.com/amanda-uhl-newsletter-signup

I won't share your information with anyone else, and I'll only email you a quick message whenever new books come out or go on sale.

If you did enjoy *The Icing on the Cake*, I'd be so thankful if you'd write a review online. Getting feedback from readers helps to persuade others to pick up my book for the first time. It's one of the biggest gifts you could give me.

Until next time,
Amanda Uhl